OPERATION
FREAKSHOW

OPERATION FREAKSHOW

A Novel

Ray Fisher | Dave Koco

HANNACROIX CREEK BOOKS, INC.
Stamford, Connecticut

The co-authors wish to credit artist John Ball, photographer Justin Tate, and a special thank you to Jeff Yager for discovering us and providing us with a stage to tell our stories.

Interior design by Scribe Freelance

Published by:
Hannacroix Creek Books, Inc.
1127 High Ridge Road, #110, Stamford, CT 06905 USA
http://www.hannacroixcreekbooks.com
hannacroix@aol.com

Follow us on Twitter: @hannacroixcreek
Library of Congress Control Number: 2016938184
ISBN: 978-1-938998-45-4 (trade paperback)

This book is dedicated to all those with scars from their childhood that will never heal. For those who know real monsters don't come from under the bed, they stumble in the late hours of the night and steal your innocence. Freakshow is not a hero for the masses, they would never understand, but to us, he is the hero we dream to be.

—DAVE KOCO

It is an error to believe that vengeance is but useless cruelty.... We avenge ourselves only upon what has done us evil, and what has done us evil is always dangerous.

—EMILE DURKHEIM

I.

The Holy Bible is tattered. Upon closer observation, one can see that this particular Bible is bound in calf hide, not any of that faux leather crap they try to bind the sacred scripture with now. On the spine, the fading glimmer of the letters *K, J,* and *V* are visible. Having seen decades of use, and passing through countless hands, it is now missing its back cover. It boasts less the testament of God and more a testament of its own ever-increasing lackluster.

A woman holds this sacred scripture in a dimly-lit room. She's sandwiched between her husband and a reading light that sits atop a cheap nightstand overburdened with dog-eared gossip magazines, tobacco ash, fast food wrappers, and moldy cheese dip. The couple, the book, the reading light, the nightstand—everything in this room, in affect—seems to complement one another, a compliment that extends beyond the borders of this room to the rest of the domicile. All things of which through years of abuse, misuse, ignorance, and neglect now shamelessly is put on display for those to behold.

The stained blankets strewn across the bed begin to stir as the husband makes what can only be described as an ambiguous moan. Without knowing the couple's circumstances, one might almost arrive at the conclusion that he is in pain.

The husband lets out a sigh of frustration through his

obscenely large nostrils and reaches over to grab his wife's sagging freckled breasts. She smacks his hand away and continues to read, though she can no longer concentrate. There will be no more reading tonight.

"I'm horny and you're my wife," he reactively sputters at the rejection. He shoots her a glance of contempt, adding, "Last I checked, part of your job is to suck my dick."

She ignores him. He reaches behind her head and grabs a fistful of her frayed hair. She lets out a yelp and fights to free herself. He tugs on her hair with so much force she can hear it being torn from her scalp. He shoves her head downward. The stench emitting from her husband's crotch is more pungent than the spore-dispatching cheese dip on her bedside table.

"I'm not in the mood... I've got a headache." She manages to cry out between her gasps for the stale bedroom air.

"You always have a fucking headache, bitch."

Her expression knots into a ball.

"Don't call me a bitch!" she screams back.

She breaks herself away. Clutching the Bible, she falls back into her pillow just as her husband swings his hand toward her face. A loud crack emitting from behind her pierces through the room and everything seems to jolt up with excitement. She looks up and sees her husband's closed fist against the headboard. He curses through clenched teeth as his free hand darts at the book pressed against her chest. Before she has any time to react, the book is being hurled into the darkness of the room. A soft thud is heard. Her husband pulls his hand away from the lacquered slats. His knuckles are raw and becoming flushed. He forces himself onto her pelvis. Using his knees, he slowly pries her legs open.

"Please don't!" she pleads.

A genuine fear is in her eyes. She would have been much better off if she had not dodged his swing. Still struggling to free herself, she is consequentially backhanded in the mouth with his injured hand. She stops moving. She feels so stupid. Things would have been over so much quicker if she just didn't struggle. A trickle of warmth descends her cheek. To think, there once was a time when she would have willingly had sex with her now smelly-crotched abuser.

He grunts, "Fuck you, you bitch. I'm fucking you no matter what. Who pays the fucking bills around here? Me! I'm the man."

Her eyes slowly well up with tears and everything becomes a blur. She looks toward the nightstand. Anything to take her mind off this ordeal. She is bone dry and the pain is unbearable.

"Who's the fucking man?" he asks her with an eye of satisfaction. He places his leathery hands around her neck and squeezes.

"Get wet you old hag. It's like fucking my grandmother down there."

He presses his lips together and sucks his cheeks in. His tongue sweeps the inside of his mouth for lubricant. He searches behind his tonsils for any available moisture, but is only met with a dry inflammation that he has done so well, up until now, to ignore. He undulates his jaw and then ejects a thin frothy substance into his hand. The discolored saliva, mucous, and food particles pooling in his palm is a meager portion at best. Disappointed as he is, this will have to do. He massages his concoction into her groin like it were a savory ham being prepared for a roast. He attempts once more to fully penetrate her, but cannot. As much as he tries to force his way in, his penis only yields and bends. He braces the shaft with his fist in a last ditch effort for success, only to fail once more.

Blood begins to trickle out of a small tear in her vagina.

The applied lubricant, having now dried completely, leaves a curious sour aroma behind. Finally giving up, he decides to pull out, his sticky foreskin catching on her dry labia as his phallus retreats.

"I'm sorry," she says, acknowledging her husband's frustration.

He can't stay erect for much longer.

"You sure are sorry. Finish the job."

Pressure is relieved on her trachea as he shifts his hand towards the back of her head. Yanking her head forward, he begins to smother her face with his engorged penis. Her hot exhalation on his glans makes him giddy with excitement. Horrified, she makes a muffled cry and pulls away. The bed feels wet. She looks down and sees her inner thighs smeared with blood, her husband's pubic hair and scrotum bare flecks and patches of red offset from her injuries.

"Oh, that's it, bitch. You some kind of Holy Roller? You too good to suck me off? You Bible-thumping whore!"

She falls off the bed in a fright. Grabbing a frayed blanket on the floor, she scoots to the corner of the room.

"Please," she says, taking a breath. "Please, no more."

"I'm getting my dick wet one way or another! And seeing how you have a case of grandma pussy, which obviously comes with a headache..."

He halts mid-sentence. Ignoring his appearance, he drags himself to the edge of bed and while massaging his injured hand, stands up with a renewed conviction.

"I'll look elsewhere."

She jumps up from the corner and grabs at the mattress, pulling herself toward him.

"I'll do it! I'm sorry! I'll do it!"

"Too late bitch," he states with disinterest.

The floor groans under his weight as he leaves the room.

He possesses a limp, which causes him to move with a subtle unevenness. There is a punched out hollow wooden door leaning on the wall adjacent to the doorway. It has been removed from its hinges since she once tried to lock herself in this room. The sound of her husband's sticky feet adhering and then pulling away from the vinyl flooring becomes fainter. She looks in the direction of where she thinks she heard the soft thud earlier. She begins to crawl, but her movement is impaired by the tender throbbing sensation between her legs. Moving slowly through the filth of discarded tissues and overdue utility bill envelopes that are strewn across the floor, she makes her way to the far side of the room. Looking straight ahead she can see it, near a half-empty bottle of generic dark cola, the Word of God, lying face down in his soiled work shirt. Its final page reflects in a glow, standing out in stark contrast to its surroundings. She outstretches her hand.

In a much smaller room, a boy nearly oblivious to his surroundings, grips action figures in each hand and bashes them together repeatedly. Within his peripheral vision, the reverse side of a Worldwide Wrestling Federation blanket pulled over his head, the top of a bare mattress, action figures, and himself. He sits hunched over cross-legged, a flashlight positioned between his legs, pointing upward. His constant fidgeting creates a perpetual change of his shadow. It grows and shrinks, at times almost completely engulfing his surroundings in darkness only to retreat a moment later. He makes peculiar sounds, imitating the howls and taunts of grown men fighting in his soft whispers.

Behind him lies a small spiral-bound notepad with a fighter's bracket crudely sketched onto it reading "Tonight: Bam Bam Bigelow vs. Capt. Kamata." Further names are scribbled on the paper, but the writing is illegible. The boy is in the middle of positioning Captain Kamata for an aerial maneuver as a loud crack pulls attention away from the match. He jolts up and grabs for his flashlight. Without missing a beat, he depresses the button, cloaking the entire room in darkness. Moving slowly, he pokes his head out from the blanket. The bombast poster of Manuel el Monsturo Jr., a popular Mexican luchador, looks down at him from the wall holding his CMLL championship belt.

His mattress reverberates with the sound of popping springs. He slows his breathing and listens intently for any further noises coming from the house. After a long break of absolute silence, muffled cries start coming through the walls. His heart races. The pulsating is felt first in his chest, then spreads to his stomach. The sensation travels down his leg slowly, slithering downward to his feet like a lazy worm. It then makes its way up, through his neck, and towards his face. It passes behind his eye like rising mercury and finally peaks at the top of his head.

A throbbing in his temples grows and the faint cries seeping into the room are overpowered with the sound of his own thundering heartbeat. A tickle coming from somewhere below his intestinal wall notifies him of the need to purge his bladder. He tries to move his legs, but can no longer figure out how to do so. Do the mechanics involved in standing up initially take place in the feet, knees, or hips? The room seems suspended in time with him frozen to the bed. He becomes conscious of a sharp pain in his back and concludes that he must be lying atop his spiral-bound notebook. He wishes he could just go to sleep, but can't remember how to do that either. He thinks he can hear the soft padding of feet coming from the hall though he cannot tell if the sound is growing or shrinking. With his own pulse a deafening drumbeat in his ear, he can't be absolutely certain if he heard anything at all. He takes in a breath and holds it. Focusing his auditory faculties directly outside his door, he can now confirm the footsteps. A lumbering now immediately outside his room causes him to lose his breath.

He shuts his eyes and tries to project himself to the hall. In what condition is this fumbling terror? What does it want tonight?

The creature outside his door permits him a short moment of silence. Then, with a burst of thunder, his bedroom door flies inward. The letters comprising his name, which hang on the door, rattle like bones. He opens his eyes just enough to see the naked silhouette of his father standing in the doorway.

"You sleeping?" his father asks.

The covers are pulled up to his nose. His father may just ignore him this time.

"Mike!"

He pulls the covers down to his chest and fakes lethargy as he answers.

"I'm sleeping Dad. What do you want?"

Mike's soft cries, through his father's intermittent grunts, are audible from across the hallway. His mother, curled in the corner, tugs the polyester blanket pitted from cigarette embers over her shoulders and clasps the leather-bound relic in her arms.

"Remember not the sins of my youth, nor my transgressions: according to thy mercy remember thou me for thy goodness' sake, O Lord," she repeatedly whispers in hope of being answered.

II.

Twenty-five years later.

A jet black SUV is parked in front of a two-story home with faded azure vinyl siding. Aside from a very light scratch in the SUV's driver's side door, due to someone carelessly handling the keys, the vehicle is seemingly spotless. A young man covered in tattoos sits in the passenger's seat. His hair is of a very peculiar color. One isn't sure whether to classify the hue as a red or an orange—it could be either—but it certainly isn't anything natural.

He has a voice with just enough nasal acoustics to be mistaken as pubescent. His clean-shaven face only adds to any already held suspicion of his immaturity as those who sell him tobacco frequently request that he present his identification. The young man's fitting nickname, Fish, is perhaps to some an even further indicator of his inexperience.

A man sitting next to Fish in the driver's seat is comparatively very ordinary. He is 33, just shy a decade older than his partner sitting shotgun. He wears a cabbie hat that was most likely purchased at a discount store as one can discern from the shoddy stitching. The only thing that doesn't compliment his ordinariness is the gaudy jogging suit that he wears. Although also purchased at the same discount store as his hat, the cerulean-colored ensemble, coupled with its synthetic sheen and what looks to be a fresh mustard stain on his right thigh, create an optically-disturbing effect for anyone caring to look at him. His keys dangle from the ignition. A circular white button with the name *Ringo* decorates his key ring. He drums his fingers against the steering wheel anxiously as the two wait for one more person to join them. Fish looks upward to the second story of the house they are parked in front of.

"Hurry up dude. Let's get this shit over with!" Fish calls out impatiently with a shrill overtone.

Just as Fish begins scrutinizing one of the second floor windows for movement, a monstrous shadow is diffused over the blinds, and the room suddenly goes dark. A door slams from somewhere inside the building and its echoes are carried across the street. The front door flies open and a tall figure strides down the stoop. His stature is intimidating to most, standing no less than six and a half feet high. A large portion of the man's muscle has receded under a layer of fat, but this only adds more mass to his already-frightening appearance. The skin on his arms is stained with the ink of tattoo artists, done at different times by different people in different places who had different things in mind when they took the needle to him. Nothing sensible can be made out from the hotchpotch of band names, mythical creatures, sexual innuendos, fictional characters, and idiomatic expressions in foreign—if not dead—languages scribbled into his arm. Compelled to ridicule but suppressed by fright, one can only stand in dumb amazement at this bleached-blond graffiti-covered barbarian.

Nearly tripping over an overlooked obstruction at the very bottom, the towering figure leaps over the last few steps.

He stops and looks behind to see what caught his foot.

The obstruction stirs, slowly growing; it begins to take the shape of a young girl. Her hair color is very plain brown. A hormonal imbalance due to her overwhelming consumption of calories leaves her with enough facial hair to put most boys of the same age to shame. Her size is massive, and it stresses her naturally petite skeletal frame, causing constant pain in her lower joints. Gravity is her oppressor. Her demeanor, needless to say, is rarely anything other than melancholic. She is moping.

A disembodied voice from within the building yells out to the tattooed man.

"Be careful dumbass!"

He scans the house's lower windows and sees one partially open. Eying it, he shouts back an apology.

"Sorry!"

Ignoring the two eagerly waiting men in the SUV, he turns toward the girl.

"What's wrong Betty?"

She responds in a barely audible tone.

"My uncle won't give me money for ballet."

"Just ask Ana for the money. She'll give it to you," he coolly responds...

Concluding that this advice is more than sufficient, he begins to walk away with an air of accomplishment.

The tearful girl calls out to him.

"He said I'm too fat to be seen in public! He said I would make the family look like fat fools!"

The towering man stops in step and curses the Creator under his breath. Apprehensively, he turns his attention back to the continuously morphing mass addressing him. He slowly approaches her, hoping not to upset her any further with improperly-calculated advice. He crouches beside her, his left knee pops under his weight. He addresses Betty with sincerity.

"Who cares what others think? So what if you're a big girl? If daytime TV has taught me anything—and it hasn't—it's that you have two paths you can take. You can work hard and when you grow up you will be hot and can tell all the boys who made fun of you to fuck off, or... you can cry on my front steps and give up and be the fat bitch that needs a crane to get out of her house."

"You really think I can be the hot girl one day?" she asks, sounding slightly hopeful.

"Sure!" he quickly responds. He would like nothing more than to wrap this consultation up within the next minute. "I mean, no one ever would have thought Ana would be the hot chick she is today."

Betty looks to him smiling and replies, "Ana is beautiful."

A window squeaks open from behind them. Ana, a woman with blue streaks in her onyx black hair, props her arms up on the windowsill and sticks her upper body out of the building. Her breasts are plump and nearly hanging out of her low-cut shirt. Her extended arms propped up on the window put pressure on either side, squeezing them oblong as she bends over further to get a good look at the two conversing. Her lipstick is a shade of dark blue. Everything else is black—the manicured nails, her eyeliner, mascara, sculpted eyebrows, and earrings. She has no observable dermatic inconsistencies. She smiles at Betty, showing off her flawless teeth. Arguably, Ana's one and only and greatest shortcoming is her absolute lack of refinement.

"I'll teach you how to be a hottie, toots," she says to Betty through a piece of bubblegum in her mouth.

Ana's sudden appearance causes unrestrained ululating from the two men in the SUV. They watch in fervor as her half-visible figure turns and twists. Fish turns to Ringo in excitement.

"I would own that pussy! I mean really fucking own it. Get in those guts and pound the shit out of her."

Ana places her open hand next to her mouth. "I can hear you!" she shouts to the SUV.

Fish blushes in shame.

Ringo scoffs at Fish's freshly-sanguine complexion before shouting out the window.

"Hey Freakshow, are you almost done with princess tub-tub?"

The tattoo-covered man seems irritated and answers back.

"Fish, Ringo, do me a favor... and shut the fuck up!"

He consolingly puts his arm around Betty. He can't stick around much longer.

"Betty, I've gotta go. Ana can help you out."

He pats Betty on the back and then dashes toward the SUV, approaching the comfortably-seated Fish.

"Shotgun bitch."

He swings the passenger side door open and ejects Fish into the back with little difficulty.

III.

Mike Bua stands in front of a ticket booth holding onto the hands of Maki. Constant announcements over the speakers allow them seldom a moment of silence to reflect on their situation. Mike, a tall attractive man with commendable physique and excellent hygiene, is not the sort of person you would expect to see getting sentimental. The discharge from both of their tear ducts is a leaden weight on their lower eyelids.

Mike Bua speaks in a calm tone.

"Please, don't leave. We can get past this."

Maki can feel her chest tightening. Her eyes are no longer able to support the volume of fluid being flushed into them. They overflow.

Maki's communication skills in English are more than sufficient. An impressive level of erudition in vocabulary alone provides her command and versatility in many subjects and topics, but what she makes up in one, she lacks in another. Her accent is still befuddled with poorly-pronounced consonant combinations and intonational errors. More than acceptable in an urban setting, however, anyone living in rural areas would be quickly nauseated by this petite Asian's cacophonic English. Studious, yet not pragmatic, her study materials consisted of books, not of real conversation with people.

She looks down at Mike's large hands cradling hers. Her conscious thought operates entirely in Japanese.

"I will always love you Mike, but we can't, and never, will get through this."

Upon hearing this, Mike's eyes are freshly supplied with warm fluid. He is angered by his body's physiological response to sadness as a potent dose of adrenaline is released. His hands begin to shiver from the stress. His disposition has him considering whether or not he should rip the ticket counter off from the floor. He blinks with rapidity in hopes of dispelling the tears in his eyes. He feels not only shame when he cries, but humiliation as well. If anyone he knew were to see him in this state, he would be mortified. In his state, simple eye contact from a stranger could spark a regrettably violent outburst. Mike struggles to regain control. His breathing becomes spasmodic.

His voice cracks.

"I'm so sorry."

"I know you are," Maki replies.

"I will always love you and always be there for you," he assures her.

Maki wipes her tears away with her palms, wraps her arms around Mike, and plants a kiss on his cheek.

"I know," she softly says into his ear.

She slowly approaches the ticket counter, wheeling what little luggage she has behind her. It is all she carries with her now. Everything else was sent out weeks ago. Mike watches with now bloodshot eyes. His legs are quaking. He needs a drink to relax his senses.

IV.

A digital clock is recessed in the dashboard. It was manufactured to appeal to more traditional tastes, but it is merely a parody of true craftsmanship. The second hand plods across its face in silence. The passing seconds slowly dissolve to black as the illuminated indicator flickers onward, measuring time with more accuracy than a common user can even begin to appreciate. It has no notches and no numerical markings. If you were to open it, you would find neither springs nor cogs. This quasi-analog chronometer, being installed in this particular automobile, was tailored for the "classical taste with a modern touch" demographic. The design is highly impractical. Unless the minute hand is falling exactly on a quarter division of the hour, it's damn near impossible to read the exact minute.

The clock reads something around ten-forty.

Ringo, Freakshow, and Fish are seated in the SUV. It is parked and the engine is off. The static atmosphere of the suburbs at night invokes an apathy in the trio. Their senses long for excitement. Ringo gazes bleary-eyed into the face of the clock's second indicator pulsating around in circles. Fish lies down on the back seat and rhythmically bounces a small rubber ball against the ceiling. Freakshow sits with his eyes closed and arms crossed as if meditating.

Ringo's hypnotic state is broken by the unremitting thumps being made against the headliner. He turns to look back. A small strip of orange cast from a streetlamp is like a color-reactive liquid spilt on Fish's torso.

"Fish, you are driving me fucking insane with that goddamn ball! Act like this isn't your first rodeo, kid!"

Ringo whacks Fish in his thigh. Fish responds with a sudden jolt of offensive force from his leg. The vehicle begins to rock as they flail in fury, throwing blind punches and kicks at one another. In the narrow space of the cabin nothing connects.

Freakshow's voice cuts in.

"I'm about to boogie cock you fools, like I do when Ana acts up."

The two refrain from their antics and look to each other in confusion.

"You'll do what?" Fish asks.

Ringo sees the preemptive opportunity and manages to get a final swing in, which is deflected off of Fish's knee. Ringo fixes his posture and twisted clothing, then turns to Freakshow.

"What did you just say?"

"What, you guys don't know what a boogie cock is?"

"I do," Fish proudly states.

"Then what the hell is it champ?" Ringo asks, sucking his teeth.

"It's when, ahh... You know, when you punch someone in the balls," Fish says, sounding very unsure.

"That's a bang cock," Freakshow quickly corrects just as Ringo butts in with what he feels is a very important fact, followed by a rhetorical question.

"Fish, you're a retard. Why the fuck would a dude want to punch himself in the nuts to get back at a girl?"

Fish reflects for a moment, and then decides to follow up with his own question.

"Then what's a boogie cock?"

Freakshow clears his throat.

"First, you gotta make sure your victim is dead asleep, preferably facedown. You sneak into her room and if she isn't in position already you can either wait, or if she's a real deep sleeper, you can position her yourself. Then you start rubbing one out."

Fish, smiles and sits upright. Adjusting his pants, he comments, "Man, I already rub one out every night to Ana."

"Shut the fuck up Fish and let the man finish his story," Ringo interjects.

Freakshow continues, "You get real close to her face and right before you cum, you give her a real hard smack in the ass."

Grinning, he mimes the act by smacking his right hand open-palmed into his left, creating a high decibel slap that is quickly absorbed into the fabric-lined interior of the vehicle. "If you time it right, you'll blow a load in her face right as she opens her eyes. Then you yell BOOGIE COCK!"

The story ends. Ringo has a look of confusion on his face. As the comic imagery of such a genius prank sinks in, his diaphragm begins to spasm and he finds himself roaring in low-pitched guffaws. Freakshow chuckles to himself as Fish giggles lightly in the backseat.

"Boogie cock," he says cutting through Ringo's laughter. "That is fucking brilliant!"

V.

Blinking neon lights infinitely divide as they bounce off the multitude of reflective car hoods, windows, and mirrors. Mike Bua sits in his car, parked outside a place marked Sal's Arabian Nights. His car reflects the ostentatious display, a grand welcome to customers. All the cars parked here have adopted the colorful properties of the monstrous sign. They look like large shiny chameleons positioned over a grid. Smaller neon indicators hanging in the only window the place has advertise the various brands of alcoholic beverages the establishment carries. Mike, slouching in the driver's seat, grips onto the neck of a bottle. As he raises it to his lips to finish it off, it dribbles down his chin and falls upon his shirt, landing very near a badge that hangs around his neck. A photograph of a small dark-haired girl is placed behind the steering wheel, hiding the speedometer.

Mike opens his car door. The dome light fails to come on. It has been burnt out for some time. He closes the door behind him, not bothering to lock it, and walks toward the entrance of the building. As he opens the door, the sound of blaring hair metal arrests his senses. A mulatto man wearing a shirt one size too small stands by the door with his arms crossed, wearing a stern expression. He's trying entirely too hard to look intimidating.

The man looks to Mike's chest, acknowledges the badge, and nods his head in a gesture of goodwill, as if there were some unspoken understanding between those who occupy various positions of authority. Mike is visibly annoyed by the bouncer's false notion of camaraderie between them. He should have left his badge in the car. Unfortunately, he's entirely too drunk to give a shit about anything anymore.

A small corridor ending with a tacky transparent beaded curtain leads him to the main room. Passing the curtain, he turns immediately to the right and takes a seat at the bar's empty counter. Adjusting himself on the stool, he orders a beer from the dismal-looking bartender. Her makeup, on top of the cold lighting, disguise her age fairly well. Anyone intoxicated under normal conditions certainly wouldn't be able to guess anywhere near her true age. Her breasts have a youthful perkiness and look very well maintained. Aside from a small scar visible at an angle on either side, they are practically perfect. The bar stools look brand new and a blue ambient lighting has been recently installed along the underside of the counter; not yet steeped in the atmosphere of thick smoke and alcohol laden air. Up front men clamor for an encore of a performer, who now having gathered her tips, exits the stage. Capacity is at fifty percent. Not bad for a weekday.

Mike reaches in his pocket and pulls out the photograph. His hand gently cradles the picture to discourage prying eyes. The girl in the photo wears a white floral-patterned dress. His inner ear floods with a viscous soup that drowns out all sound. He closes his eyes in an effort to recall the moment when the picture was taken. A sudden sharpness in his chest shoots up his spine. As his heartbeat quickens, his legs are locked with tension. He shuts his eyes and works to slow his breathing. The pain slowly begins to subside and Mike regains control of his senses. The bartender, being bored and wanting to earn a decent tip, disregards Mike's sullen mood and approaches him.

"Should you be wearing that while drinking?" she asks, pointing to the leather inlaid with a shield hanging from his neck.

"Huh?" Mike wasn't paying the bartender the slightest attention. "Whatever..." he responds, wishing to return to his stupor.

The bartender employs her flawed rationale. Figuring that a police officer could use advice from a former stripper, she leans down on the counter to get eye contact with him and addresses him once more.

"I'm saying, it could be dangerous or against the rules or something."

"Hey Breasty McBreastalot, how about you shut the fuck up and get me another one of these?" Mike swills his near empty bottle of beer in the air.

She steps aside, revealing a glass door refrigerator directly behind her. She opens a bottle and slides it in front of him. Deciding it would be better to stop bringing up the badge, she changes the subject. Catching a glimpse of the photograph in his hand, she tries again.

"Who's the little girl?"

He draws his listless eyes to hers.

"It was my daughter."

"Was...?"

Mike jumps up from his stool and sends it flying behind him. He grabs the bartender by her top, nearly spilling her tits out onto the bar counter. The bouncer notices and quickly advances towards Mike, but not quite sure of the protocol in subduing police officers, he keeps a distance and simply yells out empty threats.

Mike wears a pinched expression of hatred on his face. He speaks fervently.

"Don't you fucking talk to me ever again. You're just a fucking whore. A no-good whore. You think you're not because you serve me drinks and ask me questions, but you're wrong. You are just as big of a whore as the girls on stage. Maybe you're even a bigger whore because it would be way easier to get a blowjob from you then from them."

After finishing his thought, Mike releases her in revelation of his severely-stressed mental state.

A different voice carrying a thick accent booms from behind him.

"Do we have a fucking problem?"

Mike turns around to a new face. A tall and thin man with discolored tape over the bridge of his nose shifts his weight from his left leg to his right. His skin is dark and his left eyelid hangs down farther than his right. He wears an old tweed suit that's fraying at the cuffs. Mike becomes aware of a spicy odor that seems to be emanating from this ethnic-looking man's twinkling pores.

"Who the fuck are you?" he asks.

"I'm Sal."

There is a short pause after his name, inserted for dramatic effect.

"I'm the fucking guy who owns all this and will kick you the fuck out, assface."

His accent is thick, his phrasing choppy. He still needs to work on his insults, but, nevertheless, he gets his point across. His eyes are drawn to the flickering yellow seal hanging from Mike's neck. He changes his demeanor.

"I'm sorry. I didn't realize that you were one of the boys. Is there a problem here at my fine establishment, officer?"

"No Sal. There's no problem," the bartender says,

answering for Mike as she adjusts her top.

Mike speaks for himself. "Yeah, we've got a problem. Where the hell are all the good-looking bartenders tonight?"

The bartender scowls and walks to the far end of the bar with an unnecessary force in her step, making it certain to all how upset she is.

Mike calls to her. "Now, how about a fucking drink, whore!"

Sal maneuvers behind the counter, fetches a bottle from the fridge, and opens it. He speaks in a consoling tone and he places it in front of Mike.

"This one is on me, pal."

"Why?" Mike questions on the offensive.

"Because I said so," Sal says, pushing the bottle an extra inch toward Mike.

Sal walks toward the bartender and puts his arm around her. Words are exchanged between them but cannot be understood by Mike through the din of customers and loudly-reverberating speakers. Body language would strongly suggest that Sal is coaching her, probably in customer service.

Mike slowly opens his palm and becomes lost in the photograph once more.

VI.

Ana and Betty relax on a sofa together. The room they occupy is painted white with a decorative trim of green ivy along the ceiling. There is a floor lamp next to the sofa with a single globose paper lamp shade on top. It filters out specific waves of light, bathing the quaint room in peach. There is a pinball machine in the far corner. A large oak coffee table with a glass top sits in front of them. A potent smell emanates from three neat piles of bagged marijuana placed atop the table.

Betty gazes in awe. Their asymmetrical shape and positioning leave a strong aesthetic impression on her. The natural green hues contrasts with the glass tabletop taking on the peach color of the ceiling it reflects. It's a simple beauty that cannot be expressed in words. She feels as if she has reached a greater understanding of things. Her thoughts encompass both the simple and profound. She opens her mouth and speaks with brevity.

"I fucking love this place."

"Hey," Ana responds in surprise. You're not supposed to be talking like that."

Betty forces a cheeky smile. Ana looks at her ridiculous expression and starts chuckling to herself. Betty joins in.

The wall directly in front of them is lined with three big-screen televisions. The center screen flickers with images of a cheaply-produced local commercial. A mustachioed business owner with a Polish family name seems to be lost in all the surplus furniture at his store. Pictures of living room and dining room sets play like a slideshow on the green screen behind him. He swings his arms in bewilderment at the incredibly low prices. He frantically reads off the names and brands of items to be liquidated. His voice doesn't project and sounds digitally enhanced. He is a very poor salesman. Despite the incredibly-affordable mattresses, they are all too repelled by this local celebrity's buffoonery. The commercial only leaves them feeling embarrassed. Suddenly, a discretionary warning shows on the screen.

"The show is on," Ana says with excitement.

The television is entirely too loud. The screen fades to black and a narrator's voice cuts through the void of the screen.

"Previously on *Lost*..."

Betty looks euphoric as she cuddles against Ana.

"I love this show."

VII.

The engine of the SUV has now cooled completely. Freakshow stares out onto the uniform lawn of one of the neighborhood's residents. Ringo is currently attending to an itch under his left armpit as Fish dozes off in the backseat. Freakshow decides to break the silence, seeking Ringo's advice with something that has been bothering him for some time.

"You think Sal is still pissed off at me?" he asks.

"Oh, fuck yeah," Ringo sluggardly replies as he stifles a belch. "You broke his nose, on top of the other shit-kicking you gave him, just because he tried to get a peek at Ana's goods."

Fish, overhearing the conversation, sits up with a look of intrigue. He pushes his shoulders against the seat. Lifting his waist, he plunges both of his hands into the pockets of his trousers and retrieves a crumpled sandwich bag containing a stubby joint and some discarded seeds. Reaching inside, he takes the joint out, positions it in his curled lips, and produces a transparent purple lighter. Igniting and inhaling, he watches on as the dialoguing silhouettes of Ringo and Freakshow against the front windshield create a cinematic illusion.

Freakshow continues.

"Yeah, but he has to understand, no one touches Ana. No one."

"I don't see the big deal with you Show. She's a stripper! I can't figure how she can be the only girl who doesn't fucking flash her pussy on stage. How does she even work there?"

"Send him a fruit basket Freakshow!" Fish arbitrarily ejaculates, uncertain of what prompted such a solution.

Taken aback by the overenthusiastic interjection, the two look back at Fish in unison.

"What the fuck are you talking about?" Ringo asks.

Fish tentatively pleads his case. "Listen, you got Sal sitting in his filthy one desk office. He's ready to conduct interviews with girls who don't know they're about to sell their souls. Maybe he's in a pissy mood because some deal didn't go through as expected."

He breaks for an obnoxiously long drag and jars the smoke in his lungs. "So... Sal's muscle walks in, not escorting in the next interview, but with an armful of fuckin' fruit."

Fish exhales, cloaking himself in the white ether. "He's clueless as to whom the sender is. He'll looks at the card and it'll say, 'Sorry dude. Freakshow.'"

He snorts as he attempts to arrest his laughter. A smile breaks out over his two listener's faces. Fish regains some level of control over his senses and continues.

"Way I see it, that motherfucker has two options."

"What's that?" Freakshow asks, humoring Fish.

"Well, either he gets a chuckle and the heat is gone, or he'll call to you and say 'Go fuck yourself.'"

"What?" Ringo's asks in confusion.

Fish continues.

"If he calls you, you tell him that it was a joke and that he should go fuck himself. Shit!" Fish flicks his hand, casting away the shortened glowing joint under Ringo's seat.

"Motherfucker! Pick that shit up!" Ringo shouts, reaching back swinging his arms.

Fish, drawing his legs up to avoid Ringo's assault, sucks

on his thumb and index finger to soothe his burn.

"I hate to admit it, but that might be your best idea ever," Freakshow ambiguously states through the reensuing hijinks.

VIII.

Mike has been frozen in his chair for the past hour. Finishing off another beer, he waves his arm to get the attention of the fake-breasted bartender at the other end of the counter. His hand feels lifeless, swaying like a reed at the mercy of a breeze. The bartender begrudgingly walks toward him. Getting another bottle from the glass refrigerator, she places it in front of him and walks away. She moves so beautifully now. There is no unnecessary motion of her mouth, straining of vocal chords, or energy wasted in trying to attain eye contact.

A foul smell suddenly penetrates the air accompanied with a drink-heavy breath. Someone's head, or for purpose of a better visualization, a broken and tangled nest of hair housing a large spotted egg, materializes in the seat next to Mike.

"Hey pal!" it says. The man whom the egg belongs to grunts involuntarily after overexerting himself in speech. He must be too drunk to have noticed Mike's badge.

The bartender gestures to the man, trying to call him down to the other end of the counter. He ignores her and points his fat finger at the picture Mike still holds.

"That's one attractive little girl you got there. I got one at home. She's no looker like yours. Mine is a bit of a porker," he says, finishing off with a chortle.

Mike acknowledges the man's clueless and intoxicated state, and asks as politely as he can.

"I just want to be left alone."

"Listen, miss fatty wants to be a ballerina of all things... or something like that."

His arm outstretches and swings around to rest on Mike's shoulder.

Mike grabs the man's limb and throws him to the ground in a debilitating judo move. A surge of blood reaches Mike's head. He feels the absolute need to take a seat once more. As he is doing so, security quickly pounces on the man lying on the floor and pulls him to his feet.

"What the fuck did I do?" the man yells. His grizzled hair dances in the path of an overhead air duct as he is dragged and thrown out the door.

Mike's head throbs with the constant circulating of his thinned blood. He grips the edge of the counter in an effort to halt his capsizing inner ear. He shuts his eyes and beckons to the bartender to provide him with another beer, although he can't be sure if she's looking or not.

"Hey Holmes," a voice calls out.

Mike keeps his eyes closed and hopes whoever is speaking is not addressing him.

"Hey Holmes, I'm talking to you."

The voice is louder now. A vein running over Mike's left temple dilates.

"I'm talkin' to you, esé! I think it's messed up with what happen with you and Jose."

Mike, employing the aid of his brow, manages to lift open his eyelids. The bar slowly comes into focus. Pushing his hands off the counter, he spins himself around, still not excluding the possibility that the voice is not even directed at him.

"You listening to me?"

Mike raises his head to see a young man of Latino persuasion—though he assumes to be Mexican—with a shaved head and exquisitely cropped facial hair. Surrounding him are what look like his siblings—all wearing their pants in the same manner, all having the same over-sized shirts, and all wearing some sort of glittering-earlobe accessory. Scanning their physique, and not troubling himself with exact size numbers, Mike hopes none of them are carrying any weapons.

"You wear that because you think it makes you look tough?" the voice says, gesturing at Mike's chest with a wave.

Perhaps a fight is exactly what Mike Bua needs at this point. He doubts he'll be able to handle them all should they rush him at once. He closes his hand, careful not to crease the photograph it holds.

"You ever get tired of being a stereotype?" Mike asks, trying to be antagonizing.

Mike's chest caves and he flies backward as the bar counter greets him just above his kidneys. His reaction time is lagging terribly. He can't even remember how much he has had to drink tonight. Just as Mike begins to ask himself who in the hell Jose even is, he feels a jolt in his stomach. He drops down on one knee and tries to regain a lost breath. He can hear the bouncer hollering in the background. Whoever threw that punch knew how to lock their wrist. The pain is a little more than he expected. Mike keeps his head down and silently rebukes himself. It feels like the better half of what he's imbibed this evening is trying to make its way back up his esophagus. He grimaces and tries to keep it down. It would be a shame to waste anything.

"Hit me again and I'll break your arm," he says, with overconfident swagger.

Mike Bua can hear their mocking laughter, though he

doesn't bother himself with looking up.

"You fucking believe this guy?" someone exclaims from the back.

Someone comes at him with a punch, but he sees it coming this time. He grabs at the attacker's wrist with both hands and guides the appendage into a hyperextended position, rolling onto his back in the process. The photograph is smothered between his hand and the assailant's dark-skinned arm. A sound not unlike the thick pop of firewood is heard. A harsh cry of pain follows and the entire room seems to go silent. Mike can't even hear the bouncer anymore. Mike drags his body upright. Very confused glances are exchanged among the remaining members before it is unanimously decided, through body language, that they should jump him all together. The beating is one of impromptu discord.

Mike, gripping onto his photograph, blindly swings his elbows, trying to push through them. His cumbersome legs catch on something. Something cold and very hard stings his cheekbone. His head reels from the impact. Gravity seems to be exerted on his side now. He can see the filthy dark-brown flooring of the club running for miles. He holds his hands up to his face. He wants nothing more than to be lost in the photograph once more, but the frenzy of heels and outsoles pummeling his body keep him lucid.

IX.

The television is turned off. Betty's fidgeting is at no end. She decides it is better to stand up and pace around the room than to disturb a dozing Ana. This would be an appropriate time to utilize the recently purchased Guilded Ages pinball machine in the corner. Perhaps it would take her mind off of things. If only the sound card installed simulated something other than army war cries, clashing steel, and roaring dragons. There is an unsightly indentation on the couch cushion where Betty always sits. She asks herself why no one bothers to rotate the cushions. Her toes wiggle involuntarily, a reminder of why she got up in the first place.

Ana opens her eyes.

"Maybe you should stop smoking. You don't seem right," she says, noticing Betty's anxious state.

"Ana," Betty responds in apprehension, "I've gotta tell you something."

"What's up, twitchy?" Ana asks, not picking up on the subtle change in her friend's tone.

"I'm moving soon." Betty lets the gravity sink in before proceeding. "But I don't wanna go. I want to move in with you and Freakshow and stay here forever. Well, not forever, but you know."

Ana makes a gesture for Betty to sit down, but Betty

shakes her head in disagreement. Moisture begins beading on her sloped forehead.

Ana, remaining seated, grasps Betty's hand.

"Calm down Betty. Why and when are you moving?"

"I'm pregnant, and my uncle doesn't want us to stay here anymore." Betty feels a slight relief in the atmosphere.

"You mean your uncle that used to touch you?"

Ana wishes to follow up with the sensational question of who the father is, but Betty starts venting.

"Jose says that I'm a whore! He says he doesn't want our 'freaky white trash' neighbors to laugh at us. He started throwing things at me. He said we're going to Mexico to visit his sister." Betty's hand turns cold in Ana's grip. "He wants me to get an abortion!"

The room is still.

Tears running off Betty's pallid complexion drop onto her companion's bare arm. Ana stands up and embraces Betty's clammy rotund body.

"I'm sorry Betty." Ana can't seem to articulate words anymore. "I don't know what to say. How about... I know, you stay the night and we can talk to Freakshow when he gets back in. He'll know what to do."

At first Betty refrains from giving any signs of understanding. Then, pressing her face against Ana's shoulder, she softly reassures herself.

"Yeah, Freakshow's a good guy. He'll know what to do."

X.

Fish lays down, his body imitating a viscous fluid. A force of gaseous weight on his chest causes his ribcage to slowly collapse. An exasperated sigh flees his lungs.

"Man, I'm so fucking bored. Why don't we just go in there and kill everyone?"

Freakshow searches for Fish's countenance in the rearview mirror, only to realize that his partner is once again lying down and out of sight.

"Calm down Sniper Joe," he says to his seemingly invisible counterpart. "Last time I checked, your short-ass has never killed anyone."

"I will one day," Fish inhales. "I'm not scared."

Ringo mutters something to Freakshow, which is unintelligible to Fish in the back. Freakshow lets out a low-pitched snigger which is cut short by a barely-audible shout coming from somewhere in the neighborhood. Ringo's ears tense, trying to pinpoint the direction of the voice. He hesitates to swallow, fearing his attuned ears will lose the frequency forever.

Freakshow scans the row of expensively-constructed homes for movement. Fish, unaware of any sound but perceiving an abnormality, flings his torso upright. Resting his hands on the front headrests, he peers out the windshield. A heavy wooden door slams shut. All three of them now sit frozen with eyes fixated on a dark figure shifting on a lawn.

Ringo speaks in a near whisper.

"Well, well. What the fuck is this?"

"Our lucky break," Freakshow replies.

Slowly taking shape, a man swings his arms in a tantrum. Fabric dangles from his waist and stirs in the breeze with every uproarious gesture. He raises a clenched fist in a paroxysm of anger. Inflating his chest, he spins on a heel to face the house.

"I'm going to lock her in her room forever!" he wails.

A female's silhouette shifts in the doorway. An illumination from deeper inside the house outlines her voluptuous curves. An inappropriately thin nightgown cloaking her seems to dissolve into the luminescence. She looks to the figure traipsing over the lawn and addresses it in a pleading fashion.

"Do you even know where she is?" She waits for an answer until understanding that he's probably not listening. "Please, don't do anything stupid. Think of the election!"

Her voice is sultry and cracks under strain of excess volume. She is incapable of calling the figure back should it leave the threshold of the lawn.

"I'm going to fucking kill him!" he answers back in a slur.

Drunken with rage, he storms across the lawn onto the ashen-grey pavement. His feet patter against the concrete in an arrhythmic fashion. Hanging suspenders are reset onto his shoulders and an awkward hand attempts to rebutton an opened dress shirt.

Fish watches intently and his heart begins to race.

The muffled jingle of keys is followed by the sound of rigid lock tumblers. An unlatching is heard and a door opens casting light on the man—middle-aged, slightly disheveled, with an exceptionally youthful hairline. He stands aside a silver Escalade and quickly scans his surroundings before climbing in. The door shuts and a smooth mechanical whirring resonates into the hollow suburb. The silver vehicle begins to pull away.

Fish cups a hand over his mouth and pushes a thumb down, miming a radio transmitter. His opposite hand juts out an index finger, pointing at the large silver box on wheels gliding ever so further away. "Follow that car!" he confidently commands in a very poor impersonation of a Prohibition Era detective.

"Godammit Fish..," Ringo starts.

Fish drops his finger and throws himself back into his seat.

"I know, I know. I'll shut the fuck up."

Ringo has the headlights off. He does his best to keep a distance with the Escalade. They wind through the confusingly-constructed grid of American suburbia. Streets curve around and sometimes run parallel to themselves. It's an extremely tedious route and at times almost seems as if the man driving the Escalade is aware he is being followed; if not, just a product of pure paranoia. This developed area is massive, or at least seems so. Ringo can't be sure whether they're encountering new areas or doubling over. The houses have no distinguishable features from one another, and are set so far back that one can hardly read the addresses which are impractically spelled out in alphabet anyway.

The Escalade, ignoring a stop sign, turns right onto a slightly-wider road. Ringo flicks on his headlights and continues to shadow the vehicle, maintaining a seven-second distance buffer. Soft suburban light posts give way to the harsh and aged yellow beams of highway lights. Vacant lots turn into empty fields as the landscape ebbs in the night. The patch of highway they travel gradually becomes more familiar.

The Escalade gives off a bright red sheen and disappears from the road. Ringo decelerates and searches out the driver's side window for the detour.

"At least we know where he's going," Fish proudly deduces.

A dirt road stretches out to their left and the flicker of bouncing tail lights is visible. Ringo pulls onto the path and switches to his lowest lumen setting. The further down the road they go, the more the wooded area asserts itself around their vehicle. At first it was mere twigs, then as towering trunks that blot out the night firmament. A ravine on either side that tapers and widens acts as a funneling abyss and doesn't afford them the leeway to turn around. Broken glass occasionally glimmers on the leaf littered road. From farther up, a fire reaches its long arm of warmth into the woods. In about one-hundred feet ahead the road will open up towards the lake, a popular destination for neighborhood teenagers looking to escape the rigamarole of study and part-time jobs.

A road on the opposite side of the lake has fallen into disuse since one of the old bridges collapsed. Appropriately dubbed "The Bridge to Nowhere," its remnants, just beyond the bonfire, go about twenty paces over the water before dropping off. Fish once recalls having hanged a stray cat from one of the wooden bridge's lower trusses a few summers ago. The Escalade pushes onward to the lake, throwing up dust in its wake. Being slowly engulfed by the growing light of the bonfire, it disappears entirely. The ravine which has guided the vehicle up to this point begins to shallow out. Freakshow reaches over to unfasten his seat belt and turns to Ringo.

"Pull over and wait here," he says.

"Why?" Fish contends in the backseat.

"Dipshit, they have to come back this way," Freakshow

curtly answers.

Ringo turns off the lights and steers the SUV over to the right side.

Freakshow sits massaging his shoulders quietly.

A clamoring of adolescents is heard shortly afterward, along with the tempest of car doors slamming and glass shattering. Engines rev and speed past the stealthily hidden SUV that Freakshow, Ringo, and Fish occupy. The rhythmic beating of the flames is snuffed out in an instant with a toppled cooler. The woods go black and a creeping miasma of smoke and dust trails behind the remaining cars that speed up the path.

XI.

Voices become less panoramic, growing more focused with every passing moment. Mike Bua's vision is horribly blurred, operating at the evolutionary equivalent of a planarian. He is only able to distinguish light and dark. His face feels warm and wet. He rubs his thumb in an affirming way over the photograph, still cradled in his half-closed fist. A large shadow inches near his face and the overpowering smell of shoe polish strikes his olfactory.

"I said let up on him! I think he's had enough," Sal shouts in his Middle-Eastern heavy English. "C'mon, you don't wreck my place and you can hang out here. Remember our deal! I cut you guys enough slack already!"

Mike is grabbed under each arm and pulled up with much effort. His head lolls from side to side. The arms release him onto his stool. Mike clumsily places his palm on his face and draws it down slowly. Luckily enough, they managed to spare his face. Thank goodness; the warm and wet sensation is only the phlegm and spittle of his attackers.

A gully makes its way down from Mike's head as suds begin to form in his hair. Urine, he thinks. Remembering that he is in fact propped up, and unless someone climbed up onto the counter and has an abnormally cool bladder, the only other logical explanation would be that this is his leftover beer. The aroma from the stream running over his nose confirms this. Finally, the clacking of an empty glass against the counter dispels his worries completely.

Not an entirely horrible ordeal. Mike's visual disorientation is mostly due to his severe intoxication and getting strangers' bodily fluids in his eyes. No permanent damage from the beating, as far as he can tell. The residual pain in his cheekbone seems to be his most serious infliction.

Chuckles from the slightly-disappointed group of hoodlums fade away. Mike's eyes slowly adjust once more to his surroundings. His reflection in the refrigerator's glass door on the other side of the counter catches his attention. He looks a lot better than he feels. The booze poured over his head moments ago washed most of the phlegm off and refreshed his complexion. There are a few tender areas around his ribcage and shoulders, but it's nothing that isn't normally draped in clothing anyway. The last thing he needs is questions being raised at work. He regains some of his composure and tries not to dwell too much on the embarrassment. Perhaps he can still redeem himself.

Still observing himself in the glass door, Mike leans in and waves his empty bottle in the air. In his pathetic state, he has no trouble getting the bartender's attention now. She approaches him with a subtle bounce in her step.

"What happened to your last bottle?" she asks.

Mike senses sarcasm. He fixes his posture and replies in bold volume.

"A bunch of Spics spilled my last drink."

Someone answers back, though Mike cannot recognize from which direction.

"Some motherfuckers never learn!" the voice says.

How many are there? Mike regrets not counting heads during his first encounter. They must be spread out all over the establishment. A small army of treading feet are heard moving toward him and the smell of shoe polish breaches the air once more. Mike waits for someone's thick accent to cut through the aggression in the room. He just doesn't know whose it's gonna be.

Sal speaks.

"Liability gentlemen! Take it outside!"

Mike slowly pivots on his stool to be face to face with his antagonists. They approach him, looking absolutely ridiculous—from the exaggerated swinging of their shoulders to the way they all seem to purposely turn out their forearms to show off their tattoos. These men only know how to handle themselves in group situations—intimidation tactics at best—but there is no substance. As these thoughts are running through Mike's head, he feels someone strike his hand.

"She's fucking hot!" one of them proclaims, holding up the photograph that was just in Mike's grasp.

Mike lunges for the photo with reckless abandon, but he is quickly subdued by two younger members of the group on each side. They hold him back. The picture is passed off to an older member who turns to smile at Mike in triumph.

"What are you, man? Some kind of child-toucher?"

The lips of everyone around Mike curl like paper catching a flame. They let out a roar of laughter, commending their senior.

"I don't blame you... I would fuck her until she called me daddy."

Making a lascivious gesture with his mouth, he takes the photograph and rubs it over his south of the border penis housed in domestically-manufactured jeans.

Mike struggles to regain control of his appendages.

"Gentlemen, outside!" Sal shouts from somewhere.

"I think you broke my friend's arm, esé."

A man—who from Mike's perspective looks like everyone else—steps forward. An unnatural curvature in his elbow cues the gasps of horror from some of the more inexperienced members of the group. Everyone else starts on a nervous low-pitched chuckling.

"See what you did to my friend? You like this?"

The photo is held up in the air, as if it were the decapitated head of a conquered chief of some opposing tribe. Rotating his shoulders, the gang leader makes two one-hundred-and-eighty-degree swoops of his arm, turning to his comrades around him. The man gripping onto Mike's right arm releases a single burst of laughter. The sound swims into Mike's ear canal and buries itself there. With a single movement, the man seeming to be leader, raises his opposite hand and shears the photograph with the skill of a cleaver. The deafening roar of hooting and ridicule in a foreign language at an unclockable syllabic rate plow through Mike's skull. He throws the grip of weight off his arms and charges at the man holding the cleft photographic paper. Mike hurls his fist like it were an iron ball and chain.

The Mexican looks forward in contest. Mike's fist connects. It pulverizes his nose and continues to travel with just enough inertia to meet the cheekbone. The opposing force of compact interwoven tissue halts Mike's fist. Absorbing extra energy, the man's bone cracks vertically up to the eye-socket. The two torn pieces of glossy paper fly out of the man's grasp as he throws his hands to his face. A primordial gurgle leaves through a useless darkened red stump on the front of his face. Blood mixed with mucous and powdered bone clog his throat as it attempts to flow downward.

Mike frantically scratches at the floor, his hands

spattered with blood, his breathing spasmodic. The room is vibrating with energy. He hears something cut through the thunder of the room. His head cocks forward with a violent jolt and darkness envelops his senses.

XII.

A phone rings.

Betty's lipid body pulls with an upward force, straightening her spine and correcting her posture. She blurts out words instinctively to no one in particular.

"Please don't pick it up," Betty says.

Ana stands and proceeds to walk to the corner of the room where a phone is mounted on the wall.

"I have to Betty," Ana replies solemnly. "It might be Show."

The handset's beige spiral cord hangs down an inch off from the floor and is tangled on itself with numerous kinks in the wire from pinching and overstretching.

"Don't you have caller ID or something?" Betty asks. Her brow furrows with worry.

Ana ignores Betty's question and lifts the receiver off its port. The nearly hollow plastic almost floats in her hands. She presses the wax-clogged speaker holes to her ear.

"What up?"

"Send Betty home now," Jose says, speaking with the slur of an apathetic jaw. His overall tone is friendly, if not somewhat inebriated.

Ana pauses, thinking of something to say.

"Is it cool if she stays the night?" she asks, speaking into the transmitter, struggling to maintain a strident tone. She tries her best to fake a smile as she looks to Betty.

"We have a big day ahead of us tomorrow, so, no. Send her home please," Jose replies, sounding exhausted. It almost sounds like he is fishing for pity.

"Ahh, she's actually already sleeping."

"Then wake her ass up and send her home!"

Jose's tone quickly changes as he throws all formalities out. The illusion of an acquaintanceship between the two quickly vanishes. Ana struggles to hold onto the phone.

"Look, it's really late. Can't she just stay the night? Then I can have Show give her a ride home in the morning."

"Listen here, you gothic freak fuck. I don't know what that no good bitch has told you, but you send her home right now or I might just have to let out your dirty little secret."

Ana wants to break the phone into a thousand pieces. Her hand holds the receiver like a vice. She wishes for nothing more than the person on the other side of the line to die. Ana becomes aware of a low volume static scratching across the lines. Jose fiddles with something that sounds like pebbles on the other side.

"Now, you wouldn't like that," Jose says as he releases his final words in triumph.

Ana forfeits her voice. She doesn't know what to say anymore.

"You understand, freak?"

The kitchen refrigerator clicks on and the sound of pebbles is heard again over the line.

Ana cautiously replies, "I understand."

Betty's palms place pressure on her eyes in an effort to try and confine her tears.

Ana hangs up the phone and returns to the couch.

"I'm really sorry Betty. You've gotta go home."

Betty is hunched over. She pouts to her knees.

"Please, let me stay."

"I'm sorry. You have to go. He already knows you're here. And, well... you know."

Betty hyper-salivates. Her lips droop, glistening with drool. She slowly brings her bottom lip up to her central incisors. Her pronunciation is lethargic, exaggerated, and stressed on the fricative. Defeat pervades the air.

"Ff-uck."

Ana moves her hand towards Betty.

"Here, take my cell phone and call me if anything happens."

Betty takes the outdated egg-shaped cellular phone out of Ana's hand and places it in the pocket of her hooded sweatshirt.

"I wish I could live with you guys, that's all. I mean..." Betty pauses for a moment. "I'll stop by tomorrow."

Ana rubs Betty's back, hoping it is of some consolation. She tries to push confidence into her voice and reassure Betty.

"Be strong, baby. How bad can it really be? He's your uncle after all. He loves you, right?"

Betty wipes her palms onto her pants, staining her large thighs with tears. She stands up, grabs her backpack, and exits Ana's room in silence.

XIII.

"Everybody, don't forget your gloves," says Freakshow with eyes fixed to the path. "Especially you Fish, your prints, your responsibility."

This is Fish's second time hearing this. "I know. I know."

The Escalade rolls onto the dirt road, the vulcanized rubber giving off a hollow pop at every obstructing pebble. The disheveled man sits in the driver's seat trying to fix his hair. He gives rebuking gestures with one hand while steering with the other. Locks of waving blonde hair sit atop the head of a comparatively smaller person in the passenger's seat. A girl, leaving her head down, releases several wails that vibrate through the vehicle and momentarily cancel out the engine's humming.

"Oh, this should be good," Ringo says, squinting his eyes. He readjusts his grip on the steering wheel.

Fish's heart races. As Freakshow takes a breath to speak, his wet lips give off a small smack that prompts everyone for orders.

"Game on," he declares.

Ringo's foot levers onto the gas. The SUV, and the three seated within it, cut onto the road revealing themselves.

The man slams on his breaks and the Escalade skids to a halt. He barely misses a collision.

Freakshow flies out of the vehicle with Ringo and Fish behind. Their guns are pulled out, aimed roughly at the Escalade's front windshield. They aren't concerned with aim right now; they only intend to show that they're serious. Freakshow wastes no time. He is calm and professional.

"Get the fuck outta the car!" he flatly commands.

Ringo steps forward, his cerulean outfit blindingly reflects the cluster of LED's in the headlights. Focusing his gun on the driver, he shimmies over to the passenger's side and flings the door open. The girl screams in fright. She violently kicks and scratches, though her still-fastened seat belt retards her movement. Ringo, bearing her attacks, reaches over with his left hand to unbuckle her. She knocks his hat off, revealing his thinning pate.

"Bitch, get out of the fucking car!" he yells at her in fury.

"Please!" the man screams, his breath staggered. "Just take whatever you want! Just leave us alone!"

An advancing Freakshow unlatches the driver's side door and pushes his gun against the man's head.

"Not today bro," he responds.

Freakshow violently yanks the conveniently-unbuckled man out from the Escalade, turns him around, and handcuffs him. Fish's gun rests in his slightly-tremoring hand.

Ringo whistles with giddiness as he wrestles the sexually-developing girl out of the vehicle and onto her feet. He forces both wrists behind her. Then, clasping them in a single fist, he latches cold steel just below her hands.

Freakshow calls out to Fish. "Fish, go park the cars in the woods."

"Fuck, why me?"

"Goddammit!" Ringo snaps in frustration. "Shut the fuck up and park the cars in the goddamn woods! Jesus Fucking Christ!"

Ringo, with one hand resting on the girl's restraints, points his pistol toward the far side of the road, indicating direction.

Freakshow and Ringo dig their firearms into the captive's backs. They guide the father and daughter to the thick woods in procession.

A set of headlights from the road behind them briefly flood their surroundings in white before swinging around and disappearing.

XIV.

Fish stumbles through the tortuous system of roots and moss-covered rocks lying upon the forest floor. They nip at his toes and claw at his ankles as he tries to navigate the utterly-black environment. He stops intermittently to catch his breath and listen for any sounds that could lead him in the right direction. No one brought flashlights, making his chances of success in finding anything near impossible. He extends his hands outward, level with his face. His pistol is tucked in his pants. The position of his arms, stiff posture, and mechanical movement of his legs are akin to some monstrous chimera from a Gothic fiction.

A splashing noise bounces off the trees. A chilling sensation fills Fish's sneaker and he immediately lifts his leaden foot out of the water. Recoiling in disgust, a warm putrid odor greets his face. He spins, loses his balance, and falls backward, his hands sinking into the gritty moisture of rotting leaves. Amid the commotion, an outline of a man suddenly appears just beyond the disfigured and swollen tree trunks, rising from the water. Observing Fish's situation, an all too familiar voice reprimands him.

"You fucking retard."

"You could have waited for me!" Fish answers to Ringo. "There's a chance I could've been lost out here forever, douche bag!"

"Fish, shut the fuck up!" Ringo replies.

Freakshow's diminutive voice sounds from somewhere farther up the woods.

"Both of you shut the fuck up and keep walking."

Fish picks himself back up. Just now realizing he does not have any gloves on, he sloshes his hands on the surface of the swamp three to four times to rinse off any excess matter collected on them. He bows his head down and sniffs his wet hands, winces at the odious smell clinging to them, then briskly walks to catch up with Ringo, Freakshow, and the two captives.

The girl sobs, looking to the forest floor as she marches forward. The handsome middle-aged gentleman's shirt is spotted with soil. His shoulder is marked with the bark of the trees he's been brushing up against. A small twig bearing a leaf is snagged on his pant leg. With Fish rejoining the group, the man seizes the opportune moment to restate his plea.

"Please, you don't have to do this." He discreetly tries to direct his voice at Fish. "Whatever you are being paid, I will double it!"

Freakshow interrupts before Fish has a chance to consider the man's offer.

"It don't work like that," he says, irritated. He shoves the man forward, reversing his step.

Ringo walks with his gun held up against the helpless girl's shoulder blade. He chuckles to himself. "This fucking guy watches way too much TV."

The man suddenly adopts a displeased demeanor and turns his head to Ringo.

"Don't you know who the fuck I am?" he asks, narrowing his eyes in defiance.

Freakshow quashes the man's attempt at pleading his

case once again.

"I don't need to know who you are. I just have a job to do."

The man's renewed conviction is quickly dispelled by Freakshow's immovable will. He feels smaller than he has ever felt before. Hope is being exsanguinated from his body. He takes six paces and his legs can move no more. Hyperventilating, he falls to his knees. His right knee lands on a sharp rock, but his nerves fail in communicating this to him.

Everyone stops in step and turns to spectate as Ringo goads the man on.

"Oh great. Here come the waterworks."

The man's face is soaked with water. His eyes are puckered and his chin shriveled. Snot flows into his mouth only to be ejected with the excess saliva running off his bottom lip. Spittle trails down his shirt.

"Please don't," he says, hardly intelligible. "I'll do anything. Please just let me and my little girl go."

He struggles to gain a breath.

"I'll do anything."

"How old is this fine piece of ass?" Ringo taunts the man by grabbing the daughter's taut right buttock. The man is horrified.

The daughter whimpers, not knowing whether or not to answer, but the blunt silence is more than she can bear. Her voice is thin and weak.

"Sixteen."

Ringo reaches over and cups her immature breasts in his hand. He scissors her nipple between his index and middle finger, fondling her gently, and enjoying himself to a great extent.

"Man, it should be illegal for a sixteen-year-old to look this fucking hot!"

The man summons a strength buried within himself and lets out a shriek.

"I'll fucking kill you!"

He darts forward with a gashed knee toward Ringo, but is quickly whipped by Freakshow's pistol-bearing hand. His head falls flat upon the uneven forest floor, sending a single dull pulse through the ground that is received by everyone's feet.

Freakshow reprimands Ringo.

"Ringo, knock it the fuck off!"

Ringo removes his hand from the girl's breast and looks to Fish.

"All I'm saying is if it's illegal to fuck a girl that looks this fucking hot, they should put 'em on an island away from me."

Freakshow slowly swivels his neck and surveys the surroundings.

"This spot will have to do."

Freakshow pulls the still sobbing man up by his collar onto his knees. He presses the barrel of the gun straight down against the top of the man's skull.

XV.

Betty stands frozen on the small concrete landing in front of 19 Hooverville Drive. The concrete landing is crumbling and rounding at the edges. There is a single black-painted iron railing that runs to her left. It is bolted into the concrete at three points—two of the points being secure, and the bottom third being chewed away by rust. The slightest touch sends it wobbling like a spring. At the bottom of the steps, there is a cracked plastic pot that used to hold a flowering Lamprocapnos. Now, the parched soil sitting in the pot is fused together by dead upturned roots. It flowers no longer.

It is dark and very late. Betty questions herself, like she always does, as to why she came home in the first place. The torn screen entrance opens, casting a light on Betty. Her uncle stands at the half-open doorway holding a bag of ice to his face. Printed on the bag is a smiling cartoon polar bear wearing a muffler sitting atop a floe as snowflakes fall all around.

Betty takes notice of a discolored patch of skin near her uncle's cheekbone. She doesn't question it. She pretends not to take notice of his injuries altogether and averts her eyes, though perhaps too suddenly. Wheezing, her uncle moves his heavy body out of the way to make way for hers. Betty enters the trailer and shuts the door behind her.

The trailer hisses and creaks with any shift of weight, swaying and gurgling like some giant gastric mechanism.

Betty walks towards her room, hoping to get to sleep as soon as she can.

"What did you tell those freaks?"

She stops. Her uncle's words are carried into the void of the now silent trailer.

"They're not freaks," she replies, then pauses. "They're my friends."

"Those freaks? You're friends? They make the homos look normal!"

Uncle Jose spits at the air in disgust. He proceeds in a low solemn tone.

"What did you tell them?"

Betty refuses to acknowledge her uncle's gaze and looks towards his feet as she responds.

"Nothing."

She looks to the wall.

The oak clock hanging there is broken. It has been stuck with its hands pointing at twenty of nine for ages now. Atop the oak clock sits cheaply-bought ceramic cherubs about to kiss. The trailer violently pops and groans once more as Uncle Jose storms toward her and fists her hair in his swollen hands.

"You're a fuckin' liar!"

He throws her on the floor and whips the bag of ice relentlessly at her face. Betty screams for her life. Her mouth fills with the taste of blood. She feels a gap in her teeth that wasn't there before as she slowly loses consciousness.

XVI.

Mike Bua slouches in a crudely-stitched tweed chair. He always thought the chartreuse yellow and green color combination to be garish. The two chairs positioned in front of the metal desk remain, not due to lack of funding, but of the captain's own aesthetic leanings. Numerous stains of uncertain origin—but most likely from coffee—spot the chairs making them resemble sickened giraffes. Mike applies generous pressure to an ice pack he holds against the back of his head. Aside from the gentle rustling of papers, the office is quiet, allowing his headache to slowly subside.

"Mike?" a voice calls out.

Mike groggily draws his chin away from his chest and looks up to his captain. A head of peppered hair sits atop the shoulders of a squat man who carries himself with an air of military dignity, a man whom most would assume is not an occupant of this particular office. He holds a thick manila folder in his hands. Paper clips and sticky notes protrude from the file like quills.

Mike's lolling head looks as if it were about to capsize. He manages a monosyllabic response.

"Huh?"

The Captain slams his fist on the desk. Mike's head perks up. He would have more success trying to balance a bowling ball on his index finger. The bag of ice falls out of his hand and lands somewhere behind him.

"You're so goddamn drunk you can't even keep your head up."

Mike wishes to ask what the time is, but instead he replies, "I'm cool, man."

"No, you are not cool at all!"

The Captain plops the fattened file in front of Mike.

"What the hell am I going to do with you? Do you like making me look like a goddamn fool?"

The Captain waits for a response or gesture of acknowledgment from Mike.

Mike keeps his hand pressed against the back of his head, unaware of the fumbled bag of ice.

"Mike, no matter how much you drink or try to get your ass kicked, your little girl is not coming back."

A sentimentality is now evident in the Captain's voice.

"Listen Mike," he continues. "You're a great detective. One of the best, if not *the* best. You are a good man, but you've gotta get your shit together."

Mike looks toward the Captain, but his eyes trail off toward the dust-coated plaques and the certificates hanging on the sun-bleached wood paneled wall.

The Captain simplifies his speech.

"Mike, what would you do if you were me?"

Timed particularly well with the Captain's ending monologue, a second person's voice, whom Mike is very familiar with, cuts in.

"Hey, Mike," says Matt Mashburn. "We need you. We have a homicide."

Matt is leaning into the room with his hand propped against the doorway. The last remnants of his boyish red hair are visible at the top of the high and tight cut he sports. His voice radiates with optimism and calls back the throbbing pain in Mike's head.

Mike doesn't want to turn around, as he points his chin to the ceiling, replying with sarcasm, "Of course *we* do."

His words float into the air and are dispersed evenly throughout the Captain's office.

"Get a goddamn grip," The Captain says.

Matt is confused as to whom is being addressed. Perhaps now is not a good time. He straightens his arm and slowly inches himself out of the doorway.

"Are we done here, Captain?"

Mike summons his energy and begins to hoist himself out of the tweed chair.

The Captain eyes Mike up and down, with a look of hopeless defeat.

"Yeah, get out of here."

Mike keeps his left hand on the wooden armrest of the chair as he swings his body towards the door. He looks down, sees the bag of ice, and retrieves it with his free hand.

"Mike!" the Captain calls out once more. "I think this goes without saying: no more drinking."

As Mike Bua crosses the threshold of the doorway, he turns to smirk at the Captain.

"Who's been drinking?" Mike asks.

XVII.

"Please don't. I'll do anything," the father cries.

The situation has taken a turn for the pathetic. Fluid is being spewed forth from nearly every orifice on the man's face. Dirt is smeared across his forehead and the crotch of his trousers is soaked with urine.

"Anything?" Freakshow singingly jests.

Ringo turns to Fish and rolls his eyes.

"Oh, great. Here comes the homo shit," he announces, unamused.

The girl straightens her posture as Ringo casually makes the sexual inference. His words carry the grim reality of her present situation.

Fish leans gently onto his right foot. Water gushes out from the thick cushion in his shoe, bathing his toes in a froth of decaying particles. He tries to recall any information regarding leeches that he may have learned about, and turns to Freakshow with a worried look.

"C'mon Show. Stop messing around and let's get this over with."

Freakshow reassures Fish.

"I got this."

Then, turning back to the man, he makes an attempt to negotiate.

"Okay, here's the deal. I'm going to kill you no matter what, but, if you suck me off, right here, right now... I won't harm your daughter."

There is a long pause for thought. The man's heavy panting fills the air. Any saliva that was in his mouth is gone now. His tongue swells and his throat contracts. The inside of his mouth turns to cardboard.

The man makes a dry rattle as he clears his throat. Refusing to look up, he speaks, his fragile voice cracking.

"How do I know you are telling the truth?"

Freakshow fires his weapon level with the man's face. The booming recedes deep into the forest and is quickly dampened to silence. The man recoils in pain. His daughter cries out. A stabbing sensation in his ears causes him to writhe on his knees. His body contorts in cruel exorcism and he slouches over in exhaustion. A low gurgle leaves his throat. Ringo, and Fish look on. The daughter sobs as moments pass. Hunched over, the body still swells and shrinks with breath. The man cries into the crunching leaves under his face. Realizing that he is still very much alive, he sits up and scans hastily over his body. There is no blood, not even a wound. Gradually becoming reoriented with his surroundings, he looks over himself once more. Befuddled, he searches the faces of those around him.

Freakshow speaks.

"I don't think you have much of a choice."

Freakshow keeps his gun held firmly against the man's head and unbuckles himself with a single hand. He pops a button off and slowly draws his zipper down.

"I would do what he says," Ringo states, discerningly.

The man looks up to the tattooed behemoth threading his organ through checkered boxers. He tries to get a good look at Freakshow's face, but then questions the sense in such a wish. The man is beyond confused, beyond hopeless, and the inside of his mouth feels like parched earth.

Unable to move amid what he is witnessing, Fish desperately tries to make eye contact with Ringo or Freakshow. He wants to raise his voice in protest, but all that comes out is a quivering utterance lacking any tact whatsoever. He fails to enunciate even the first word properly.

"W-w-w-w why? Why are we doing this?"

"Calm down, little buddy," Ringo replies in a whisper, as not to disturb the ongoing perverse ritual.

"Please don't hurt my daughter!" The man cries, though he can't seem to properly manipulate the muscles in his mouth. Every vocalization is now a struggle. The friction of his dry tongue catches on the roof of his mouth, paining him. He looks to his daughter.

"Please sweetie, please remember, I'll always love you."

Salty mucous dribbles into his mouth, refreshing the tip of his tongue.

"Remember the good times, not this..."

Ringo's taunting is incorrigible. The man's sentimental train of thought is rudely interrupted.

"T-T-T-Today junior!"

Sobbing, the man inches his face towards Freakshow's crotch. Fish turns his head in revulsion. The daughter tries to look away, but Ringo braces her chin to maintain a line of sight with her father.

A swelling cannon of gunshot sounds once more and the man on his knees falls to his side. Fish opens his eyes and examines the body from where he stands. Though it is dark, he can see that there is clearly no more movement. The body lays lifeless.

"You know, you're a sick fuck," Ringo commends Freakshow, who is busy adjusting his clothes, making himself presentable once more.

Fish is in relief and shock for more reasons than he can bother to analyze at the given time. His palms are glistening with perspiration. His shoe is still drenched in the concoction of the swamp.

"Yo, let's get the fuck outta here, guys," Fish says. He wonders if perhaps he could have said something even more reasonable, more perspicuous, something that would yield a more immediate effect. He tries once more. "Let's, ah... let's just go!"

"Freakshow had his fun," Ringo interjects.

He kicks the back of the girl's knee dropping her to the ground. "Now, it's my turn."

The ridiculous smile drawn across his face is only surpassed by his awful clothing preference. With his hat now gone, the exposed hairless crown atop his head makes him look very much like a circus clown. For some reason, his name seems more befitting than ever.

"I'm gonna fuck this little whore all night long," he mutters to himself between clenched teeth.

"C'mon dude. She's only sixteen," Fish uneasily replies.

Freakshow redirects his attention, and his pistol, towards the immediate threat that currently manifests itself in the form of his own partner, Ringo. He casually lifts his weapon and aims for his grinning accomplice's shoulder. Ringo sees metal glint from the corner of his eye.

Freakshow draws a breath for calm, though he coincidentally perfects his aim in the process.

"No, you're not," he says in fortitude.

Ringo stands upright, wearing an expression of confusion. He looks to Freakshow, then to Fish, then back to Freakshow.

"What the fuck?" Ringo says in exasperation. "Are you

for fucking real?"

"I'm for real."

"Oh, okay. Okay. Let me get this straight. You can have old man river over there blow you, but I can't fuck this teenage whore?"

"The man kept his word and I plan on doing the same."

"The motherfucker didn't even do it!" Ringo explodes.

"He was going to."

"How the fuck do you know?" Ringo shouts in wild furor.

"I just know."

Ringo's testosterone-driven biological imperative clouds his rational thinking. His argument is disconnected, inconsistent, and contradicts itself. Fish, taking a brief note of this, uses the valuable break in conversation to try and pull Ringo back to reason. Again, his anxiety gets the better of his oratory.

"Guys! Let's..." No wonder they take me for a retard, he thinks to himself. "Let's just get the fuck out of here. Let's go..." He fails to take a full breath and continues. "We can leave now. The job is done, guys. Let's go."

Ringo grits his teeth.

"Fish, will you just shut the fuck up?"

Freakshow doesn't ease his stance at all. He needs to let Ringo know that he means business. Ringo lets out a long sigh and drops his shoulders in acquittal.

"Okay... Okay, okay. I won't rape the bitch, but there is no way I am letting her leave."

Ringo brings up his weapon and pulls the girl's head back by her hair.

"Don't!" Freakshow warns, and cocks his weapon. "Ringo, don't fucking do it."

Fish's trembling hand anxiously claws at the back of his

shirt. He grasps for the pistol tucked snugly into his waistline. In a fluid motion, he propels his arm around him and points it directly at Ringo's chest. Unfortunately, Fish's praiseworthy actions go largely unnoticed by the two, busily honed into one another's body language.

Ringo's lips quiver under strain. He addresses Freakshow. "Fuck you, Mike."

Ringo's finger depresses the crescent-shaped trigger. A flash of light. The girl's head cocks forward and a dark mist made barely visible by the night sky ejects from her skull.

A second flash of light.

Fish stares down the barrel of his gun as Ringo tumbles backward. Ringo's wide-eyed look is one of pure surprise. His blooming palms release the weight of the pistol, vanishing it into the nearby foliage. Now laying on his back, Ringo presses an open hand on his shoulder. His fingers wrap around to the back, trying to identify an exit wound, if any. Still holding his gun up, Fish is frozen in disbelief. His mind cannot seem to catch up with the unpredictability of the events unfolding before him.

"You fucking shot me, motherfucker!" Ringo forces out as much volume as he can muster.

Freakshow has an indecipherable expression on his face as he inches his weapon down. His mouth slowly opens.

"Fuck you."

Fish tries to read Freakshow's countenance to no success. He seems so detached from the situation.

"That's not my name," Freakshow calmly says.

XVIII.

Nineteen Hooverville Drive, at night.

A rookie police officer props up the crime scene tape for a passing Mike Bua as he clambers into the trailer. First responding officers are being questioned by a concerned-looking Matt Mashburn. Matt scratches the side of his dry-shaved head with the end of his ballpoint pen as he curiously looks down at his small top-bound spiral notebook.

The trailer pops loudly with activity as officers with whom Mike isn't even acquainted with shift from room to room. Mike can feel a fresh delivery of blood being sent to his head with every heartbeat. He acknowledges a few unpleasant looks from the other officers, no doubt picking up on the fermented stench he is wearing.

He scans the room, trying to internalize what he can in his current mental state. An antique oak clock no longer seeming to be in use hangs from the wall reading twenty to nine. There are flea market knickknacks, collapsible furniture, made from pressboard and cheap malleable pipe, a chewed out recliner, and frozen dinners that have been licked clean. His nose follows the lingering pulp of mildew coming from the back of the wheeled home. A young male officer exits the bathroom, covering his mouth with a white linen handkerchief. He quickly grazes past Mike before making his way through the narrow hall.

Mike turns into the bathroom.

A large bloated mass lays lifeless in the tub. Oversized jeans and underwear are pulled down around the ankles joining them like fetters. A light grey pullover hoodie is stained with blood around the collar. A white plastic bag of a popular discount store franchise World-Mart covers the head and concaves to the opening of a gaping maw that was gulping for air. Mike squats down closer.

Bruises with differentiating hues blot her corpulent legs. Small burns no greater in diameter than a pencil are randomly dotted up and down the inside of the thighs growing greater in number as they near her crotch. Cigarettes, Mike thinks, although they could be anything. Some look quite old being healed over and suggest that the abuse has been taking place for years. After another minute of scrutinizing, Mike exits the room. Habitually reaching for his cigarettes from the front pocket of his jacket, he stops himself and instead scratches the side of his stubbled face. He draws his hand over his mouth and down his chin. Stopping, he looks upward and speaks.

"Where were you on this one asshole?"

Turning his head back, the glint of a brazen rectangular frame in the hall catches Mike's eye. As he walks further, a framed cross-stitching bearing a quote from Leviticus adorns what would have been an unsightly space of peeling wall to his left. Mike, now standing in front of the tarnishing photo frame, squints his eyes as a dim familiarity creeps onto him. He flips through the index of his memory. In the photograph, a portly Hispanic man smiles through bottle lens glasses. His dark hair is thin on top with remaining thick uncropped tufts on the sides decorating the man's head like a diadem. Judging from the granular quality, this picture must have been taken at least three decades ago, but the face couldn't have changed much. The features are so distinct. Mike curses his mental ability as he shuts his eyes and furrows his brow. Then: cognizance.

"Fuck!"

Mike slams his fist into the picture, shattering the glass and shaking the trailer. Half-concerned officers look down the hall to understand the cause of the commotion. Shards of glass burrow into the back of Mike's hand. Small ribbons of skin lazily hang off his knuckles. Matt runs toward Mike, wearing the same look of concern on his face from before.

"What? What's up?" he worryingly asks.

"I saw this fucking guy tonight!" Mike blurts out.

"Where?"

"At fucking Sal's!"

"The strip bar, *Sal's*?" Matt asks, smirking.

"What the hell are you smiling about? He tried to play buddy-buddy with me and talked shit about his niece." Mike is dripping blood all over the crime scene. He quickly cradles his hand in his unzipped jacket. "I should've fucking killed him when I had the chance."

Matt speaks slowly, like one would speak to a child. He wants Mike to understand the situation more clearly, which may be an impossibility given his alcohol-induced state of stimulation. Bringing Mike down was a very stupid move by the Captain.

"Look, Jose Santos is a suspect, but we can't be certain of anything yet. Let's not jump to conclusions."

Mike thrusts Matt aside and curses through his teeth as he storms out of the trailer in agitation.

XIX.

Ringo's hand vices his shoulder as he sucks for air through his teeth. Fish never imagined that a gunshot wound to an upper extremity could be as painful as Ringo makes it look. He slowly walks over to Ringo and kneels over his body.

"You fucking shot me, Show. No fucking way! You fucking shot me. How fucking unprofessional is that? I'm working with trigger-happy amateur cocksuckers here... Fuck you guys! Fuck you Freakshow!"

Ringo squeezes his eyelids together and replenishes his lungs with the chilled wooded air.

"This is the last time I work with you two motherfuckers. We're done professionally!"

Fish, though exhausted, ekes out reserved strength and extends his arms towards his perpetually unpleasant and wounded partner, lifting him.

"C'mon, let's go," Fish says.

"Just shut the fuck up and just get my ass outta here!"

Fish deliberately lets his arms go limp. Ringo falls to the ground, rolling onto his side, grunting in pain.

"Tell me to shut the fuck up again!" Fish quips.

Ringo scoffs in disbelief. "Oh shit. Now you've got the balls. You been sitting there all fucking night like a bitch. I had to save your incompetent fuckin' ass from getting lost in the woods. All of a sudden I'm shot by fucking psycho over there and you grow a set."

Fish grows visibly disconcerted. He ruffles his brow and lets off a barrage of invectives.

"No! You shut the fuck up. I'm tired of all your jokes about me being a pussy, and I'm tired of you telling me to shut the fuck up all the time! I have something to contribute to this group, too. I have good fucking ideas too, so *you* shut the fuck up!" Fish drums the heels of his hands against his temples and begins pacing in circles whilst muttering something about Ringo to himself.

Something about Fish seems horribly off. A nervous tic, unnoticeable to Ringo, in the index finger of the hand still holding the gun sets a small alarm off in the silently-observing Freakshow. Fish stops in step and menacingly cranes his neck at Ringo. "Is that all you have to say, huh: shut the fuck up?"

"Look Fish, I'm sorry, I didn't know it was like that," Ringo says in a subdued tone.

Fish's hands drop away from his temples. "Look. It's cool. It just makes me fucking crazy mad." Relieved, he walks towards Ringo, every right step answering in a soft squish. As Fish crouches down to pick up his partner, Ringo whispers to him.

"Hey, Fish?"

Fish turns an ear towards Ringo's soft voice. He leans in, waiting to be privy to words of gratification that perhaps Ringo is too proud to utter aloud.

A thick grinding sound from Ringo's throat is followed by the hot splatter of ooze in Fish's ear.

"Shut the fuck up!"

Ringo's screaming shreds through the phlegm and saliva lodged in Fish's ear.

Fish shoves Ringo to the ground by his injured shoulder.

He swiftly throws his head back and returns the favor by using Ringo's face as a spittoon.

"No! *You* shut the fuck up! You shut the fuck up!"

Fish's antsy index finger snuggles upon the concave of the gun's trigger.

"You shut the fuck up!" Fish squeezes the trigger twice.

Ringo stares pie-eyed toward the treetops as his broken teeth are tumbled through the blood welling up from a sizable hole in his throat.

"You shut the fuck up!" Fish squeezes once more.

"You shut the fuck up!"

Three more shots are fired before the metallic clicking of Fish's revolver tells him that he is finished. The six gunshot wounds to the face make Ringo now unrecognizable, which is not to say that he is unidentifiable. His jaw is unhinged and his left cheekbone seems to have collapsed under its newly porous properties, being grotesquely misshapen. Ringo's eyes retain a permanent look of surprise that stare out somewhere among the boughs of the trees. The eerie silence now begins to pervade Fish's sensibility. A pang of guilt insists that he say something to dispel the morbid serenity.

"Who's fuckin' afraid *now*?" Fish addresses the body, his voice wavering as feelings of uncertainty in his irreversible actions grow.

The three bodies lie arranged in a macabre obtuseness. The air is laden with blood. Fish is entirely at a loss for what to do. He cannot seem to pull his own eyes away from Ringo's, as if expecting a final rejoinder to be expelled from the tumid hole that was a functioning mouth only a few moments before.

"It's time to go," Freakshow says, fetching Ringo's weapon from the bushes. "Fish, I'll need your gun as well. You wait over there," he says, pointing to a thick trunked tree surrounded by an orgy of surfacing roots.

Fish hands his gun to Freakshow and heads for the fattened-brown stalk penetrating the heavens. Fine dark specks dispersed over the back of his hands smear as he runs his thumb over the knuckles of his fingers. In the foreground, Freakshow furtively rearranges the exanimate trio.

XX.

Morning.

Ana lies asleep on the sofa, cradling a floppy cushion in her thin arms. She opens her eyes slowly at a rapping at her door. She must have fallen asleep as soon as Betty went home last night. The rapping gets louder as Ana takes her time with sitting up and fixing her hair. She didn't have time to brush her teeth last night and feels very much inclined not to answer, whoever this particular visitor is.

"Show? Is that you?" she calls.

The knocking continues. Ana sees the living room light is still on, betraying her presence within the house. She hopes that it's not another stalker-weirdo from work.

"Who is it?" she groggily asks.

"Police ma'am. We have a few questions we'd like to ask," the opposite side of the door answers.

Ana shoots upward and lunges herself at the table, sweeping the neatly-packaged bags of marijuana into her arms and throwing them under the couch cushions.

"I'll be there in a second!" she says with lost breath.

The knocks immediately stop and a heavy silence falls upon the room. The officers are surely listening for any peculiar sounds coming from within the home. Any damn excuse to barge in without a warrant. Ana hopes that she at least remembered to lock the door.

Without a lost movement, she rips the socks off of her feet, wipes any further traces of cannabis from the glass table, and then buries her socks into a crack in the sofa.

"Sorry, I'm coming!" she says just as the rapping begins once more.

She takes a deep breath and regains composure as she unlocks the door. She leaves the chain fastened for her own legal safety. She cautiously cracks the door as far as the chain will allow. Two officers stand before her. One has what looks to be a clear freezer bag pinched between his upheld fingers. It contains her cellular phone.

"Morning. I am Detective Bua and this is Officer Mashburn. We just have to ask you a few questions."

Their badges are clearly visible and the handsome man speaking seems vaguely familiar.

Mike Bua steps back, trying to get a better look at Ana through the crack. Claiming to be a detective, his alcohol-laden breath and thickly bandaged hand understandably arouse her suspicion. However, the marked cruiser parked on the street would have to make them official. Why else would they have her phone? Ana gets an inevitably queasy feeling in her gut.

"Have you been drinking?" Ana asks Detective Bua.

"Yeah, it's been a rough night," Detective Bua says as he glances past Ana, trying to peek inside.

Ana quickly shifts herself to block his view.

"You know, your place doesn't smell entirely legal, if you catch my drift. We can do this the easy way, or the hard way. Now, I have good excuse to kick down this door if I have to. Or perhaps you'd like to unlock it and invite us in like a civilized human being?"

Ana looks to both Detective Bua and Officer Mashburn

before closing the door. The brief sound of sliding metal is followed by the door reopening and a barefoot Ana standing before the officers. Her toe nails are chipping a midnight blue polish.

"Thank you," Officer Mashburn says to Ana as he and Detective Bua invite themselves in. Ana's wrinkled skirt seems to wave him a greeting. Mashburn's eyes are helplessly locked to Ana's exposed areas of skin. Ana, conscious of Mashburn's gaze, adjusts her skirt to discourage his indulging.

"What is your relationship to a Bethany Santos?" the detective asks Ana before she even has a chance to close the door behind them. Ana can feel vomit slowly creeping its way up from her stomach.

XXI.

Midday.

Mike Bua very much needs a shower, whether it be a hot or cold one. He is very much tempted to jump into a lake, should one present itself before him. Since he was pulled into the Captain's office around midnight, he's been trying to purge his alcohol-ridden system with the unpalatable coffee they keep on hand at the station. His mouth is drying up fast and he needs something other than a diuretic to keep himself moving. He wipes off some oil collecting on his nose with his forefinger and thumb. The greasy coating on his fingers is then transferred to his pant leg with a few carelessly-made swipes. Mike reaches to grab the steering wheel as a left turn is executed with the kind of finesse you'd expect from a detective.

Matt Mashburn sits besides Mike. "Are you sure you're good to drive?" he asks, looking worried.

Mike doesn't answer.

Matt has nitrile gloved himself and is quite eager to search Ana's phone for what he thinks may be any incriminating evidence. "That Ana chick is pretty hot, huh?" he asks expecting an agreeable response from Mike.

"If you're into that kind of thing..."

Matt frowns at first, though too occupied with the

thought of discovering a treasure trove of explicit personal data. A smile returns to his face and he continues to rifle through the digitally-preserved photographs.

"Who isn't into a little freak like this?"

He seems more to be reassuring himself than formulating a question for Mike. An obviously agitated Matt leafs through some bikini photos of Ana with great care. In various shots, tattoos suggestively covered by a blue top housing Ana's large breasts peek out from the sides.

Matt begins thinking aloud.

"Jeez, do you think those are real? If they are, that is one fantastic job. I've got every angle here proving there are no scars. An architect couldn't design something this perfect. Those are some smooth milky tits..."

Disheartened by a one-sided conversation, Matt tries to further persuade. He holds the phone up to the steering wheel. The screen displays Ana playfully posing in a bikini. A chuckling Matt adds a creative caption for the photo: "This is the type of girl that would have no problems licking the sweat off your balls and then eating your asshole!"

Mike only pretends to look at the phone and obstinately replies. "Very professional Matt."

He pauses as a single cough relieves a tickle in his throat. "Well, maybe next time you should ask her out."

The decelerating cruiser enters a parking lot and effortlessly navigates to the nearest empty accommodation.

"We can do that?" Matt asks, his excited voice curving up an octave.

XXII.

The door is unlocked.

"Ana? You home? You're not going to believe the fuckin' night we had."

Freakshow takes an exaggerated stride into Ana's living room, holding a brown paper bag stuffed with warm hamburgers and fries. Fish follows behind, gripping a cup holder that cradles three extra-large beverages in their assigned quadrants. He is freshly showered and newly clothed. Before shutting the door behind him, he breaths the air, casually stirring it with his nose. A smile draws across his face.

The spherical shade of the floor lamp at this hour casts an eerie phosphorescence on a darker corner of the room. Ana is normally not so careless with electricity. Fish wraps his lips around a straw of the only cup from which one protrudes. His cheeks shrink back into his head. A dark fizzing liquid immediately runs up the short tube and is plunged into his mouth. The movement of a shadow from the dining area prompts Freakshow to quietly draw his pistol. Fish's cheeks pop back out as he watches Freakshow walk towards the back of the house in guarded sidestep.

Taking into consideration that the dining room goes widely unused, it is quite filthy. A dinner table in the center of the room is only visible by its legs. A large pile of old clothing and toys is heaped atop the table. Four chairs encircling the table catch anything spilling from the top. School worksheets from an unknown date clutter the floor. A vacuum cleaner with a snapped handle is propped in the far corner and unpacked dishware lies inside a nest of newspaper padding among other still sealed mover's boxes. Ana sits on the floor, cross-legged, with a wad of black-spotted tissues crumpled in her fist. Mascara is smeared on her cheeks.

"Ana!" Freakshow announces with relief. He sets the pistol and brown paper bag on the floor. His large figure cumbersomely squats down to mirror Ana's posture. He places his hands on each of her knees. "Jesus Christ, Ana, I almost shot your ass! What the fuck happened?"

Fish pops his fiery head in the doorway.

"Whoa, what the fuck is going on over here?"

"Bett—" Ana says stopping involuntarily to suck in a staggered breath. "Betty was murdered by her spic uncle!" She draws the wad of damp tissues up to her face to catch the falling tears.

"Are you for fucking real? Why the fuck would he do that?"

Freakshow is lost in the incongruence. He moves inward to embrace Ana.

"Who the fuck is Betty?" Fish asks, chewing on his soda straw.

Freakshow puts Ana on an emotional standby as he turns to Fish to answer. "Betty was the girl crying on the porch yesterday."

"Oh... You mean Princess Tub-Tub McBeardsley?"

"Her fucking name was Betty!" Ana growls, reaching for the bag containing everyone's lunch and hurls it at Fish. He flinches. The bag misses. It malforms on impact against the doorway and plops to the floor sounding off in a dull crinkle.

"Fish, Ana was close to Betty. Do you mind?" Freakshow placidly states.

Fish fetches the bag off the floor and peers into it with the readiness of a diver standing on a platform. He angles the bag, searching for his sandwich. His feet lead him back into the living room. The television clicks on.

Ana shudders as she reaches for the hands resting on her shoulders.

"A detective was here...," she starts.

"Fuck, the police were here?" Freakshow mutters. "We're going to have to move again."

"Fucker, do you mind?" Ana says wearing a bilious expression.

"I'm sorry, you go on babe."

"She was pregnant."

"Who? Betty?" Freakshow exclaims.

"She was... Her spic uncle was forcing her to go to Mexico and she didn't want to go and I didn't want her to either. I told her to crash for the night and that you'd know what to do."

Ana begins pacing her words.

"Then he called. He told me to send her home. I had to. He said he would tell everyone about... you-know-what."

"You guys got some kinda secret or something?" Fish asks, standing in the doorway.

"What the fuck? Fish, shut the fuck up! What is wrong with you?!" Ana rages.

"Hun, I don't think you should be telling Fish to shut the fuck up anytime soon." Freakshow forewarns.

"Why the fuck not?" Ana asks, furious.

"I just wanted to know if you guys had any hot sauce."

Fish squats down to look at the rubbish on the floor.

"Hey! Is this your old artwork, Show?"

He picks up a page torn from a spiral bound notebook with a masked wrestler ready to fly off the ropes in a crayoned two-dimensional ring.

"Careful with that. It's one of my masterpieces. Hot sauce is in the top left cupboard. Can you give us a few, Fish?"

Fish exits the room once more. Shortly afterward, the pop of a wooden cupboard from the kitchen runs through the wall. Freakshow and Ana wait a few more seconds to be certain of their privacy before continuing.

"Babe, you need to calm down. Tell me what happened next."

"I let her borrow the cell phone you got me. That's how they found me."

Ana clenches her hands into fists and throws them in her lap.

"I told you we need a burner phone, Ana!"

"Damn it, Show! You're not listening! She was suffocated. God Show, I think the baby may have been Jose's. I knew he wouldn't stop touching her, drunk or not! Betty was probably just afraid to tell me."

"Fuck," Freakshow says, glancing around to make sure Fish is out of earshot.

"The worst part is, last night, when she was worried, I told her that it can't be that bad."

Ana reaches for the tissue box behind her, but it is empty and only resounds in a stiff cardboard call as her fingernails scrape at the bottom. She ends up settling on the previously used ball of wet tissue and dabs it on her face.

"Hey, I don't wanna hear any of that shit. This isn't your fault, Ana," Freakshow says, lightly shaking Ana's shoulders.

"No, but that fucker is on the run."

An action figure abandoned under one of the dining chairs catches Freakshow's eye for a moment. He pensively stares at Ana's tear-stained top.

"Listen, we'll get him before anyone else does," Freakshow says with confidence that Ana finds hard not to believe in. "Do you know where he may be?"

Ana nods, holding the stained ball of tissue to her eye.

"Let's go then. Get a pair of pants."

Freakshow stands up, grabs a shirt off the dining table, and walks toward the living room where Fish mindlessly surfs through the overabundant selection of daytime programming.

"Fish, we've gotta go."

Ana slowly picks herself up from the dining room floor, her legs stinging with fresh circulating blood.

The clothes on the dining table have been upset. A large crater from something displaced reveals a very scratched tabletop that dips down in the center from the stress of weight. Ana limps, with legs half asleep, into the living room carrying a large black duffel bag with both hands. It swings only a few inches off the floor before she drops it completely winded.

"What's going on?" Fish asks, standing up.

Freakshow changes to a long-sleeved shirt as he replies, "Work."

XXIII.

If anything was going to make the day worse for Mike, it would have been having to sit back down in one of those god-awful stained tweed chairs listening to the Captain drone on about work performance and proper behavior while on the job. That was, in fact, exactly what was happening at the moment, this time without the blissful buffering effect of inebriation. The Captain paces incessantly behind his cadet grey metal desk. His august gestures and facial expressions have been carefully rehearsed. Despite this, his clearly flustered state creates an amusing effect. Barraging Mike in reproof, the Captain's mouth flaps like a flag caught in a violent gale. One would only need to ink his borders and float word bubbles overhead to create a comic strip worthy of syndication.

The Captain, using his finger to stab at the air, points at Mike's bandaged hand. Mike props his elbow on the armrest and holds his arm upright. He can feel the blood rushing out of his swollen hand.

"So you're going to suspend me?" Mike interrupts. "With all these fucking crooked cops, you're going to suspend me? Is that what you're telling me, Jack?"

"Mike, only if you choose not to visit the shrink. I've been letting you slide for too long."

Bua directs a stony gaze toward the ceiling and whispers something through his lips.

"Mike?" The Captain places his hands on the desk and leans in, to catch what Mike is saying to himself. "Mike, are you listening? What'll it be?"

Peeling his eyes from the ceiling, Mike looks to the Captain. "All right. I'll talk to the fucking shrink. I'll tell her everything. Like how your wife is a cokehead and has genital herpes that you gave her. I'll tell the shrink how Mr. Straight Arrow Captain received the aforementioned herpes when he went to Atlantic City and paid to fuck a black whore!"

The Captain becomes unnerved with Mike's vociferousness, but is too proud to ask Mike to keep his voice down.

"Is this really the path you are going to choose, Bua? Because if I go down, you're coming with me. IAB will leave no stone unturned once you decide to open Pandora's box."

That may very well be the best outcome, Mike thinks to himself as he shakes his head in betrayal and gaits heavily out of the office.

"Goddammit, see the shrink Mike!" repeats the Captain in hopes that this argument will somehow, in the end, bring a favorable outcome for himself.

XXIV.

Sal's Arabian Nights. The establishment is officially closed during the day, which isn't to say there aren't more sinister dealings taking place here outside of normal operating hours. Ana hasn't shown up for work in the past two weeks. The daylight brightens up the parking lot, revealing the tarred wasteland in its entirety. Minute shards of broken glass flicker like small gems trapped within the countless fissures of the aging asphalt. Foreign fluids on the lot sit exposed to the balmy midday sun. Paper waste consisting of receipts and torn lottery tickets are whisked away by a gentle breeze, drifting behind precast concrete parking curbs.

Two oxidizing beaters are parked by the entrance, one omitting the cooling clicks of recent use. Ana recognizes neither. Going past them, she pulls down on the handle of the steel door, gives a gentle tug, and walks inside. Opening up to what Sal officially designates as the "lobby," it is more realistically identified as a corridor, serving as nothing more than a funnel for arriving customers, leading them down to an opening which empties into the main hall.

Various notices on state law and a meticulously detailed club policy are adhered to the wall. Sal always takes the liberty to mention his many attempts at framing any and all juridical documents, for reasons of appearing official, and always blaming his thwarted noble deeds on some rambunctious meathead of a customer with weak constitution, who, for having taken personal offense at being ejected from the club, decides to rip down things hanging from the wall.

A squat man with a shaved head, whom Ana doesn't recognize, approaches unwelcomingly, waving his arms.

"No, no, no. No fucking way. Sal doesn't want you here," the man says in his hoarse voice, shooing her away with immediacy.

Grabbing her above the elbow, he pulls her near the exit. Ana compacts a fist and swings around, throwing it at his jaw. The black painted cinder blocks that line the club's interior seem to suck the man in. He flies backwards, bumping his head against the unforgiving wall. Ana anticipates on him getting back up, but he does not.

Ana parts the beaded curtain at the end of the corridor and peeks into the club. With no one within her line of sight, she slows her breathing and listens intently. The stillness of the room carries to her familiar voices. Having determined how safe the area is, Ana turns towards the entrance, pushes the door open, and beckons to a black SUV idling in the center of the lot.

XXV.

Ana holds the door open as Freakshow and Fish pass the threshold of the sidewalk and into the club. The door closes behind them. As Ana wipes the handle down, Fish pulls on his black leather gloves, giving them a final tug at the wrist before closing his fist in a dramatic display of adroitness. Freakshow, avoiding theatrics, dons simple white latex, making him look the more sinister of the two. A wrinkled pair of extra-large gloves are passed to Ana who puts them on without hesitation.

Freakshow lowers himself to his knees and drags the black duffel bag in front of everyone. Fish's eyes dilate as Freakshow grabs the tab of the zipper. With a monotone purr the teeth slowly part, opening into an inky gulf. Freakshow's monstrous white vestured hands reach into the blackness, surely to produce something of extraordinary visceral wonder. A momentary twinkle from within has Fish on the edge of excitement. Anticlimactically, two silver snub nose revolvers perching atop Freakshow's hands emerge and are carelessly passed on to Fish, who stares at his hands in stupefaction.

"This is it?" he inquires.

The question is regarded as immaterial as the squat man lying unconscious on the floor, and is ignored entirely.

Fish turns, facing the beaded entrance leading to the

main room as Freakshow busies himself with rummaging through the bag. He is conducting the dissonant clacks of metal and plastic rubbing against the textured canvas.

A door swings open from somewhere within the room. Freakshow doubles sifting through the disarray of weapons in the bag. A man's laugh echoes in the hollow room. Sounding footsteps moving neither nearer nor farther keep a metronomic tempo.

Suddenly, a loud boom arrests everyone's attention. Ana throws her hands over her ears and mouths something to Freakshow and Fish. The large latex gloves sag off her fingers. The booming dies away into a murmur as the three anxiously collect their senses.

"Goddammit!" a man with an afternoon liquor slur yells from within the room.

"Sorry!" a man with a higher pitched voice replies.

"Learn how to run the sound!"

In the background, grinding guitars and drums swell to a tolerable volume, proceeded by the shuffling of moving tables and chairs.

"Nearly shit myself," Fish comments.

Freakshow yanks a tangled black vest from the bag and swings it around his barreled chest to put it on. Exposed magazines hang out from its shallow pockets, surprisingly not falling out. Freakshow swiftly pats down the vest, running through a checklist in his head. Fish, averting his eyes to the wall, now takes notice of a large assault rifle leaning up against it. Although Freakshow has never been the type to splurge on weapons, this is clearly something special. It is obviously modified, though beyond the jungle camo patterned stock Fish cannot be sure of how.

"Where the fuck's Denny?" the man struggling with his speech voluminously sounds off.

A new voice, farther off, responds.

"That fucker thinks he has to go outside for a smoke."

Banter proceeds between the three currently faceless men as Ana and Fish keep their ears open for an announcement that perhaps one of them will make an attempt to look for the unconscious bouncer. Freakshow pays it no attention. He retrieves his weapon leaning against the wall and balances it in his arms as if he were embracing an old friend.

"Don't you have any pipe bombs or shit?" Fish whispers to Freakshow. "You gotta gimme something better than these."

"Fish, you're trigger happy," Freakshow stoically answers, handing his pistol to Ana.

"I know. That's why I'm saying. The pipe bombs...," Fish says in a defeated murmur.

Freakshow and Ana huddle near the beaded curtain dangling from the end of the corridor. Fish follows, though looking down at his disappointing arsenal as he does so.

"Okay sweeties, show us what ya got," a man from the other room shouts.

The music pauses momentarily before switching to a different track. Fractured pink and green lights bleed into the corridor and dance on the walls. The ferocious wail of an electric guitar blasts through the speakers.

Ana's hands shake betraying her emotional state. Freakshow flashes her a concerned look.

"I'm fine. Just gimme a sec," Ana says. Placing her hands on her knees, Ana purses her lips and relaxes her diaphragm. Freakshow and Fish watch impatiently as her head rises and ebbs. Finishing, Ana sprightly throws her arms in the air with a refreshed expression on her face.

"By the way, where the hell is Ringo?" she asks.

XXVI.

The door is open. Officer Mashburn gently taps his knuckles on the frame as a measure of politeness.

"Captain, can I ask you something?"

The Captain breaks a stony gaze he was holding with a round glass paperweight on his desk and looks at Mashburn.

"Shoot kid."

"Why do you let him talk to you like that?"

"Who?" the Captain asks, knowing very well who is being signified.

"Bua," Mashburn says treading lightly into the office. "The guys just wanna know why you put up with his shit.'

The Captain picks up the paperweight and turns it in his hand, scrutinizing the tiny bubbles suspended within. "Because Mashburn, unlike every other cop I know, I've never seen Bua have any fear, I'm talking ever."

"Bravery? He gets to do what he wants because he is brave? Captain, the guy is a mess! He nearly got himself killed from sheer stupidity last night! Need I point out he's an alcoholic? To think he goes out in public representing the force is..."

The Captain raises his hand, shushing Mashburn.

"I know things are rough for him now. He'll come around. You know, a while back, before you were here, Bua turned down a big promotion so he could spend time with his family."

"Captain, I'm understanding, but you need to at least suspen-"

"I'm not finished goddammit!" the Captain's shouts. A maturing displeasure from within him forces his bottom lip out like a shelf. His jowls sag off his face like melting wax from a candle. "Don't ever tell me what I *need* to do! Bua is more competent than anyone else on this force! Do you even realize that?"

Though his expression remains largely unchanged, the Captain's barking tone gradually subsides to sentimental rhetoric.

"Bua is the only reason I'm sitting at this goddamn desk today. Hell, he's the only reason that I'm alive and able to sit anywhere."

XXVII.

"There's gotta be at least four men in the room now. Two, maybe three girls on stage," Freakshow briefs.

A vent in the ceiling propels cool air onto the beads, sending them swaying. That, along with the laughter of men in the background and music turned up, envelops the entire club in an artificial seismic wave. Freakshow squats by the curtain, trying to view the stage while keeping his head out of the threshold of detection, a nearly impossible feat.

"Hey, Show," Fish calls, tapping on Freakshow's shoulder. "You know what you should do from now on?"

"What?" Freakshow asks, sensing something of immense unimportance about to be divulged by Fish.

"Start using a catchphrase and one-liners."

"Sure...," Freakshow says, not the least bit interested. He needlessly continues to occupy himself with spying into the club in an effort to passively discourage any further propositions.

Fish continues, unimpeded.

"For example, you could use something like, 'It's Showtime!' or , 'You guys wanted to see a show?' You can use frea-"

"Yeah, that's fucking great," Ana angrily interrupts. "We're here to wreak payback on a guy who molested and killed his niece and your main concern is fantasy action hero wordplay?"

Fish nearly stutters. "We're not really gonna kill him, are we? I mean, we're not getting paid or anything for this."

"Shut up. This one is *pro bono*; we're doing this as a favor." Freakshow stands and states orders of action. "Ana, you're staying here, right? Fish, get your head in the game and let's go. Game on!"

He disappears into the club. The beads swing wildly in his wake. Fish hastily follows.

"Get on the ground! Everybody get down now!" Freakshow sounds off in a war cry.

Fish jumps out with gusto, directing his silver revolvers to the ceiling and pulls the triggers once each in alternation. The guns buck in his hands.

A cry of terror is heard from the stage. Men pinching tightly-rolled bills up to their noses fall into booths for cover. Freakshow, startled by the unexpected gunfire, turns to Fish while keeping an eye on the room.

"Fish, what the fuck? You don't just start shooting!"

"I thought that was the plan!"

"No! No, that's not the fucking plan at all!"

A body snakes closer to a door in the rear of the club.

Freakshow makes a fresh declaration with his assault rifle and fires a warning shot at the rear door, signing it with a silver crater. The threatening roar of the much-larger sounding weapon cues the hysterical blubbering of someone on the stage.

"Nobody fucking move, fuckfaces!" Freakshow shouts.

"Don't move you fucking idiot!" someone yells from inside a booth.

Fish lowers his voice so as not to call attention to their general lack of planning, as well as his personal lack of experience.

"So, what *is* the plan?" Fish putters through the side of

his mouth. He detects a hint of worry in Freakshow's expression.

"Just ask for Betty's uncle and-"

"You know what he looks like, right?" Fish presses.

"Jeez, typical fat Mexican, or Dominican? Balding? Short?"

"Everyone I just saw duck behind these booths looks like a typical fat Mexican, or Dominican; balding and short. What's his name?"

Freakshow looks to the stage at a dancer trying to raise her head.

Fish fires a warning shot. The dancer throws her head back down sobbing.

"Fuck! Cover this shit real quick," Freakshow says as he does an about-face, flings the curtain aside, and returns to the corridor.

The swinging beads lap against the wall.

Ana sits across from the unconscious bouncer, musing as she traces the pistol with a finger.

"Ana, we're gonna need you," Freakshow says adopting a pleading tone.

"No fucking way!" Ana resists.

"C'mon babe, please?"

"I don't know if I'm ready for this yet. I promised myself I would never go back in there."

"Ana, we have no idea what the fuck this Uncle Jose guy looks like. You *need* to help us out."

Ana clenches her pistol with a flushed red hand and slowly rises as she hangs her head in discouragement.

"Thanks babe," Freakshow says, accompanying his verbal gratitude with a patronizing rub on her back.

"So, you guys came to see *the show*, right?" Fish broadcasts over the room as Freakshow reappears with Ana trailing behind.

Freakshow testingly glares at Fish.

"All right. All right. Your call. I just wanted to try it out," Fish concedes, shrinking back.

As expected, there was no resistance. Freakshow, Ana, and Fish manage to conduct a swift and uneventful sweep of the room.

Men: 5
Women: 3
Weapons: none

This is nobody's first time here and the layout of the club is simple enough as is. A spacious arrangement; booths run on either side of the room with round tables and accompanying chairs scattered in between. The stage up the front has a walkway that stretches out to the middle of the room. A bar in the back marks where they recently entered. A double door emergency exit on the right wall is chained and fastened with a padlock. A door adjacent left to the stage leads to the restroom, office, storage, and dressing room. A space to the right of the stage is occupied by sound equipment. Single bottom-latch windows opening outward run along the upper portion of the walls and allow ample lighting in.

Fish threateningly directs his revolvers at a group of four men huddled into a booth. Freakshow herds a man near the stage's adjacent door over to the right side of the room with the others. The flustered man marches with hands upraised in surrender as he nervously clings to a small plastic bag containing unidentifiable paraphernalia. Three strippers are sat at the edge of the stage; one hysterical, two in a drug-induced torpor.

Ana, with much chagrin, discloses to Freakshow and

Fish, "I've never seen any of these people before."

"What?" Freakshow asks in disbelief. Deciding to posit a more specific question, he follows up with: "You mean, he's not here?"

"I *mean*," Ana sticks sarcastically, "I don't fucking see him."

Fish hopes to cue an instant response. "So?"

Freakshow jumps for the stage and throws the crying stripper face down. He rests his heavy leather boot on her skull and points the gun toward her face. She offers no physical resistance to his interrogation techniques. He bends forward and hangs his face over hers.

"Hey beautiful, did you see a fat Mexican fucker by the name of…"

She cries in protest.

"Please don't hurt me. I'm just trying to get some money to finish school and take care of my baby!"

"But of course you are," Freakshow concurs. "Ana, fuckshisname?"

"Jose," she says with an indifference.

Fish has a fit. "No fucking way! We have no plan! All we got is some fat Mexican's name! This is starting to become really stupid!"

"Starting? I think we passed stupid a long time ago," Ana agrees under her breath.

Freakshow eases the pressure on the bawling woman's skull as he turns to quell disorder within his own ranks.

"You two please, *please* shut the fuck up! Ana, you said that fat fuck Jose comes here all the time, right? Just let me think for a sec."

"I think he's in the restroom," the meek voice from under the boot divulges.

Freakshow throws his hands to high heaven. "Thank you

God! Fish, check it out."

Ana slumps into a chair. Drawing a bent cigarette from her pocket, she places it in her eager lips, and with an unsteady hand, ignites it. Fish, dragging his feet, crosses the labyrinth of cocked tables and chairs. He momentarily stops before the door, observing the fresh bullet insignia near the handle. Armed with the dual snub nose revolvers, he unskillfully pushes down on the handle, hooks the door with his toes, and kicks it open.

XXVIII.

Fish doggedly slips into the small room. A door in front of him is marked with two blue geometric figures: a circle sitting atop an inverted triangle. Another door to his right hanging slightly heavier from its hinges has a bolt lock above a simple pull handle. The door is unmarked, but it must lead to an existing office, dressing room, and lavatory for the opposite sex.

He stares at the light grain wood comprising the bathroom door. Maybe Fish will manage to get lucky. Maybe Jose didn't hear jack shit behind the double doors and will walk his mug straight into the opposite end of one of the two silver barrels. Fish could catch him by surprise and be finished with it quick, but those odds are very slim. Fish waits in anticipation for any sound of movement. Could he even be trusted to make a kill on his own? Maybe he can at least catch Jose defenseless with his portly frame stuck in the window attempting to scuttle through it.

But the bathroom is silent.

Fish pushes the door open, sending off a loud squeak.

The bathroom is doused in a retroactive seafoam green that heavily impresses itself on the eyes. An overflowing trash can sits by the door. Four urinals and four stalls. The walls are etched with dirty jokes and the mirrors are smeared with what

Fish hopes is crusted liquid soap. A brown buildup gathers along the edges of the wall, especially concentrated in the corners, and the paint: wherever it isn't peeling it leaves a venous trail of fine fractures. All four stall doors are closed. Fish cannot recall whether the doors were always closed or not. He's watched entirely too many movies to not appreciate the kicking-down-the-stall-doors trope used in countless action films. Fish wonders, if Jose is in fact hiding in this room, perhaps he would favor a peaceful surrender.

"Yo, anyone in here?"

Careful not to lose his balance, he squats to peek under the stalls. No presence is visible. Upon getting back up, Fish loses some balance and braces himself with his hand, touching a wet spot on the floor. He silently gags and grabs for a paper towel to remove the mysterious liquid from his outer palm. At least they are well stocked, Fish thinks. He tosses the brown paper towel to the floor. Thinking himself extremely clever, he refuses to be claimed as another victim of a well-known Hollywood they-never-hide-in-the-stalls-closest-to-the-exit folly and walks to the farthest stall instead.

He kicks the first door in with his heel. Easy enough, as he has seen Freakshow do it countless times. The door flies in on loose hinges. A hole big enough for a fist to pass through punctures the stall divider. This must be someone's idea of a sick joke, Fish thinks. Phone numbers of people unknown to Fish are scribbled around a waist high socket. In uppercase letters the words "glory hole" are artfully inked over the aperture. An endearing Kilroy looks on from the opposite wall.

"But they're always in the end stall," Fish mouths, shaking his head in disappointment.

Moving to the next stall, he kicks the door in. This side of the hole bears lascivious taunts and testimony of sexual activity scrawled in black and blue ink. Crude pictures of the male organ embellished by numerous contributors over time serve as an unofficial public record of wantonness.

"Jose?" he calls out.

Moving to the third door, he kicks it down. Nothing.

"What the fuck am I doing? This is fucking stupid. He's not even here," Fish says in frustration. He smites the last door open with the butt of his gun, and regrettably lets his guard down. At that very instant, a remarkably fat man with a dour countenance charges out with an extended arm. His open palm crashes against Fish's face and forces him to the floor. Disoriented, Fish looks to the door just as the brown gingham bulk flees the bathroom.

"Show!" Fish yells, trying to penetrate the walls.

XXIX.

Finally, a shower. Mike Bua hops into an unmarked police vehicle and pulls out of the garage. The engine on this cruiser sounds like absolute shit, he thinks to himself. Mike hasn't been home for days. Having considered the situation at home as of late, sleeping at the precinct and dozing off at bars always seemed the more favorable option.

Mike reaches into his coat pocket and runs his fingers over the reassuring glossy texture of the photo torn in two. Maki's plane would have touched down by now. Mike resists an urge to try and contact her. Even if he did, what would they have to talk about? Putting down the windows, the wind whips through his damp hair. Approaching an on ramp, he slowly applies pressure to the accelerator, impelling the air faster and faster throughout the vehicle. A small voice begins to sound from the center console: dispatch. He reaches down to tweak the volume.

"Sal's Arabian Nights, shots fired."

Mike sends a reply that he's on it. Flashing his dashboard lights, he throws his weight on the gas. The nauseated transmission sounds off in a dry heave. Surrounding automobiles take shelter on the right lane as he bursts through traffic.

"Looks like the shrink will have to wait," he says to

himself, his words being ripped apart in the roar of circulating air.

XXX.

The clunky bullet-indented door knocks against the wall as Jose flies into the main room. He bounds toward the exit in diagonal strides. Ana, spotting him, parts her mouth in disillusionment. Her cigarette subsequently falls, scattering embers across the table. She leaps up and charges at him. Intercepting him mid-stride, she redirects all his forward momentum and plows him into an empty booth, his head nearly sharing the same fate as that of the bouncer's.

Fish enters the room hunched over from pain. Using the backside of his thumb, he applies intermittent pressure whilst alternating nostrils to quell what he deduces to be an oncoming nosebleed. Breathing heavily through his mouth, he witnesses the latter half of Ana's tackle and lets out with a resounding "holy shit."

Freakshow belts out new instructions.

"Everybody get the fuck out now!"

The five sordid men quickly pocket their paraphernalia and run for the exit. The slobbering stripper, suddenly aloof at the prospect of having to head out in broad daylight in her manner of dress, shamefully collects herself and sulks away. The final two torpid strippers, with oblique nipples stretched over their beach ball breasts, exchange a few words as they mechanically collect loose bills sprinkled across the floor and stage.

Ana pincers her legs around Jose's chest, immobilizing his arms. He reeks of halitosis and cat urine. Still wielding a pistol, Ana soars her fists high above her head and hurls them downward pummeling his face in rancor. Jose's body squirms, violently trying to escape the merciless blows. He frees his arms and darts them forward in an attempt to wrestle the weapon from Ana. He clamps both hands around her wrist and digs his fingers into her tendons. Ana's grip weakens. The gun slips from her hands and falls into the void of the booth's floor. Jose releases her arm and ducks his head under the tabletop.

Ana desperately searches for any instrument to inflict more damage on José. Her eyes move to the tabletop. An empty and oversized glass ashtray invitingly sits atop. Her grip chokes the heavy circular glass as if to pulverize it. Losing all control, she begins wildly thrashing Jose as he tries to reach for the fumbled weapon. He moans in pain through the wet thumping. His complexion forfeits most of its solid property, becomes increasingly discolored, and assumes qualities not altogether differing from an over-ripened fruit. An amalgamation of bodily fluids egressing through broken tissue seem to purge his impurities. Ana smashes the thick glass just above his cheekbone. The convex bone yields like warm clay. Jose looks up at Ana in bewilderment. His hemorrhaging right eye is grotesquely recessed in its redesigned socket. Adrenaline receding, Ana backs off of Jose as Freakshow and Fish try to get a look at the damage.

Jose begins to chuckle lightly, but cuts himself off, his face's structural integrity being in no condition to afford him the luxury of laughter. Retiring the use of his jaw, Jose speaks employing only his tongue and lips.

"You hit like a faggot," he gurgles.

Freakshow raises his assault rifle.

"No!" Ana protests. "Let him suffer."

Blood, tissue, and loose hairs dangle from the glass bludgeon. Jose deflates as a breath flees his fat body. His body slowly molds to the booth as if becoming permanently affixed to it. Ana waits in anticipation for his last breath, that gurgling indicator of expiration. Her fingers relax and release the ashtray, letting it fall in a dead thud upon the floor.

"Ahh... Freakshow?" Fish hesitantly confides. His nasal voice is more distinct with the clotting blood depositing in his sinuses. "I don't wanna keep being that guy, but we really have to go."

Ana fishes her pistol out from under the booth table with the swoop of a leg.

XXXI.

The heavy steel door mewls in protest as Ana carelessly throws it open in panic. Freakshow follows from behind with Fish shadowing even further back, toting the tonnage of weaponry, the two silver revolvers tucked into his rear waist.

Freakshow, looking to the distance, manages a five-second forewarning with a simple "fuck."

Fish drops the bag. He and Ana straighten their backs, attempting to match Freakshow's height as they trace his gaze.

"Fuck," Ana repeats.

A straining engine sounds off from up the road. A fourth generation turtle blue Grand Am sucking in roadside litter with its slipstream barrels toward them on the otherwise vacant highway. Freakshow fires his weapon as the sedan skids onto the lot. He orders Ana and Fish down as he lets off a few more cathartic rounds, shooting out the headlights and obliterating the windshield.

Freakshow reloads.

The Grand Am's doors pop open in synchronicity. Two men tumble out of the front, return fire, and seek cover on the far side of the vehicle. A third larger and foppishly-dressed man lumbers out of the back, cursing at the top of his lungs through the gunfire. On the lot for cover, only one of the previously-parked sunburnt beaters remain: an Oldsmobile.

Taking safety from the line of fire, Ana crouches and heads as far back as the rear bumper. Fish follows behind, dragging the heavy duffel bag. Freakshow acknowledges his size vulnerability and hunches down to take cover as well. Shots seize from the Grand Am amidst inarticulate orders.

"Stop fucking shooting! I said stop fucking shooting!"

It's Sal.

Sal is settled in a seated position with his back against the car. His breath is thick. The inside of his suit is sweltering. Lightly kneading the bridge of his nose with his forefinger, he yanks down on the knot of his necktie, easing his airway. "You no-good motherfuckers! How dare you? Nearly busting my nose wasn't enough? Now you have to go and shoot up my place?!"

Talking certainly won't make this situation any more solvent, but Freakshow answers anyway, back against the Olds, his words travel in the opposite direction.

"It's not like that, Sal! It wasn't supposed to go down like this!"

"You tell me how the fuck it was supposed to go down! You ruined my fuckin' car!" Sal's screams growing ever choleric.

Fish's sweating hands tap Freakshow on the shoulder.

"Show, you should tell him about the fruit basket."

"Not now Fish," Freakshow curtly responds.

Sal goes off on a winded diatribe, elaborating on the audacity of the three who think they can "just barge in" to a "respectable place of business" and "play vigilante." He goes so far as to claim himself a victim of racism, threatening with litigation, and guaranteeing their continued suffering by asserting his influence even within prison walls, that is, if he "chooses" to let them live. He finishes off with a, "I'll fuckin' kill you, Ana!"

"It's just a Grand Am, you shit!" Fish mischievously jousts.

Sal goes into a violent episode, spouting incomprehensible language, which oddly enough, they are certain is English. In his furor, his vocals start tearing on the high end.

The SUV, being far from the crossfire, sits in the center of the parking lot, undamaged. No more than two parking rows away, Ana tries to squeeze a shot in. Edging herself dangerously close to the Oldsmobile's threshold, she exposes her position.

A pistol shot comes from the Grand Am.

Ana shrieks in pain. The weight of metal in her hands is released and chinks against the asphalt. Following the origin of pain, she looks down to see her left arm has been dissected by a bullet. She uses her freed hand to cover the wound and stabilize the torn sinew. The pain makes it hard for her to apply enough pressure to retard the bleeding to any great effect. Her hand quickly becomes steeped in blood.

Responding, Freakshow darts up and clears his magazine with automatic fire, the body of his rifle rapidly cocking within its camouflaged slide. Someone on Sal's side falls. Freakshow grabs another clip from his bulging vest and reloads.

Fish nests his torso underneath the car and sends a half-dozen carefully calculated shots over to the Grand Am, disabling someone's ankle and burying two shots in Sal's posterior. There is no longer any movement from either of Sal's bodyguards.

"Fuch-you-fuch-you-fuchs!" Sal sirens off in agony. In hope of mollifying the wounds, his early onset arthritic fingers searchingly stab at his rear, but only makes the pain worse. He is on the border of tears.

Fish squinches out from under the car with improved self-esteem.

Freakshow grabs the duffel bag and slings it over his

shoulder, unencumbered. "Fish, drive. We need to get out of here," he calmly orders.

Fish runs for the vehicle as Freakshow hauls Ana in his massive arms. A steady drip of blood flows from her weakening limb. Ana tries to relay an apology to Freakshow. He responds only by politely asking her to shut up.

He aims the passenger-side doors at his partners.

"Climb in," Fish says.

Sal, still wishing to maintain his illusion of authority, pleads to Freakshow in the most apologetic manner of which he is capable.

"Mike! You fuck! Don't leave me here! Don't fucking leave me here!"

Freakshow places Ana on the backseat and hops in, closing the door behind him.

"I will fuckin' kill you! I'll fucking kill all you faggots!" Sal shouts in finality as spit sprays from his mouth like a fleeing swarm of gnats.

The black SUV peels away. Just as soon as it disappears south, a multitude of flashing blue and red lights appear coming from the opposite direction.

Two dazed strippers shielding their breasts with a fistful of crumpled singles stagger out of the club in platform high heels.

Sal gazes up to the balmy summer sky. The corners of his mouth turn upward. He lets out a couple of coughs that sound very much like laughter.

XXXII.

Fish speeds away, nervously glancing back at the slowly-vanishing specters of flashing blue and red.

"Fuck! Fuck!" Freakshow vehemently curses in the backseat. He takes off his vest and shirt, displaying the innumerable array of tattoos stratified across his chest and back. Tearing his shirt with his teeth, he ties it around Ana's arm. She grunts in discomfort.

Fish observes Ana's deathly pallor and begins nervously rocking in the driver's seat.

"We have to get to the hospital!" he reacts, trying to keep a stutter in check.

"No hospitals!" Freakshow says.

Fish, at loss of other ideas, repeats once again.

"We have t-"

"No fucking hospitals!" Freakshow yells.

The weight of the vehicle seems immense to Fish. The accelerator seems to have stiffened since they pulled out of the parking lot. The raw smell of Ana's blood seeps into Fish's clogged sinuses. He wishes to open a window, but abstains for fear of protest.

Ana's lips twitch. Freakshow kneels forward. Ana's weak voice barely carries to his ear. "Promise me you won't take me to the hospital. No one can know."

"I know Ana. I know," Freakshow whispers consolingly.

"Fucking promise me!" Ana says overexerting herself.

"I promise. Goddammit Ana, you know I wouldn't do that," Freakshow confirms.

"What is she saying?" Fish impertinently questions. "C'mon Show, where am I going here?"

Freakshow presses his ear directly over Ana's lips, relaying instructions to Fish.

"The Brazilian," says Ana, through Freakshow.

"What the fuck does that even mean?" Fish asks, puzzled.

"Keep heading south...

Twenty minutes...

Turn right on Voyager," Ana's instructs through her conduit.

"I should recognize the way from there," Freakshow adds in finality as he carefully rests his lips on Ana's pale forehead.

"Jeez, is she even gonna make it?" Fish poses to himself.

XXXIII.

Late midday, Sal's Arabian Nights.

It's a circus outside. A large gathering of police officers and the media in a single-concentrated spot can hardly be construed as anything else. The news outlets are unusually early this time. Mike Bua had barely finished securing the crime scene before the first flock of vans showed up.

A few fatalities, a few survivors. No one will be missed. The kind of people gathering at a place like Sal's in the middle of the day comprise a certain degree of lowness and sleaziness that normal citizens would probably lose sleep over. Many would say that someone did society a great favor here today.

Eager reporters outstretch arms and balance their microphones on extended fingers as if aiming to knock over something just out of reach on the other side of the crime scene tape. White reporter, Asian reporter, black reporter, Hispanic reporter, effeminate male reporter, and even a fat reporter. Their gender, ethnicity, physiological, and sexual leanings balance amongst each other as the ideal of political correctness. "What happened here?" "What happened inside?" and "Who was involved?" are the only questions their limited imaginations can offer. Any true deductive abilities on their part would draw them to the much more curious trail of partially-bloody footprints in size 14 combat boots that disappear in the middle of the parking lot.

As far as witnesses; two girls working the dayshift are too high to be credible or even useful in the investigation, the bouncer has a concussion, and Sal—after he tends to his comical injuries—won't be talking to anyone but his lawyer, while perhaps investing the help of other hired guns and putting a hit on whoever caused him this grievance.

Two stiffs are hauled away in body bags.

Mike steps inside to savor a moment with Jose Santos before the medical examiner carts the body off.

A mangled face attached to a multiformed body lies glued to a booth. A thick tuft of hair wrapping around his head is hardened with blood. Jose's gingham shirt is forced upward by his dangling arms, revealing a splotchy, distended, and hair-covered belly. A half-open eye is offset in his skull; orbital fracture.

Mike massages his thickly-bandaged hand in vindictive remembrance, as if his injury was directly inflicted by the currently deceased.

"At least the sick fuck got what he deserved," Mike sounds off in a bitter utterance.

XXXIV.

The smell of brine seeps into the vehicle as Fish slowly pulls to a gravel strip, the only marked parking area, running alongside a massive white row of abandoned warehouses. This area hasn't been in use for decades, not since the port relocated to the north bay. The warehouses sit like dormant giants guarding the pier. Where Fish is parked, a peeling sign adhered to the top corner of the building reads: BJJ.

"Okay, we're here. Wherever 'here' is."

Fish pulls the keys out of the ignition. Stepping out of the vehicle, he holds his hand with fingers extended horizontally to his face in an effort to visually gauge his adrenaline levels. Seeing that his gloves are still on, he yanks them off and shoves them into his back pocket. In a reversed motion, he then reaches for the empty revolvers, packed in his waist, and tosses them into the passenger's seat.

Ana looks two shades paler as a topless Freakshow pulls her out of the SUV into the daylight.

"Grab the entrance around the corner," Freakshow orders.

Fish springs ahead.

A small door within a much larger bivalve door opens with little resistance. A giant flag of Brazil hanging on the wall greets Fish as he enters. It's the only thing lit up in the room.

Enormous tires lay in disorder across the floor. Sledgehammers and rebar attached to broken concrete seem to designate a construction zone. Section pipes, sailor's rope, and giant spools lay bare in another corner. Perhaps it's an abandoned remodeling project, Fish thinks. The walls are crumbling. A single section of the wall looks as if the concrete blocks are just floating in place. Light peeks in through the cracks like a photograph negative. Aside from the single remarkable element of a pristine blue mat lying at the center of the floor, everything has fallen into disrepair.

Fish summons initiative.

"Hello?"

Answering, a small black feline stalks out of the darkness. Ignoring the fiery-headed intruder, it exits through the door as Freakshow, with Ana in arms, enters.

Not entirely discouraged by the appearance of a cat, Fish tries once more.

"Hello? Is The Brazilian here? Mr. The Brazilian are you here?"

Freakshow lays Ana down on a wobbly aluminum bench.

Pressed for time, Fish finally screams.

"Where is The Brazilian?"

A voice muffled by a thin wall answers back.

"Calm down sir. I will be there in a second!"

XXXV.

Matt Mashburn is losing his composure. His face is becoming flushed in anger and he finds it increasingly difficult to find something to do with his hands. He starts fiddling incessantly with his peaked cap like a distracted child as he anxiously waits for a pause in the Captain's haranguing. Matt would love to squeeze a word in in his own defense. To think that a few allusions to Detective Mike Bua's instability and character flaws circulating around the station can lead you in the Captain's office.

Finally, the opportunity for Matt to speak arises.

"What the hell is that supposed to mean, Captain? I have great character. A man of honor. I'm a decorated officer for Chris' sake! What the hell does Bua ever do except get drunk and embarrass the force?"

"Decorated *military*, not a police officer,"the Captain gladly corrects. "But they give medals and ribbons out like goddamn candy now. You know what we had to do back in my day to earn a...? Never mind."

The Captain backtracks to his unfinished thread of thought.

"All right, honor boy. Who was your first bust?"

Matt was prepared for this. He deliberately responds in a flat tone, not wishing to reveal a stricken nerve.

"My brother," he says, adding a "and I think I did the right thing."

Matt's suddenly indifferent demeanor makes it all too easy for the Captain. Mashburn reads like a book.

The Captain continues to string him along.

"Wha'd you bust him for?"

"Selling drugs."

"You caught him selling marijuana *and*...," the Captain gladly corrects Matt's misleading choice for words.

Matt continues flatly.

"And sleeping with a 14-year old girl."

"Ouch," the Captain says, wincing in an obnoxious display of unprofessionalism.

Matt, becoming more upset, disregards formalities and loses his flat tone.

"What's your point?"

"When did you make that bust?"

"Two years ago."

The Captain is becoming irritated by Mashburn's constantly evasive responses, not sure whether they are deliberate or accidental.

"Not how *long ago*. How much time did you have in?"

"A few weeks."

"Damn! That sounds like some goddamn rookie wanted a bust, so he turned in his own goddamn family," the Captain eagerly disparages.

"That's not the situation!"

"So you never knew about his problems? But after being a cop for a goddamn week, bang, you solve the case?"

Matt rotates the peaked cap in his hands, not knowing how to respond to such a direct query. His mouth parts, but is unaccompanied by any sound.

The Captain peevishly raises an eyebrow at Matt's

attempt at a counter-argument before freely continuing.

"That's what I thought. I think I'll stick with Mike taking lead on these cases, but I've got a job for you Ratburn. You can report directly to me on how Bua is doing every day."

"Can I go now sir?"

Matt finds it difficult to keep eye contact.

The Captain ignores Matt and finishes his thought.

"You see what I did there? I called you *Rat*burn, because you're a rat. Now *that's* a good one."

The lack of the Captain's professionalism is appalling.

"I'm going to leave now, sir!" Matt says, excusing himself.

"Good idea!"

XXXVI.

To say that Mike Bua is being insolent would be greatly understating his current mood. He is seated.

"Fuck this shit. Fuck you. Who the fuck do you think you are to ask me about my daughter?"

"I'm just trying to help," the woman answers.

"You want to help? Never fucking mention my daughter again."

"Okay, what do *you* want to talk about?" she asks amiably.

Not this. Not this shit. Not all this education hanging on the wall in dark-stained frames. Not these repeating wooden tones accented in the large file cabinets, the sofa, bookshelves, lamp, and writing utensils. Nor the pistachio-green rug resembling bile with its beige tassels slowly wearing away from trafficking feet. All that's missing is that bestselling motivational poster with the cat hanging from a branch and maybe an assortment of plush toys to project feelings onto.

Mike reaches into his pocket for cigarettes that aren't there. A middle-aged woman wearing glasses with auburn curls cascading to her shoulders smiles at Mike Bua.

"Michael?" she calls, her voice echoing maternal seduction.

Mike wonders if this is how she gets all her patients to

talk, if this is her big secret, playing on the male analysand's oedipal conflicts. She opens you up, you make a conscious connection, and the session ends with you either weeping into her lap or suckling at her breast in regressed glory, no better off than you were when you first came in. Mike makes eye contact and begins to speak.

"Okay, we'll talk. Let's talk about how my captain's wife is a cokehead and has herpes."

She leans forward from behind her desk.

"We're here to talk about you, Michael."

Mike keeps himself distracted.

"It's Mike. Wait, wait, I didn't tell you the punchline. *He* gave *her* the herpes."

"Didn't your wife recently leave you?"

Mike can't stand the firmness of the brown leather sofa.

"She didn't leave me. She just had to go back home to her country. We still love each other, it's just that... Well, it's complicated," he says, showing a hairline fracture in his psyche.

"When did she go back home?"

Mike looks to the desk. A laser-etched glass name plaque sits just off the corner at a fifteen degree angle.

"I see you're Jewish," he observes.

"Do you have a problem with Jews?" she asks in an indifferent tone.

"No, it's just that you don't look Jewish. Do you believe in God?"

"Do *you* believe in God?"

"Fuck God."

Her expression remains unchanged.

"You don't believe in God then?"

"I believe in him. I believe he's a power-hungry prick that does no good for anyone."

"Aren't you mistaking God with Satan?" she asks.

"The devil and God. They are one," Mike states.

"But Jews don't believe in the devil. He's only a metaphor for evil, not a sentient being like in Christianity."

"Okay, well it works your way too then. Look, every miracle can be explained by science, right?"

"What about manna falling from the sky?"

"Okay, smartass. Not taking into account the laughably-absurd circumstances where prepared food precipitates from the heavens, every miracle in the Bible can be explained by science, right? What does God always end up doing? Shitting on the parade. Like when he decided to fuck everyone but Noah and his family riding that ark while holding the key to humanity's continuation. God has it made. And everyone he decides to save, guaranteed employment with his PR company."

"PR?"

"Oh yeah, the motherfucker has great PR! Think about it. One family lives out of the millions that die, and they call it a miracle!"

Mike rubs his thick bandages, surprised not to have been asked about the proverbial elephant in the room yet.

"Look, just follow me on this," he says, putting his arm down. "One out of a million is a failure. What if *you* treated a million crazy fucktards but only managed to save one?"

"You're trying to say I'd be a failure?"

"Exactly. Hell, any cop having that kind of record, they'd stone him!"

"How Biblically apropos," she says, conjoining her hands.

Mike eases his back against the sofa.

"Jeez, I didn't know they still made these psych sofas. Do they sell to you guys exclusively or something?"

The woman stands up, displaying her profile. The trim

bridge of her nose evenly slopes downward and gracefully rounds off at the tip. Her nostrils are like a child's—near perfect circles unmarked with blemish scars or freckles. She leans on her desk.

"Very neat, huh?" she says proudly. "Actually, that's not a chaise lounge. It's an antique fainting couch that I had reupholstered."

"What?" Mike responds, not comprehending her language. Nothing could have prepared his intellect for her erudition in European furniture history.

"Fainting couches were popular among women who felt themselves out of breath because their corsets would cut off circulation, or at least that's one of the two popular theories."

"Oh, what's the other?"

"Four words: pelvic massage house calls," she says with an even spacing between the first three words.

"Intriguing," Mike replies unfazed.

"Do you consider yourself a good person, Mike?"

"There is no purpose in being a good person. I never drank or did drugs before. I practically had everything..."

"Like Job did?"

"What the fuck? Are you offering psychiatric counseling or religious? Look, all I know is if, or when, I get to meet my maker, I'm going to punch him in the fucking throat."

Mike looks to his clenched fist's paling knuckles.

"Never drank or did drugs *before*?" she questioningly proceeds. "Implying that you do drugs now?"

"Middle-class drugs," Mike says shrugging. "You know, the kind that you'll be writing me a prescription for later."

XXXVII.

Fish anxiously paces.

"Well, I hope this guy knows what he's doing. Show, you sure you don't wanna take her to a fucking doctor?"

"No doctors," Ana's voice creaks. This is the first time Fish has actually heard her speak since they left Sal's. He questions Freakshow's constant forfeiture in answering for himself.

"Fuck, where is this guy?" Fish asks as his pacing draws him nearer and nearer to the reflective mat.

"Don't you dare disturb my mat!" a lazily-spoken man words off from the opposite end of the room.

Fish jumps at the sudden introduction.

A dark-skinned man stands tall as he walks across the mat barefoot. He holds a pair of rubber sandals and is clothed in nothing more than a white towel snugged around his waist. The limited light casting on his thin yet toned body casts small rippling shadows that dance over his abdomen.

"You'd better be a fucking doctor," Fish replies.

The tall man throws his sandals down to the floor and assigns a foot into each.

"Oh, I'm no doctor," the Brazilian flatly replies while keeping his eyes on Ana.

As the Brazilian approaches, Freakshow steps back,

allowing an examination to commence.

The Brazilian squats down and indecipherably whispers to Ana. The back of his head is sparkling with moisture caught in his tight curly hair.

"Were you just in the shower?" Fish asks, though feeling somewhat silly after not receiving a response to such an obviously-deducible fact.

The thin man removes Freakshow's bloodied shirt tied around Ana's arm as blood instantly begins seeping out of a fissure. He turns to Freakshow, addressing him as Michael, and asks him to hold Ana's arm up and to apply pressure.

Freakshow follows his instructions.

The Brazilian steps to an unlit corner of the room for a minute, leaving Freakshow and Fish clueless as to the situation. Ana's labored breathing and sanguine discharge inject a raw dankness into the stale atmosphere of the warehouse. The Brazilian returns with a pail filled with water and a clean dressing. He once again squats next to Ana and inspects her wound with Freakshow assisting.

The Brazilian, disregarding Fish, adjusts his volume to an attendant Freakshow at his side.

"This is very bad bro. It's her brachial artery," he says gravely.

Fish, leaning in, overhears the surreptitious exchange between the two.

"What the fuck? Artery?"

Fish throws his hands to his head in protest trying to come to terms with the situation.

"She needs to see a real doctor or she's gonna bleed out and die!" says Fish.

"You need to keep your cool little man!" the Brazilian shouts.

Ana clears a lump in her throat.

"I'm not going to see the doctor. Just drop it Fish." she says. Her eyes are shut with a force that indicate tremendous pain.

"That is it! I've had enough!" Fish tirades. "Everything and everyone has to be hush-hush. There is some secret bullshit going on here and I need to know what it is right now! And Show's not fucking saying anything! Ana, you need to go to the hospital or you're gonna die! Am I the only fucking sane person here?"

Fish catapults his leg forward and jettisons a fragment of concrete to the other side of the room. It hits the flag and plops onto the mat.

The Brazilian's temper is lost.

"Go get that fucking rock before I choke the life out of you!" the Brazilian says.

Fish looks to Freakshow, seeking reinforcement, but receives none.

"You'd better get that rock, Fish," Freakshow says in languor.

"Disrespectful motherfucker. I told you not to disturb my mats!" the Brazilian roars. "And don't you walk on there with shoes!"

Fish, deciding not to remove his shoes out of laziness, crawls on his knees a few blue rectangles away to retrieve the forsaken fragment, all the while mocking the Brazilian in a whisper. He spins on all fours and returns with the rock in hand.

"This is bullshit! What the fuck is going on here? What secret is worth Ana's life?"

"What are you? A fucking child? Calm down," Freakshow says, retaining his indifference.

"No, I will not calm down! She is going to die and you bring her to a gym!" Fish retorts. "Fuckin' Ringo, now this!

I'm tired of this third-wheel bullshit! You don't fucking tell me anything. I can only be pushed so far. Ringo was asking for it and you know it! That's why you didn't bother stopping me!"

Freakshow stands up, ready to address the situation with force. Fish retreats a step back, shaking his head in incredulity, and continues.

"Then we had to chase some fat fucking Mexican. All I wanted to do is eat my fucking sandwich!"

Fish's eyes are watering.

"Ringo killed that fucking girl last night! In cold blood! She wasn't even the hit. She was sixteen for fuckssake! You didn't even fucking stop him, *Mike*!"

Freakshow looks down to his closed hands, baffled as to how to handle the nagging partner who barely meets the credentials to be a sidekick. He turns his palms and stretches his fingers. A thin coat of blood dries, leaving the creases of his skin as splintering threads of white. Coagulating maroon is deposited into the furrows of his fingernails. Freakshow looks to the Brazilian, to which the Brazilian cocks his head, sharing the same look of uncertainty on how to proceed.

Ana breaks the silence in a sort of forced vigor.

"It's okay. It's okay," she says, her strength lessening with every word that leaves.

Freakshow nods.

"I hope you're not saying this just because you're going to die soon," the Brazilian says in a pessimistic joke of very poor taste.

Ana ignores the comment and calls Fish forward. He draws near her with immense curiosity.

"There's no easy way to say this," she starts off in exordium.

"Ana's a tranny, my brother," the Brazilian tersely states,

offering a sudden relief.

Fish's face turns a shade lighter at the revelation. A fleeing breath pushes through his constricted airway and exits his mouth. His pupils flare. His gaze is locked into Ana's. His head feels lighter than air, as if ready to detach from his body and float upward. The piece of concrete still in his hands falls upon the floor. Nearly forgetting where the exit was located, Fish drags his feet outside.

"He's taking it better than I thought," says the Brazilian.

XXXVIII.

The psychiatrist produces a sterling silver writing utensil from her desk and begins penning something down. Mike hopes it's a prescription.

"So what about your wife? You said she recently went back home?"

"No, you said that," Mike rectifies.

Deciding to finally make himself comfortable in the provided furniture, he puts his feet up and reclines.

"Sorry, you're correct. I said that."

"Yes, you did."

"Did she recently go back home?" the psychiatrist says, treading lightly with her wording.

"Yes."

"When did she go back?"

"Yesterday."

"That is recent."

"Yeah, I don't wanna talk about it. You got a cigarette? I'm dying over here."

She points to a small sign mounted on the corner of her desk that discourages smoking in the room. "Well, what about the past?" she quickly posits, not wishing to lose any momentum.

"What about it?"

"Is there anything you'd like to do differently with her?"

"Aren't you trying to beat around the bush with what is essentially the same question you just asked me, rephrased?"

"Perhaps, perhaps not," she replies.

The doctor departs her desk and decides to keep Mike company from an brown leather armchair positioned across from him. She adjusts her seat and crosses her legs. "Well, contrary to popular belief, hindsight is not always twenty-twenty. And it helps to talk about the past. Let's say you could go back and make a change."

"Are you alluding to time travel, doc?"

"Please, call me Joanna, and not necessarily time travel. Say you could make a conscious initiative in your mind right now concerning something in the past, and it would be realized."

"Just like that?"

"Just like that."

"Well a time-manipulating machine of some sort would have been much more exciting. You have a poor imagination Joanna."

Mike closes his eyes and kneads his injured hand.

"Well, not thinking too hard, I have something for you already," Mike says.

"Yes?"

"I would go back to when I first met her."

Mike's irises flit against the inside of his eyelids. He no longer desires a cigarette.

XXXIX.

The sun weakens with every passing minute. Fish sits on his hams, unable to maintain a decent balance. As he looks out past the docks, his body mimics the rolling motion of the waves. Fish's falling backward is only prevented by the massive outer wall of the warehouse that lightly presses against his tail bone, reminding him when to reappropriate his weight forward.

The Brazilian steps outside, wearing proper garments even though still only half of him is clothed. He dries his hands in a white towel that is free of any stain and slings it over his shoulder. He looks past the docks to the emerging evening sky. The night firmament is slowly being dragged in with the arriving tide. It is as beautiful as it is toxic. This is nothing more than a polluted bay now. Algal blooms in the preceding decades have successfully eradicated ninety percent of marine life here. Anything that managed to survive, you wouldn't want to touch, let alone eat. If it wasn't hypoxia that did them in then, it's the lesions doing them in now.

"You know, this reminds me much of Brazil, the coast," says the Brazilian. "You always see the sun rising out from the water, never sinking into it. And you always see night long before it actually arrives, creeping up over the horizon to devour you."

Fish shoots air through his teeth, purporting his disinterest.

"You going to be okay, brother?" The Brazilian asks, giving slight concern.

"Ana has a penis, right?"

Fish's irrelevant questioning agitates the Brazilian.

"You really want to get into that now? Does it even really matter?"

"And that's why she never took it all off when she worked at Sal's? I thought she was just a prude. But I never saw a fucking lump!"

"Botched reassignment. She doesn't have man parts, but she doesn't have a vagina either."

Fish eyes fall to the mud-caked gravel.

"Did *you* botch it?"

"Fuck no, that wasn't me! You gotta understand though; she had complications. Many risks are involved with those kind of procedures, even if you do go through the proper channels."

Fish closes his eyes at the discomfort of his stomach churning on empty.

"Fuck, and Show is a faggot? I looked up to him. He is one of the craziest and toughest fucks I know."

"You'll get past that superficial shit. You're practically still a fucking kid."

The Brazilian yanks his sagging pants up to his waist. He keeps his eyes focused on the shifting tide as if he were prophesying from it.

"I don't see the problem. You said you killed some guy named Ringo last night, but you feel bad about hunting down this Mexican because? They told me that Jose guy raped and killed his niece, man! You're really just upset with yourself because of your own expectations. Hot girls can have penises too. You've just never had to come to terms with that reality until now."

Fish has never heard any non-native speaker of English deliver an argument so eloquently outlined. The black cat appears and butts its head against Fish's bent knee. He offers his hand for inspection. The cat sneers as it twists its head upward, lightly sniffing the tips of Fish's fingers. It looks as if he's addressing the cat when he says, "Dude, I used to jack-off to Ana. Does that make *me* gay?"

"You know, we have a saying in Brazil: If you have a bigger penis than your tranny, you're not gay."

The Brazilian stamps the toes of his sandals into the gravel, removes the towel from his shoulder, and turns to walk back into the warehouse. The cat quickly responds by running ahead. A tattoo scripted over the Brazilian's back bridges his sculpted trapezia: *Ordem a Progresso*.

"Hey dude. Brazilian!" Fish calls.

"What?"

"How is she, he? How is Ana?"

"She's fine for now."

"Brazilian?"

"My name is Luiz, bro."

"Luiz... Was Freakshow's penis bigger than Ana's?"

"I don't know. I'm not a homo," he answers, annoyed, and steps back into the warehouse.

Dusk will set in soon.

XL.

The club is loud. The drinks are extremely expensive. You must have one in your hand at all times. Water doesn't count. Beer. She is dancing with her friend. What is she wearing? What is her friend's name? She looks lonely. I say lonely. She just doesn't have any guys around her. Guys with erections hovering for attention. But that's not why I'm singling her out. She is dancing with her friend. Why doesn't she turn around? I need to get away from this bar. She turns. She looks amazing. I'll be smooth. The music is so loud. I walk toward them like I need to get past them. I tried to slide between. What is she drinking? There's a short guy staring at me. She laughs. She consults her friend. She speaks like I can't understand what she's saying. She says American. She says it with a negative connotation. She smells so good. She thinks I don't understand. I speak. What's wrong with American? She said she doesn't date them. But she still looked interested.

"Then I said as a joke, 'Oh, that's good, because I'm a Canadian," Mike Bua says, opening his eyes and slowly focusing on the sterile white ceiling with no light fixture attached. Quickly-dying daylight dissected by the blinds is flung onto the wall in horizontal stripes.

"What would you change?" asks Joanna.

"I wouldn't have danced with her."

"Why not?"

"She deserved better. I approached her on an ego high. I don't even like clubs," Mike confesses. "I was just there. And she was just there. You can't interpret that as fate or destiny or..."

"Kismet?" Joanna suggests.

"Or Kismet," Mike finishes, not certain if that's the word he intended to use.

"In Islam, kismet implies the will of the Supreme Being."

Mike eyes, now closed, roll up in their sockets.

"Please, not this religion stuff again!"

"We have successfully established that you do believe in God, correct?"

Joanna's tone is badgering.

"So our conversation is limited to theological topics only?"

"Not theological, metaphysical."

"Speak English, please."

"What are your thoughts on predestination?"

Mike swings his hands to the cushions, flings himself off the couch in fury, and stands up.

"You've got some balls throwing that word at me! How about the girl with vaginal tears and anal fissures who was suffocated in the tub last night? She had fucking cigarette burns on her labia for fuckssake! She was carrying a fucking baby for fuckssake! My daughter is dead! My wife left me! They're trying to throw me off the force! There isn't a day that goes by where I don't think about ending it all! And you wanna talk to me about predestination? When I just fucking told you I don't believe in that fate-destiny bullshit! For someone who gets paid to listen, you do a pretty shitty job!"

Mike Bua tempests toward the door, nearly pulling it off

the hinges and exits the room.

Joanna sits silently in regret. She removes her glasses, placing them atop her lap, and pinches the light indentations left on the bridge of her evenly-sloped nose. A clock ticks on the wall.

XLI.

Fish heads back into the warehouse. Freakshow, Ana, and the Brazilian have disappeared from the room. An incandescent shard of light is cast onto the floor left of the Brazilian flag. Fish glides his feet across the floor and carefully navigates himself up to the edge of the mat. He sits down and laboriously loosens his tightly-laced sneakers. Pulling them off, he walks across the smooth and shining mat, following the yellow sliver of light.

The mat ends. Fish carelessly slips his shoes on, not to be troubled with redoing his laces, and walks down a short corridor bearing an eerie resemblance with the floor plan at Sal's. A door at the end of the hall is revealed to be the origin of the spilling light. Fish can hear the evening news through what sounds like a television with a blown speaker. The sound is muffled and clips at the slightest gain of volume in the broadcast. Lubricated hinges swing the door open with ease as he raps his knuckles on the stile.

Ana lays on a chewed-up couch with her feet elevated onto a black leather ottoman. Her complexion seems to be improving. Red peeks through the tightly-wrapped gauze on her arm. Freakshow sits, holding Ana's right hand.

Fish enters the room hanging his head in penitence.

"So? What's the plan?" he asks.

"Are you okay?" Ana asks. For some reason now her voice sounds deeper and decays on the last syllable.

"Are *you* okay?" Fish comments.

"Yeah, Luiz is very good. He improvised a shunt with some aquarium tube. I got some steroids and painkillers too."

"Sounds sophisticated," Fish says with insincerity.

He looks around the room. A trash can filled with stained bandages sits next to a recently-used workbench. A hose runs from a small white and blue tank connected to what looks like an oxygen mask stolen from a commercial airliner. A needle, dental floss, various colored bottles, and stained cotton balls lie untidied if not wholly disregarded.

"Well, I guess you knew what you were doing when you told us to bring you here," he says, respecting Ana's judgment.

"Well, this isn't exactly a permanent fix. I'm barely being held together," Ana replies.

She repositions her sinking arm onto some balding velvet throw pillows.

"Are you still gonna 'own that pussy?'" she asks, studying Fish's expression.

Freakshow keeps his eyes glued to the television.

"Look, I understand why you didn't want to tell me. No offense to either of you, but I'm just gonna pretend that I don't know."

Ana shrugs.

"Fair enough."

Fish looks to the television screen. The top right corner is discolored with green. The clipping volume shakes the loose plastic shell that houses the fifteen inch cathode ray tube. Closed captioning is turned on. An inexperienced local news channel correspondent tentatively holds the microphone, repeating the same thing he's been repeating for the last few hours: that there have been no new developments in the grisly shooting involving local business owner Sal Solak.

"No mention of Jose, I see." Fish critiques over the streaming captions. "So what the fuck is our plan?"

"There is no plan. We're just gonna sit tight," Freakshow says, his eyelids drooping from exhaustion.

A picture of Sal Solak taken nearly half a decade ago is fed to the screen. He's wearing the exact same tweed suit, though with much less wear. The bandage on his nose is gone. His hair is a little longer and curls up at his ears. His vibrant eyes are looking off from the camera lens. His mouth is congenially curved upward.

"That's the most misleading photo I've ever seen of that fuck. I've never seen him look that respectable," Ana says, speaking mostly to herself.

Footfall from the gymnasium crescendos as the Brazilian whisks into the room and heads toward a desk on the opposite wall with a sun-bleached computer monitor sitting atop. He ransacks through a stack of curling papers and lets off a heavy sigh of approval as he rolls a document in his hand and hurriedly exits the room.

"Luiz?" Fish calls.

"Yeah. It's hooked up to the internet!" the Brazilian shouts back in an astounding conjecture.

Fish looks under the tabletop to a much newer-looking black horizontal tower nestled into a side panel. It is blinking blue with activity. He seats himself on the curving mesh of the ergonomically designed seat and depresses a button, firing up the monitor. A black background has multicolored pipes randomly snaking across the screen at ninety degree angles. Fish delicately searches through the upset papers for a keyboard and mouse. Something catching underneath the papers sends a stack of jewel cases sitting next to the monitor nearly toppling over. He catches it mid-fall.

Ana giggles. "Yeah, try not to destroy the place."

The screen flashes to its desktop wallpaper. A fictional gang from a popular video game series poses with guns in the foreground of a giant watermarked developer logo. The awakened CPU fan with blades caked in fine dust sings in a high note. Fish straightens the stack of jewel cases. Following two thin black cords snaking out from a plastic grommet, he lures in the keyboard and mouse buried under the debris of order forms and griffonaged memos. He opens the minimized browser. Ignoring an already opened popular sports page, Fish clicks the homepage button and begins to type.

The television interrupts with a local new bulletin.

"This just in: new developments in the shooting involving local businessman Sal Solak. Local police have released video footage of the three shooters. We would like to warn you that what we are about to show you may disturb some of our viewers."

Fish stops short of sending his query entered into the search bar before the television pulls everyone's attention in the room. Grainy footage dubbed from a VHS shows a not-yet injured Ana, towering Freakshow, and Fish from a diagonal rooftop shot exiting the front door of Sal's Arabian Nights. They fire at something off screen and then duck behind an Oldsmobile. The video is slowed down, frozen, and then enhanced. Fish's heart palpitates at wondering how close and clearly they'll zoom in to any of these frames. The final stills used are less than flattering and hardly distinguishable. Regardless, Fish feels the onset of vertigo.

"Jesus Christ! How did they get that?" he gasps in disbelief.

"You didn't see the security camera mounted on top of Sal's?" Freakshow asks in trumping disbelief.

"I always thought that that was fake! Like a dummy

camera!" Fish yells, becoming once more conscious of his stomach churning on empty. "When does anything ever happen there that Sal needs security cameras?"

"What about that time that those three people stormed in and killed a pedophile-murderer that was hiding there?" Ana says jocularly pulling her lips taut across her face.

"Shut the fuck up!" Fish yells again.

"Goddamn Fish. Calm down. Those stills are shit," she adds, only slightly noting Fish's genuine state of distress.

A yellow ten-digit number shows on the screen. "If you have any information on the shooters, please contact local police with the number provided. Also, if you see news happening in your neighborhood, or have a story you'd like us to report, contact us at..."

"Jeez, Show, are you trying to get us sent to prison?" Fish's pores excrete with worry. "Maybe you don't mind fucking guys but I'm not trying to spend the rest of my life getting raped in a prison. What the fuck are we gonna do?"

"You had better watch your fucking mouth!" Freakshow threatens.

"Show, look at us."

Fish throws his hand in an unbridled gesture to the television.

He continues, "Some fucking giant with bleached hair and tattoos, a big-titty goth chick with tattoos, and some fucking dude! They're gonna fuckin' I.D. us! Fuck, you didn't even kill Sal!"

"Sal won't talk," Freakshow asserts. "Sal never talks. Hell, Sal's entire reputation is built on the fact that he never talks!"

"Dude, we are fucked! They're gonna find out about Ringo and that wannabe lawmaker you knocked off! They're gonna find out about everything!" Fish squeaks, his erratic voice unable to hold a steady note for more than one syllable.

Fish's head is spinning. He plops himself on the support of the computer chair. A lump in his throat swells and gradually works its way upward to his uvula. He closes his eyes whilst gripping the armrests. Something material, something of substance and external of his evanescing sanity. The room tilts him backward. Someone shouts, "Jesus Christ."

The chair is sucked out of his hands and all physical sensation rescinds as he falls out of consciousness.

XLII.

Fish opens his eyes to the subdued popping and crackling of the television speaker at near mute. Light floods his vision.

"Yo brother, are you okay?" Luiz asks, aiming a penlight while dragging Fish's eyelids open. "You've been through a lot today. You should try to rest."

Just as soon as the Brazilian has spoken, Fish defiantly inclines himself and swings his legs off from the workbench.

"I'm fine. I'm fine," he says to himself.

Gravity increases the circulation to his lower extremities. He feels his feet growing heavier. He runs a discreet diagnostic by gliding his fingers over jaw, chin, cheekbone, and brow checking for any abnormalities.

"Your face is fine, Fish!" Ana shouts from the couch, mocking what she presumes to be his vanity.

Fish wiggles his neck to test its mobility.

"What the hell was that? Anxiety attack?" Ana asks.

"Who knows? This boy has been under a lot of stress today," Luiz answers as he clicks his penlight off. "And that's only from what I've *personally* witnessed."

Fish hops off the workbench and maneuvers back to the office chair, letting himself fall into it as he kicks off his untied shoes. He jiggles the mouse with his hand, dissipating the screensaver. The text cursor blinks at the end of the query previously entered in the search bar. The confident single tap of *enter* on the keyboard instantaneously brings up a new screen bearing search results—decent speed considering the economically-crippled location that is being serviced.

"Look at this shit. We're all over the internet!" Fish exclaims in discouragement.

He leafs through the first few pages of seemingly-endless results. Stills similar to the ones featured on the evening news are replicated tenfold in the image search. Fish's incisors nip at a piece of skin dangling from his bottom lip.

"Don't get too worked up again," Luiz says as he tends to his cluttered table.

"Look at this! This is all shit they aren't reporting on TV," Fish says in vexation as he clicks on a link. Dreadful enlarged stills of Freakshow, Fish, and Ana fill up half the page. He carefully proceeds to the article.

LiveSourceLive - 1 hour ago

West End Bureau of Police are beginning to connect the dots in the homicide involving Bethany Amanda Santos, a 14-year-old girl who was found asphyxiated in her bathtub at 19 Hooverville Drive yesterday. Her uncle Jose Santos, primary suspect and also of 19 Hooverville Drive, has been identified as one of the victims in the strip club shooting which took place at Sal's Arabian Nights earlier today. Owner and operator Sal Solak is currently in stable condition and in police custody under charges of having harbored a fugitive. The three instigating shooters are still unidentified and remain at large.

Fish clicks to go back, tentatively scrolling down the daunting results, and randomly selects the next link.

The Semaphore - 30 minutes ago

Owner/operator Sal Solak of Sal's Arabian Nights (don't act like you've never been there) is in stable condition and is being questioned in an ongoing police investigation involving (guess!) another police investigation. Jose Santos of 19 Hooverville Drive, now identified as a victim in today's shooting was also wanted in the murder, and possible sexual abuse, involving his 14-year-old niece who resided with him (stay classy Jose!). The three shooters featured in the now heavily-circulated video footage are still unidentified and at large (perhaps planning their next pedo-hit *fingers crossed!). Please don't forget to like, share, comment, reshare and comment again!

The Sal footage is embedded at the end of the article. Fish finds no point in watching it again and goes to another source.

The Irate Iranian Immigrant - 10 minutes ago

That pedo-harboring Solak is the reason why we Middle Eastern immigrants have such a bad rap. I hope he fucking gets his asshole torn open in those showers at Bay Penitentiary. Rot in hell you fuck. Jose Santos fucking got what he deserved. From what I hear if the police hadn't shown up those three vigilantes could have finished the fucking job with Sal! SOLAK IS A PIECE OF SHIT AND IS GONNA GET WHAT'S COMING TO HIM! THEY SHOULD BREAK HIS FUCKING BACK AND MAKE HIM HUMBLE!!! I'LL FUCKING BE MORE THAN GLAD TO HELP THE THREE THAT BUSTED A CAP IN HIS ASS FINISH THE JOB! ALSO, THAT CHICK IN THE GROUP LOOKS HOT AS FUCK!

Fish's demeanor changes. He starts laughing, acting as if he were savoring personally-addressed fan mail. He reads his way to the bottom of the page, noting the generally positive feedback. He modifies his search, looking for more specific reports, though only to scroll to the bottom and nod approvingly at the supportive comments.

"Did you guys see this? This is fucking great! The people's court loves us," Fish says shying a smile.

"You mean the *court of public opinion*? Yeah, maybe you can start a blog and have fanboys throw money your way," Ana sarcastically states as she lifts a remote control to drown out further conversation.

"You have to see this! They fucking love us!" Fish says.

He wishes to prove he hasn't lost all reason. He pushes his chair out, stands up, clears his throat, and addresses even Luiz.

"I know I thought it was bad, but we did something great today. Last night we were the scum of the earth, and now we're heroes!"

"We? Scum of the earth? Speak for yourself, please," Freakshow says, unmoved.

Luiz guffaws from behind the workbench. Ana joins in the laughter.

"Fuckin' laugh! You know we're fucked, Show! Are we just gonna hold up in here forever?"

"What are you suggesting?" Freakshow asks, his eyes glued to the TV once more.

"Why stop with Jose?" Fish asks, holding up his index finger and pausing.

Freakshow and Ana take time to reflect on his obfuscating choice of words. Two blank stares are returned before he continues, somewhat discouraged.

Fish continues. "C'mon, people out there think we're fucking heroes. We can go out big. And maybe make a fucking change."

"Sacrificing ourselves for a difference? Like you're gonna do that?" Ana questions, with doubt.

"Why not? I'm fucked as is. I've got fucking relatives that will turn me in to the police for a small payday. Look, we have the chance to rid a small part of the world of these child molesters and abusers."

"And when did you become so righteous?" Ana asks.

"What about your arm, Ana?"

Fish mentions smoothly circumventing her digression.

He continues, "You know you're not going to see a doctor. Jeez, it's not like we weren't fucking killing people anyway! What is the argument here? Only thing that changes is that now we kill strictly on our own terms. And we're not just killing people; we're saving people too. The Joses are still out there. *Pro bono*, right Show?"

"What the fuck happened to you, Fish?" Ana asks, her jaw hanging slightly open.

Freakshow displays an unconvinced expression.

Fish can't stop fidgeting. He sits down once more and deftly rolls the chair up to the desk, stopping at his exact length of reach to the keyboard. His fingers fire across the plastic buttons. The arrow cursor flies over the screen. He quickly pulls up a map marked with red dots.

"C'mere," Fish calls.

Freakshow helps Ana up and they move toward the computer. Fish turns the monitor, offering a more accessible view for the two. He speaks with a twang, hanging long onto the first vowel for emphasis.

"A-a-all those sick fucks," says Fish. "We can save all the future Bettys."

He looks to Freakshow and Ana, waiting for their approving reactions.

"Holy shit...," Freakshow says, gawking at the innumerable red groupings of pixels plastering the map.

"Look!" Fish haughtily exclaims as he points to the screen at a discovery. "Primary address, secondary address, and employer's address. They've got everything listed on here!"

"Let's fuckin' kill them all," Freakshow coldly asserts.

"No, if we do this, we do it right," Ana says sternly. "Vigilantism allows absolutely no room for mistakes."

Fish starts, "I know A-"

"No mistakes!" Ana scolds. 'I want to make that crystal with you."

"Okay, no mistakes Ana," Fish confirms.

Luiz works by a dim light, disinfecting his instruments. He lifts his eyes, throwing them to the lambent glow of the television from across the room. The news starts. The strip club security footage plays once more on the screen as an introduction to tonight's featured story. "Incognito, friends," he says. "You're gonna need some masks."

XLIII.

It's dark now. Mike Bua pulls his unmarked cruiser up to the tall iron gates, a chain and padlock holds them securely shut. Today was one big clusterfuck. Sal tried to curry favor with some of the officers during questioning, dropping the name *Bua* a good dozen times in the interrogation. With any luck, he won't be suing the precinct for harassment and property damage. Sal didn't seem very scared though. Maybe he knows the three that made the hit won't be coming back. Maybe those two bullets in his ass were just a warning. Hell, maybe he orchestrated this whole thing, the convenience at which he was the only credible witness left alive is hardly something to overlook. Though *credible* wouldn't be the proper word, Sal has been lying through his teeth ever since he's been in custody.

Mike parks the car away from the gate so as not to attract attention. Giving himself a lenient running start, he hops and grabs the top of the ashlar wall. Digging the toes of his shoes into the narrow stone crevasses, he boosts himself up, slides horizontally over the wall, and drops to the other side.

Stones in multiform shapes rise from the soft earth like pale beacons. The moonlight sends their slender shadows stretching out, dials set out to measure an eternity. The well-maintained lawn springs his feet upward as he steps off.

Mike wanders the graveyard, feeling at ease. The pain in his injured hand resides as he nears a beveled granite headstone that casts an immaterially-small shadow onto the trimmed grass. He kneels and runs his bandaged hand over the sunken-in letters. He produces a single white rose from his pocket and lays it atop the slanted stone. It rolls, adjusting its face before catching on a pitched portion of rock.

"I'll be with you soon," he says.

Mike thrusts his hand into his coat and draws out a leather badge holder. Repositioning the rose, he rests his glistening shield on top to pin it down but does not let go. He drops his other knee and ruminates, channeling his rusting memories into the dead rock. He rests his hand over his breast pocket feeling for the rigidity of the torn photograph.

XLIV.

A black Civic pulls up to an unmarked house in a neglected part of town, mostly low income and mostly non-white. The neighborhood lacks substantial street lighting, making the black sedan nearly invisible against the night.

Fish turns a circular dial, dimming the headlights down to their daytime setting. Then, realizing how conspicuous the car still is, he decides to turn them off entirely.

"Is this the place?" he calls to Ana in the backseat.

Ana shuffles one-handedly in the absence of ample lighting and flips through a quire of staple-bound papers. Her arm rests on the large black duffel bag occupying the seat next to her. She absentmindedly pats it with her hand as if it were a companion canine. She squints as she answers.

"Well, obviously the house is unmarked. But I presume that this is it."

Freakshow concurs. "This has to be it."

Fish exhales some of his nerve.

"You ready?" he asks the two.

Ana nods.

"Put your masks on," Freakshow directs.

Ana, with her right hand only, clumsily, but without hesitation, pulls on a black mask. Her eyes peer through large black circles set within silver diagonal flames. Two residual heat stripes flow off the top of the flames and outline eyebrows that point inward with fury. A silver triangle outlines a small black hood with a slit at the bottom, exposing the pale flesh of her nostrils. Teeth lining the mouth restrict Ana's expression to a glimmering frown. Her black hair, now with twisted blue streaks, inelegantly sticks out from the bottom and lays sloppily around her shoulders.

Freakshow throws Fish a mask before pulling one over his own face. His eyes are set within the same black circles that hollow out the silver flames. Freakshow's muscular neck stretches the fibers that were meant to taper past the wearer's chin. Fish looks to his lap, picks up his mask, and rounds the fabric over his fingers to see a design identical to Freakshow's and Ana's. Fish probes the unpleasantly toothy and moody cutout of the mouth with his fingers.

"Jeez," Fish says before pulling it over his head.

Fish and Freakshow both rotate their shoulders to view a masked Ana seated in the back. The three give one another a long and vacant stare.

"You boys and your wrestling...," Ana says to Freakshow, the fabric of her mask undulating as she speaks.

"Can we run through the plan quick?" Fish asks, adjusting his speech through a stiff jaw.

"Plan?" Ana echoes to Freakshow with a grin behind her eyes.

Freakshow points the barrel of a pistol to the car ceiling and cocks it.

"When do I ever have a plan?" asks Freakshow. "I'm making this stuff up as I go."

He pulls on the puny door handle and squeezes his titanic body through the unaccommodating portal, his displaced weight rectifying the vehicle's suspension.

Fish's silver revolvers are uncomfortably positioned in his

waistband. He exits the car with a stiffened back.

"What should we do in a neighborhood like this? Should I leave the keys in the ignition?" Fish asks Ana, not wishing to embarrass himself by asking Freakshow.

"I wouldn't. Leave it unlocked though," she responds as she ducks her head out the side and closes the passenger door.

"Show, I've got the keys!" Fish reports in a rasp whisper to the distancing Freakshow.

A bicycle turned upside down with a missing wheel lies in the yard. Ana and Fish approach the house in a nimble gait that favors the ball of their foot. Moisture-ridden dolls and children's books covered in a thin layer of grit are piled beside the porch steps. Fish tiptoes past Freakshow, squats, and puts his ear up to the door. The house is silent. The eerily familiar geometry of the black keyhole seems to taunt Fish as he closes his hand around the oxidized brass knob and torques his wrist. The disengaging latch clicks. Fish tugs. Hard. The warped door pops out loudly from its no longer flush frame. Unflinchingly, Fish shoves the door open the rest of the way, hoping to avoid any stubborn grunts from the hinges.

Aside from a soft glow coming from somewhere in the back, the inside of the house is engulfed in a midnight blue. The dull vinyl flooring lit orange in the distance and a large black rectangle sitting on a low entertainment stand in a room to their right are the only discernible things they can see from the doorway.

The three orderly file inside. Rumpled clothing and pizza boxes cover the floor and announce their every footstep. Still favoring the ball of his foot, Fish guides himself along a wall as Freakshow lags behind to assist Ana. The orange vinyl floor gradually widens in Fish's view as he nears what he now can identify as a kitchen.

"What do we do if no one is here?" Fish asks.

Freakshow and Ana continue behind Fish, neither answering, though Fish is most certain they heard.

Thick curtains cover a small patch of the wall above the kitchen sink. Tangled cotton rope lies atop the counter. A door cracked open in the corner carries along the cool damp effulgence of cellar air. Fish pauses and looks at the door. A loud metallic clanging jolts his heartrate and counters his internal deliberations.

Pivoting his shoulders, he looks back to Freakshow and Ana. Even with their black and silver faces, the whites of their eyes are still as easily read as his own. Fish scans the room in panic and sees a previously-undetected door. Rushing forward, he raises his weapon, ready to encounter whatever haunts the other side.

The clanging continues. Gripping the knob with excessive strength, he turns and pulls on it, but it is stuck fast. He rattles the door in frustration, but it doesn't budge. The metal clangs increase in intensity. Freakshow hurriedly escorts Ana into the kitchen and relieves Fish. Raising his hand, he unfastens a metal slide latch and opens the door.

The metal clanging is replaced by the muffled screams of a girl huddled into the corner, hiding her face in the puffed folds of a dress. For an instant, the three, taken aback by their impeccability of timing, shoot each other another vacant expression.

Fish moves stealthily past Freakshow and busies himself with freeing the girl. "It's okay. We're not gonna hurt you."

He reaches around to undo the gnarled rope binding her hands at the back. The deep pantry is stacked to the ceiling with cans and boxed goods. The small room vibrates with a high-pitched wheezing as the girl struggles to regain lost breath through a saliva-soaked rag tied around her mouth. She squirms, foiling Fish's attempts to unbind her.

"Hey!" Fish says in anger, "I'm trying to help you."

He reaches into his pocket for a multi-tool. Unfolding a knife, he calculatingly slashes at her ankles freeing her legs.

"See?" he says, hoping his expedited actions to be ample proof of goodwill. The girl raises her legs and shoots her heels forward, kicking at Fish's groin in rapid succession. A sudden jolt of pain resounding in his abdomen has him keel over onto the pantry floor. "Fuckin' bitch!" he curses with a tightened gut.

With hands still restrained, the girl darts past Fish and into the kitchen. Unable to maintain balance, she stumbles forward, bumps headlong into Freakshow's trunk-like legs, and falls to the floor dazed, the blonde tresses toppling from her head. Fish, lurching over in pain, pulls himself out of the closet pantry. He looks in momentary confusion to a boy laying beside a blonde wig.

"What the...?" Fish proclaims.

The boy shuffles onto his bottom and kicks his feet against the vinyl floor. His heels skirl. He backs himself against the wall and looks to the three masked strangers. Freakshow takes a step forward and casually reaches around to loosen the sopping rag that chokes the boy's speech.

"Please don't hurt me!" the boy says, gagging as the cloth is removed from his mouth. He is sweating in terror.

"We're not here to hurt you," Ana calmly states bearing her single empty palm to him. "We're the good guys."

"They'll be back any minute," the boy says shuddering.

"Jeezus, they've got you in a fucking dress!" Fish thinks as he also speaks aloud.

Freakshow and Ana wish to draw Fish's attention to his own crassness, but are suddenly intervened by the slamming of a car door from outside of the house. Words spewed forth from the jovial bantering of men entering the front door are carried to the kitchen.

Ana, in a panic, drops her pistol as she rushes the boy to his feet with a single arm. She begins ushering him back toward the closet making a great deal of noise in the process. The voices stop. The kitchen light clicks on. The room looks much smaller when fully lit. Ana and the boy's eyes meet. His eyes are blue, and his hair is of tight dark brown curls. In the light, his sex is perfectly distinguishable, even if he were to wear the wig. Eye shadow is penciled on the edge of his eyelids and smeared onto the cornflower yellow dress he wears. For a moment it sounds like someone has upset a cup of water, but upon turning to the boy, the three can see urine streaming out from his blouse.

It patters on the floor like a leaking roof in a squall. Ana looks down to the light amber puddle, slowly spreading in diameter and engulfing her fallen pistol. The boys forearms and ears are covered in brown stripes of scabbing skin. Ana looks once more to his face, but he averts his eyes in shame.

"What the fuck are you doing here?" asks a man wearing a bomber jacket and hooking his thumbs into his denim pants pockets. He stands with his feet at shoulder width, looking on threateningly. In his open jacket, Freakshow spies a gun holster. Fish, holding his pistols and yet feeling completely vulnerable, waits for an action from Freakshow.

"Nigel said it was going to be just us and him. You started the graduation ceremony already!" the man says.

He sneers as he speaks. The hard skin of his cratered nose looks like a greased almond shell bobbing up and down in the center of his face.

A stout man with blue and red flannel top and denim bottom steps forward, jabbing his pointing finger of rebuke into the air.

"We paid top dollar! This kid only turns eighteen once

and we're not sharing with you three," The man says as he reaches over his chest to adjust a shouldered camera bag.

The boy's legs buckle. He mutely slips from Ana's hold and falls to the floor in his urine.

"Sorry gentlemen, there has been some horrible mistake," Ana says.

The flannelled man hooks his thumb over the nylon strap straddling his chest.

"Yeah there has," the man continues. "You are way too old for me!"

He lets off in uncouth laughter not shared by his jacketed partner.

The jacketed man flips his unbuttoned jacket open and rests his hands on his hips, flashing his weapon. "I'll ask you one more time: What the fuck are you doing here?" He flares his cratered nostrils.

In a flash, Freakshow raises his cocked pistol and knocks back the jacketed man with the force of two bullets penetrating his chest and piercing his heart. The stout man's expression turns to dread. Purple bags instantly assert themselves under his eyes. His figure seems to have miraculously thinned, drawing attention to the multiplying wrinkles on his terror-stricken face. He panics and orders his legs to go left. Realizing his path is blocked by a fresh corpse, he issues new orders for them to go right. His legs, suddenly overwhelmed with commands, fail, causing him to fall prostrate on the floor. He whimpers like an animal backed into a corner.

Fish tenses his index finger. The revolver kicks in his hand. A released round punctures the back of the man's skull. It slowly begins emptying its liquid contents.

The boy grasps at Ana's arm, wishing to escape the advancing pool of blood oozing from the stout man's head.

Ana stands him up as the freshly-expelled blood begins amalgamating with the urine on the floor.

"Look at me honey!" she frantically commands, grabbing his chin. "What is your name?"

"J-Juh-James," he answers, focusing all of his concentration.

"Who did this to you?" Ana asks loudly as if the boy were hard of hearing.

"N-N-Nuh-Nigel."

Two consecutive one-word answers; Ana decides to drop the hand cupping James' chin. "Where is Nigel?"

"Tied up."

"Where?" Ana insists.

"In his playroom," James says, indicating with a fragile finger. He points to a dark hall beyond a heap of rubbish in the dining room.

Freakshow leans his body forward for the slight visibility advantage and tries to inspect the hall from where he stands. His silver and black head could hit the ceiling if he were to jump. He turns his mischievously scowling facade to the three.

"Ana, stay here with James. Fish, come with me."

XLV.

A practically soundproof room. The originally tasked checkerboard pattern had been abandoned nearly immediately after starting the job. There simply wasn't enough corrugated foam to cover all four walls, even with utilizing the alternating pattern that saved them nearly half the money on supplies. Only a small portion of the wall retains the essence of its conception, of what could have been, of what was abandoned. Supplies and patience had both run to an end. Leftover foam squares sparsely dot the ceiling with unfulfilled purpose like weak links in a chain. The large remainder of the walls are rudimentarily slapped with thick blankets anchored up by dulling staples.

Where the windows are, if there ever were any in the room to begin with, would be anybody's guess. An anomalous door is most likely what incurred the large setback in budget for the room. It is brand new, heavy, and lined with a rubber gasket. It pulls like a freezer chest lifts, with a purpose not to close, but to seal. Freakshow and Fish step into the room, exercising extreme prejudice.

A bruised anus lacquered in lubricant and flecked with feces puckers at them from a bed on the far wall of the room. A man on all fours with leather belts securing all of his respected appendages faces away from them, swinging his head in gaiety from one side to the other. Insulated black threads run out of both ears to a portable listening device laying on the bed. The man detects human presence in the room. Perhaps it was the air pressure difference when Freakshow thrust the door open.

"Jamie, is that you? Would you be so kind as to show our guests where to sit?"

Nigel's saccharine-sweet voice falls dead onto the threshold of the noise dampening walls. He presses a button on the device hidden in his hand to stop the music.

"Jamie?" he calls once more, sensing an abnormality. He turns his collared neck to see the two masked strangers standing statuesque by the door. His sphincter tightens.

"Who the fuck are you two? Where are Ken and Edward?"

Freakshow doesn't answer and takes a single intimidating step toward the bed.

"Have you hurt Jamie?" Nigel asks, suddenly feeling as if he's not getting enough circulation to his feet. His speech doubles as Freakshow takes a second step. "Please tell me that Jamie is okay! You didn't hurt Jamie, did you?"

Freakshow takes another step. Fish remains by the door.

Nigel's lips are pasty and his body is covered in a cold sweat. The chilliness in his feet grows. His body tenses and he is soon struggling furiously to loosen the self-applied bonds. A blindfold swings from his neck. "Please, is Jamie is okay?" he continues to ask in futility.

"He'll be fine. Though I can't say the same for you," Freakshow humorlessly answers.

Nigel pinches his eyes closed and fights to feed air through his windpipe though nothing restricts it. "What are you going to do?" he asks, opening one of his eyes just enough to note Freakshow's dominant male physique.

Freakshow tucks his weapon away, reaches for a large ball gag sitting on a bureau, and teasingly swings it in the man's face.

"You are into some kinky shit..." Freakshow says. "Well so am, I you sick fuck!"

Freakshow jumps onto the bed and straddles Nigel's head. He tightens the gag to a near-snapping tension, and sets the blindfold over Nigel's eyes.

He reaches into his pocket and pulls out a pair of latex gloves. Freakshow pops the lid on a three-pound container of vegetable shortening laying at the bedside table and dips his fingers inside. Withdrawing his hand, Freakshow begins slathering the imitation lard onto Nigel's spread buttocks. Terrified by the intruder, and yet enticed by the stimulation, Nigel gasps with excitement. His penis slowly grows rigid with curiosity. He lets out a long moan. Fish's gag reflex activates.

A four-socket power strip fed from one of the walls and snaked around the ceiling light fixture dangles above the bed. A curling iron, no doubt the tool which inflicted James' striped scabs, lays on the floor. Freakshow plugs it in and turns it on. Nigel breathes ecstatically with unwitting anticipation. His insatiability is expressed in hot breaths that grow in intensity as the conductive metal of the iron grows in heat.

Freakshow, grasping the heated rod with conviction, begins to prod Nigel's turgid penis. Screams of agony are instantly absorbed into the liberally-cushioned wall. Freakshow pulls his hand back, offering the man respite from pain. The smell of burning oiled flesh stifles the room. Small moist bubbles from the burns group together on Nigel's wounded genitals. His screams subside, but never altogether stop.

Show probes the rectum next, stabbing the plastic tip in

at challenging angles and rotating slowly. Nigel's inexhaustible wailing can seemingly be controlled with this interesting application. Peeling skin catches on the scalding metal. With Fish's semblance not looking much better than Nigel's, Freakshow decides to end things quickly by driving the curling iron in up to its handle. Nigel's violent screams, which shred his throat, sound more animal than human. His thinly-coated mucous membrane sizzles against the searing metal, emitting an indescribable foulness. The bruised anus responds to the contacting heat by turning a dark shade of charred brown. Nigel's reactive convulsing shakes the bed and transfers to the floor.

Freakshow removes his septic gloves, turning them inside out. He carelessly disposes of them in the bedroom trash receptacle and walks out in silence.

Fish is frozen, staring at the white handle protruding from Nigel, debating whether or not to remove it. Nigel's inhuman screams, only interrupted by fits of hacking, has reached the point where Fish's ears have become numb to it. A fetid smoke fills the room. Able to bear the thick stench no longer, Fish exits the room and shuts the leaden door behind him, sealing the forsaken Nigel in his tomb.

XLVI.

James sits on the insulated wooden seat of his home's lidless and only toilet, with its water level so low it fails at masking the malodor of human excrement which it receives daily. He was often forced to accompany Nigel to the bathroom to stew in the choking air until Nigel had finished evacuating himself of the previous night's gluttonous revelry. Tufts of hair, bare toilet paper rolls, and waxen yellow cotton swabs scantly cover the bottom of a rubbish bin sitting on the floor beside the sink. The steady drip of the leaking tap is the only measure of time's passage. The masked female with the bandaged arm takes a moist cotton ball and gently wipes it over the edge of James' darkened eyelids. He stares long into her beautifully painted and pencilled deep-set green eyes and drops his shoulders in relaxation.

"How come you don't have a zipper?"

"Huh?" Ana returns off guard, pulling the blackening cotton ball away.

"At some of Nigel's playdates a man had a mask with a zipper for the mouth. Nigel always said he was inviting the guys over so we could all watch the game on TV because he knew I liked football."

Ana's eyes flash austere. She puffs her chest and ponders over proper diction as she rests her hands on James' knees.

"James, I know this will be difficult…" She stops, thinking of how to delicately proceed. "But you must try your best to forget everything that has happened to you at this house—Nigel, those two men, everything."

The words 'mom' and 'dad' pop into Ana's head, but only as an unpursued afterthought. She decides it's better not to question familial ties entirely for her own piece of mind.

"How long have you been here?" she continues.

James stares past Ana at the cracked latex underbelly of an old and curling shower mat.

"I can't remember ever *not* being here," he says with distant eyes.

Ana moves her hands to brush his moppy hair aside, revealing two gold butterfly earrings. "James, please, just try to forget," she emphasizes.

James' eyes drift from the floor and climb back up to the made-up deep-set green eyes that return his gaze from the other side of the mask. He pulls up on the damp dress, stirring his evaporating reek into the air. "They're not good people at all. They're monsters."

"I know."

James picks at his dress. Tears flush into his eyes. He leaps forward, wrapping his arms and legs around the kneeling Ana, nearly knocking her back. A sharp pain shoots through her tubed arm. James cries into her neck. Her wetted hair stiffens as it bundles together and lays against her skin. "They make me do bad things. You have to kill them all," James says, weeping in muffles.

Ana embraces James with both arms and begins rocking him.

"I'll see what I can do."

Two unshaded table lamps blindingly light up the living

room. Atop a brand new black entertainment stand a large plasma television screen flashes with video recapitulations of the week's highlights of athletic prowess. Freakshow stands, remote in his hands, toggling the volume. Fish sinks in the polished artificial leather of a new recliner. He passively views the footage with elbows braced on the armrest, dangling his pistol-wielding hands over either side of the chair. A large yellow delivery slip dated yesterday sits on the coffee table. A company logo heading the invoice reads *Ralph's Rent-to-Own*. It indicates a number of articles in the living room including, but not limited to, the television, entertainment stand, recliner, and coffee table. Ana walks into the room, pulling the hand of a sullen looking James behind her.

"Okay, we're ready to go."

Freakshow pinches at the fabric of his mask, pulling it outward and letting it snap back to push the cool air over his face. His speech loosens.

"We?"

"I mean *me*," Ana says, correcting her mistaken pluralization.

Freakshow depresses a button on the remote, killing the boisterous speakers and sending the screen to black. Fish hesitantly slides himself to the edge of the liberally-cushioned seat, trying to savor more of the brief luxury.

Ana turns to James.

"James, can you give us time to get off the roads before calling 911?" Ana asks. Maintaining a downward gaze, James nods his head. Ana drops to a knee, trying to read his distressed state better. "Give us an hour before you call 911. The police will be able to take care of you."

James lifts his chin, the gray smear of makeup around his eyes and pinched pink blush on his cheeks only further distorts his already maudlin expression.

"Thank you," he says, reaching forward and allowing himself to fall as he embraces Ana once again. His tight squeeze clamps the circulation in her bad arm.

Fish and Freakshow turn to leave the living room.

"And don't forget to tell the cops that Fishman saved the day," Fish hurriedly adds, jingling the keys of their getaway in his hand.

Freakshow slants his eyebrows inward, transforming them into slits, that signify his distaste. "That is the worst fucking name I have ever heard. Also, this kid is gonna take you seriously."

"Whatever," Fish says, rolling his eyes. "C'mon Ana!" he shouts over his shoulder as he and Freakshow walk out the open door.

Ana delicately removes James' fastened arms from her back and steadies her own throbbing arm before dashing out to catch up with the two.

"Wait up Freakshow!" Ana says.

The black Civic departs as silently as it came.

XLVII.

The gasping black cruiser inches forward. Its bumper overlaps the narrow walkway in front of Kelly's Stop-and-Go before finally desisting with its nauseous mechanical whir. Mike Bua steps out of the vehicle carrying two tightly-rolled bills of a double-digit denomination. His eyelids are a dark pink. Capillaries on the whites of his dry eyes are like cracks in the mud of blighted riverbed.

A driver of a blue pickup occupies pump number three. A woman with a less than flattering figure in tight jeans pumps gas into a Geo Tracker on four as a young man waits uneasily in its passenger seat. Congregating insects throw themselves in blind devotion unto the supreme fluorescent glow of rectangular lights recessed in the cantilevered ceiling. Mike pulls the grime-infused aluminum handle of the door, setting off the breezy tinging of a bell suspended from the lintel. Behind the counter a young man with blond hair that's going on a week without shaving, leans onto his elbows staring downward. He's completely engrossed in a contemporary art magazine.

Mike surrenders higher cognitive function. With his legs on autopilot, he meanders up and down the short-standing aisles in search of the bottled gold liquid he desires— condoms, chewy snacks, candy bars, potato chips, pretzels, sticky buns, and, finally, liquor. Heading back toward the register, he grabs a box cutter from the same shelf stocked with writing supplies, flashlights, and road atlases. Mike indiscreetly places the two items for purchase overtop the magazine of the engrossed employee working the register. The young man corrects his posture and exposes his nametag, which reads *Steven*. He bellicosely squints his eyes at the bottle of whiskey and box cutter rudely intruding upon his reading material.

The easily-irritated store clerk is about to raise another fuss with a customer before he lifts his eyes to Mike Bua's strained and impersonal stare. A shiver comes over Steven, which instantly cools his seething impulse. One of the bulging knuckles of his twig-like fingers loudly pops as it springs into action. Steven dexterously scans, bags, and goes through all the necessary motions—aside from age verification—required by his employer in completing a transaction.

Mike refuses his receipt and bunches up the top of the bag into his perspiring fist as he walks out the door, setting off the tinging of the bell once more. The door closes and the engine turns. Fat beams of light radiate on the brick wall of Kelly's Stop-and-Go. The terminal vehicle reverses, enlarging the harsh halogen glare on the wall before it pulls away, but not before sending another shiver through Steven. He tucks his magazine away as the driver of the blue pickup on three comes to pay. Steven politely receives the customer and completes the remainder of his shift in a state of unnerved alertness and inexplicably rediscovered courtesy.

XLVIII.

Fish drives, focusing his attention solely on the road, as Freakshow gently turns the staple-bound pages in his hand, examining each page in detail, whilst meticulously mapping out routes in his head. Strips of hardened tar sealing fractures on the weather-beaten and heavily traveled street knock the car around lightly. Freakshow and Fish's bodies sway and pop in unison. The eerie silence begins stirring a restlessness within Ana.

"What did you do to Nigel?" she asks, her anticipation of the answer only further disrupting her quiet.

Fish keeps his eyes to the road and patiently waits for Freakshow to answer. A long silence proceeds, one in which Freakshow acknowledges Ana through the rearview mirror with his darkened gaze. The nonverbalized response upsets Ana. She reaches for a ballpoint pen and tosses it over Freakshow's shoulder. It completes three full rotations in the air before catching on the exaggerated wrinkles of Freakshow's crotch zipper.

"Cross the address off at least!" she says, peeved.

Clicking the pen, Freakshow points, directing Fish to take a left. The Civic pulls into a quaint suburban street marking Hembridge. The houses are well-maintained with meticulously-trimmed bushes. Nothing is of a generic color.

The uniqueness of each individual family residing in each home is expressed by the color scheme specially selected from the paint company's suggested themes: Colonial Blue with accents of Sandalwood Beige and Sierra Red, and Heritage Yellow with Polished Walnut and Liberty White trim. Residences with trichrome gravel, inlaid stepping stones, and walkway lighting that partition the crabgrass-free lawns. Proud doctors, university professors on tenure, bankers, advertising agents, and European import car dealers. Automobiles proudly bearing alma mater bumper stickers line the driveways. This is collective conservative America's dream come to fruition. Hembridge is suburban paradise realized.

"We're gonna make one more stop since we're still good with time," Freakshow explains to Ana.

Ana contorts her face in doubt. She feels the slight sting of betrayal from not having been shared the information beforehand.

"Look, Show. I don't know what the hell you two were doing with Nigel in there. Judging by the screams I heard when you were leaving the room, we may assume that he's still alive. If James ends up going in there...," she trails off, distracted by Fish and Freakshow's visibly-dispersing attention.

Heeding the very advice she's about to dispense, she condenses her prolix speech. "All I'm saying is we need to be more efficient."

"Efficient?" Fish echoes, oblivious of the word.

Ana raises her voice to a startling level. "Yes Fish*man*, efficient! Meaning we don't have time to systematically torture every single red dot in the county!"

"Okay! Jeez Ana, calm down! We draw enough attention driving a Civic from the last century in this neighborhood. They're gonna think we're drug dealers or something."

Fish flips his attention once more to the road. "Where are we at Show?"

"This house with the Suburban," Freakshow says, pointing as he leans forward on the dashboard.

Fish pulls in parallel, blocking the slumbering Suburban's exit.

"Ana, Fish, wait here," Freakshow says, as he flees the vehicle before Fish can shift to *P* and either of them have a chance to process the incredulous orders.

Fish pivots his body, looking back to Ana in disbelief. "Did he just fucking go out there by himself?"

Ana puts down her window in an attempt to call Freakshow back, but he has already reached the doorstep. Fish puts down the passenger's side window in voyeuristic curiosity. They see Freakshow raise his finger and send a sonorous ring throughout the home. Fish picks up the printouts left on the seat to see the marked address being the residence of someone named "Jesse George Shane— Involuntary Deviate Sexual Intercourse with a Child with Serious Bodily Injury.'"

The sonorous ring is heard once again. Fish rests his arm around the passenger seat and leans over, ducking his head down to clearly view the distant doorstep. Someone's yells are carried outside through open windows on the second floor. Freakshow raises his hand and pushes the doorbell once more just for fun, before concealing his gun.

"This better be good!" a man says. The latter half of his sentence, particularly the word "good," is heard vibrantly through the now-unimpeded entrance. The ornamental door knocker creates a dull pang from the decaying swing of the door. A thin man in a bathrobe with a bristly white moustache and wisps of hair covering his head stands with his hand frozen to the doorknob, his eyes open wide with surprise. He retreats a single step to take a good look at Freakshow from head to toe with his myopic eyes.

"And what the hell are you supposed to be? Isn't it a little early for Halloween?" the man asks, disguising his growing anxiety with a light insult.

"Are you Jesse George Shane?"

The man looks on, mystified by the masked and illustrated behemoth. He confrontationally sets foot outside and pulls the door behind him. "Yes. I am. Who the hell are you? Did Tom put you up to this?"

Freakshow brings his arm up and blows a single hole in the man's head. Jesse George Shane's head cocks back. His hand releases the polished knob of the door, now partially sprayed with blood, and he falls back into his home. Freakshow casually walks toward the car, kicking at grass in the yard. Pulling the car door open, he squeezes in legs first, and comfortably adjusts himself in the seat.

Fish's heart races and his breathing is abrupt and short. Not being able to leave soon enough, he all too heavily applies the accelerator and the car peels away, screeching down the street before the passenger door even closes.

"Is that efficient enough for you?" Freakshow asks Ana with a smile he seems incapable of wiping from his face.

XLIX.

A low-sitting billboard doubly shelters Mike Bua, who is seated within the unmarked police cruiser. The annoying stirs of the engine have been silenced for a near half-hour. Late-night travelers whisk by, cleaving the thick haze that blankets the start of the highway's provisionally-mountainous terrain.

"Fuckin' shit," Mike slurs, drumming his fingers on his knee and taking a final swig from the bottle before twisting the flimsy metal cap back on. He exits the car and walks seven paces to get a better look at the billboard. He looks up to the harsh lighting directed upward, broken by the diagonal pattern of the diamond grate walkway. A towering black billboard in bold white lettering wittily remarks on the fact that the word *church* cannot be spelled without a U. A photograph of a stone Celtic cross is illuminated beside the writing. A website written on the bottom remains obscured by the catwalk's meshing aluminum lines. Mike, wishing to remain at least partially ignorant of the billboard, purposely averts his eyes as he leaves his vehicle.

The whiskey bottle is approximately three-quarters full. He only needed to take some of the edge off. He hooks his arm, propelling the bottle and its twelve-year aged contents, toward the intersecting lines of the crucifix. It is not a difficult shot by any means. The body of the bottle disintegrates, scattering glass and showering whiskey into the air. The neck and base, largely left intact, tumble and land somewhere in the brush. The label with broken glass adhering to it slowly succumbs to gravity and falls label down, on the grate, bearing its ship, double-anchor, and star crest at Mike. Distilled beverage streams down the cross and drips onto the spent vehicle's hood.

Subtracting strength from his legs, Mike plunks himself down just off from the dusty shoulder bearing the dozen tire tracks accumulated since the last rainfall. He stretches his legs, letting his toes fall to point outward. Relaxing his bloated gut, he perverts his posture by slowly slouching forward and resting his chin on his chest. Mucous pinched in his angled neck whistles with the slow intake of air.

Reaching into his pocket, he withdraws the box cutter purchased at Kelly's Stop-and-Go. The stubbornly-stiff plastic case so often used to package bladed objects was discarded even before Mike finished with his whiskey. Forcing the button down with his thumb, he releases the safety mechanism and pushes the blade out, clicking it four times before relaxing his grip. The brushed metal retains a dying glow from what little light reflects off the billboard. Mike hastily casts off his restrictive coat. The thick bandages of his right hand catch on the sleeve, pulling it inside out before he finally manages to fling it off.

In growing frustration, he slashes at his glass-cut hand wrapped in gauze, making deep cuts into his palm. The freshly-split wounds turn pale before becoming dark and overflowing rivulets. Mike holds his wrist up and watches as the blood trickles downward, following a vein on his right forearm. Having nowhere else to go upon reaching his bent elbow, it beads and drips like an administered intravenous fluid. The fine grit blown to the side of the rutty road by passing traffic over the decades repels the pooling fluid.

"I'll be with you soon," he garbles out with a twisted face.

Bringing the blade to his forearm, he makes precisely-controlled cuts that break the skin but spare his fibrous muscle.

More blood.

Mike wishes Maki were here. Anyone to plead his case for living. With both sides of an existential argument presented, perhaps he could make a more informed decision and cut himself with more conviction. But he is hesitant and doubt plagues his thoughts as much as anything else.

He pulls the box cutter away from his arm and flings in to the highway, hoping it will cause some horrendous accident in the near future. Keeping his arm up, he wraps the dusty jacket around his fresh wounds and walks with an imagined limp towards the car. Sinking into the driver's seat, he turns on the two-way radio. A voice immediately broadcasts, "All units..."

Mike twists his fingers quickly dispelling the volume. The knob clicks, indicating the power returning to its off state. Wishing he could recline in his seat, a great fatigue takes hold of Mike and he falls asleep.

L.

Hoping to relax his nerves, Fish attempts light conversation.

"You should have said 'trick-or-treat' or 'Happy Halloween motherfucker' after you shot him," says Fish. "That's what Fishman would have probably done."

"Yeah? Well, I'm not Fishman, it's not even October, and this isn't lucha libre," Freakshow says, yanking off his mask.

"What kind of fucking superpowers does Fishman have?" Ana asks affrontingly.

Fish's eyes swing to the center cup holder. A bottle of Red Stripe being cradled by the matte black plastic shifts its label toward him upon hitting a large pothole. Fish retrieves it and quickly puts it to his lips with the bottom up. The mixture of warm stagnant hops and backwash coat his tongue before being flushed with his own saliva. His uvula helps with throwing the rancid beverage down his esophagus. "I can drink like a fish!" he exclaims, making sure Ana can see his wide and forced grin in the rear-view mirror. She is not impressed.

"Yeah, I'll bet that tasted good. Also, that would make you an *alcoholic*, not a superhero."

"Not every hero needs superpowers there Incred-a-girl. Now, help me come up with a slogan and logo."

Unmotivated by the challenge, Ana ends the conversation by failing to respond. Redirecting her attention, she picks up the hit list and turns to the last scored page bearing Jesse George Shane's name. She stares at it, expecting a change in her mood, but feels only a growing fatigue. She removes her mask, permitting the stale air of the fast food remnant interior of the car to cool her perspiring face. Ana draws a line through Jesse George Shane's name and reaches for a translucent orange prescription bottle wedged tightly in her jean pockets. Not bothering to count, or even glance at her hand, she turns the container sideways, tapping three times with her finger. Cupping her hand over her mouth, the pills are swallowed with a liberal amount of stocked spit. Ana wipes her sweating philtrum with the back of her forefinger and closes her eyes, trying not to be haunted with thoughts of her shunted arm and soon inevitable end.

The studious ticking of plastic keys interrupted only by the quiet assertions of a left-clicked mouse funnel into Ana's ear and raise her to a conscious state. Fish sits at the desk of Luiz's living quarters at his BJJ gym with Freakshow hanging over his shoulder, pointing at the computer screen. Ana drowsily shifts herself, causing a loud wooden pop in the ancient sofa. Freakshow turns. Seeing Ana awake, he flashes an empty smile, for no better purpose than to reassure and calm her with an agreeable demeanor, like one would do to a child. Fish continues an ongoing conversation.

"Damn, I should have said something like 'sweet dreams' or 'nighty-night motherfucker.'"

"I notice a lot of your slogans have 'motherfucker' in them," Ana says, announcing her lucidity to Fish.

Fish keeps his eyes to the monitor. "Well, look who finally decided to get up!"

Ana pulls herself upright and inspects her bandage. The dressing has been changed.

With lack of enthusiasm for simple addition, Freakshow asks Fish, "So how many did we get?"

"Three at Nigel's place, that Shane guy in Hembridge, and the two I got in their sleep. That's seven, er... six!" Fish covers his arithmetical fumble by introducing a new topic. "Man, when the comic book comes out, we gotta make sure that all those one-liners are in there. And you gotta put in that I, The Fishman, killed them!"

Freakshow grumbles out a response. "Okay, Fish. Listen, A: There will be no comic book. B: Your lines suck. C: Y-"

The information sinks in slowly for the passively-listening Ana. She straightens her back upon shocked realization. "When did you kill two guys in their sleep?"

"When you were fucking passed out on painkillers in the car!" Fish swivels, cackling at Ana, exaggerating his laughter and even throwing his head back. He keeps his eyes slightly open to savor Ana's expression, but is distracted by the image of an unmarked house on the television, the white lead paint peeling off the clapboard walls and the overturned bicycle.

"Ho-lee shit!" Fish jumps up, reaches for the remote, and restores the volume by firmly depressing the mute button.

The speakers howl with life, but not making anything more comprehensible. Black caption bars line the bottom of the screen. An attractive woman with slitting eyes, angular eyebrows, and flowing blonde locks wears a grey suit accentuating her breasts before shallowly tapering at her waist. Her unprofessional pink manicure goes hardly unnoticed by her superiors, but is never brought up.

"Once again, this is Abby O'Neill and we're here at the scene of last night's multiple homicide. In a possible connection with the murder of Jesse George Shane of 17

Independence Parkway, apparently gunf-"

"Damn this reporter chick is fuckin' hot," Fish says, standing attentively by the television with arms crossed.

At the scene, a group of people who have been crowding together since sunrise gravitate to the front or the back, correlating with the positioning of cameras. Many are still in sleepwear. In this low-income neighborhood, many are not bothered by the trifling issue of whether one is presentable or not. This is full news coverage, and it's live. The city's news resources are focused entirely on a previously unnoticed house on a block. The opportunity to be featured on television, even if only for a moment, overshadows the need of both breakfast and education for the resident children, as so many have already forgotten to feed and prepare their family for the school day. Half-naked toddlers with ashen feet chew at their nails and cling to the legs of their parents. Parents too young to look so old, who cannot afford the luxury of clothing that properly fits or to replace their missing teeth, but often indulge on tobacco, pay-per-view, and a diet of fast food and soft drinks. The gossip drudgingly mills amongst them.

"I think he was tuchin' thah boy," someone eagerly divulges from the back.

"Yo, I seen this foo' cuttin' flahwahs all gay and shit," someone else trumpets from the back, hoping to invoke curiosity in a news correspondent.

Abby O'Neill stands at a diagonal shot of the front door from the street. A boy is escorted out, wrapped in a police blanket. Abby's bleating reaction triggers a clamor. She ducks under the police tape. The cameraman shuffles behind her. She thrusts the microphone in James' face. "What did the murderer look like?"

The single police officer escort pushes Abby back and uses himself as a barrier. "What the hell do you think you're doing? Davis, Mitchell, gimme a hand!"

The cameraman steps back and maneuvers to zoom in on James.

Abby gets her microphone as close as she can to the boy's face.

"They're not murderers! They're heroes! They saved me!" James yells.

"Fuck yeah!" Fish victoriously bellows on the opposite side of the screen. Freakshow and Ana find more amusement in watching Fish's arrogant reactions than the Channel 4 reporter's antics on screen.

"I'll have you arrested!" another officer yells over the impromptu interview.

Abby's inexorable journalist instinct triumphs over the police threats. She has successfully ascertained that there was more than just one killer. "What did *they* look like?" she speedily phrases.

"C'mon kid!" the officer shouts as James willingly drifts toward Abby's mic.

The camera falls sideways, entertaining a ground-shot of a tackling officer's unpolished shoes. Focus is lost.

"Oh snap!" someone from the crowd shouts. Concealed snickering is not picked up by the microphone.

"Just say the name, kid!" Fish cheers with a closed fist pumping in front of him.

"They looked like skulls!" James says, overexcited. His mind reels through the unspeakable events of his life up until now, and the last thing he heard as the three left last night. An arbitrary word is thrusted in his thoughts: Operation. His eyes light up.

Operation? Operation what, James thinks.

"C'mon you fuckin' kid!" Fish jeers in impatience.

James puffs up his chest. "Operation Freakshow!" he

screams.

The microphone cuts out and Abby's high heels fall back as more black unpolished shoes fill the lens. The feed is lost and rerouted to an unprepared morning co-anchor in the newsroom whose jaw hangs slightly open in astonishment. Someone off camera furiously cues him to speak.

Fish slams the remote control into the floor, breaking off the cover. The batteries fly out and scatter in different directions like suddenly illuminated cockroaches. "What the fuck? That little fuck can't get anything right! Operation Freakshow is the dumbest thing I have ever heard!"

"Yeah, because 'Operation Fishman' would sound sooo fantastic," Ana sarcastically attaches to Fish's brooding monologue.

"I kinda like the name," Freakshow stingingly adds.

"You fuckin' would!" Fish argues as the shadow of his fantasy dissipates.

"We have a bigger problem than your hero fetish," Ana says pointing to the screen.

In the newsroom, the co-anchor reads from the prompter. "Chief of Police Paul Fulara will be holding a press conference at noon regarding the recent surge of shooti-"

"Everyone will know about us," says Ana. "So, we'd better be as prepared as the rest of the people on that list."

Outside the news van, Abby O'Neill straightens her skirt as the clumsy junior camera operator meticulously checks the equipment for any damage.

"What the fuck was that, Stanley? Can't you hold the camera still for a minute, or is your family's Parkinson's deciding to show itself early?"

"I'm sorry, Abby," he says docilely. He had settled on apologizing for his incompetence long before he even knew he was going to be scolded.

"What the fuck was that shit?" she reiterates.

"I'm sorry, Abby."

"Not you Stan. That fucking kid. You saw them bring out the bags. You smelled that godawful stench."

"I think that was coming from inside the house though, Abby."

"No shit. It came from inside the house! The residents here don't smell *that* bad!"

Abby looks at her reflection in the van's oversized rear-view mirror fixed to the door. She pouts her lips and runs her fingers through her hair until it rests on her shoulders in the desired manner.

"I'm talking about 'Operation Freakshow' and that hero business. I can't make heads or tails of it."

Stanley coils the cables and signals the driver to help pack up.

Abby turns around to lean in and rests her hand on Stanley's shoulder, winning his undivided attention. The scent of her shampoo is intoxicating.

"Goddammit Stanley. I've smelled burn victims before! One of those body bags was smoking for fucksake! These Freakshow guys bust into a house, kill the adults, but leave the kid alive? And this kid isn't traumatized *at all*? Not only that, but he makes them out to be heroes on TV? And what about that story Dana beat us to yesterday? At Sal's?"

"Yeah?" Stanley passively adds, knowing that Abby isn't asking for his opinion anyway.

"That guy Jose! Don't you get it? What that kid said? *Operation* Freakshow? This is organized! I think someone is putting out hits. Who the hell is covering the Hembridge shooting?"

LI.

Mike Bua isn't certain whether it's the blazing sun hitting his eyelids, or the incessant ringing and vibrating of his mobile phone on the dashboard, that awakens him. His cuts, covered in a thin film of coagulant, have bonded with his jacket. He refuses to peel it away. Peeling it would only cause more of a mess. Squinting, his bloodied hand reaches for the phone. Not bothering to conceal his scratchy voice and heavy tongue he answers in nonchalance, "What's up?"

It's the Captain.

Having anticipated Mike's hangover, the Captain proceeds upon relaying recent developments in the Solak case. It's a short conversation which, in the end, only summarizes the fact that Chief of Police Fulara will be holding a press conference at noon, and that Mike is to attend. He will also be briefed on a child abuse case.

"Bethany Santos?" Mike inquires.

"No, this is a new one. Clean up or don't show up, Bua. If you show up smelling like anything other than a rose, I'll be sure to fire your sorry ass! And leave your goddamn two-way on!" the Captain barks before terminating the call leaving Mike's head swirling with newly-acquired information that struggles to travel through the fouled synaptic connectors of another hangover.

Mike unintentionally whiffs his acrid breath as he searches for the keys, which end up being in the ignition. Pulling off the rutty shoulder, he flips a switch, lighting up the car's grill and dashboard flashers. U-turning over the median, he steals a final look at the stained Celtic cross. He puts down his window and proudly flies his middle finger at the billboard as he speeds away.

LII.

"What do you think?" Fish asks with enthusiasm, expecting nothing less than the supportive cheers of his comrades. He shows the backside of a two-year old expense form scavenged from Luiz's desk. Sketched in ballpoint pen is the crude profile of a fish. Scribbled out on the left hand side are two previous attempts of the same image, to which he was not satisfied with the symmetry. The countless pen strokes shaping two intersecting arcs are no longer than an inch in length and give the fish a hairy appearance, almost like a flagellum, but only if one doesn't squint.

Freakshow distorts his face, worried that he's not viewing it properly. An unbearable five-second interval for Fish is quelled by Freakshow's agreeable and concise, if not altogether contrary, critique.

"I like it. It's simple, but gets to the point."

Fish scratches his chin and nods his head with bravado. It is difficult to know whether he is completely self-aware as he does this. He raises an eyebrow and looks to Ana for her expertise. She knots her brow, pointing at the illustration accusingly.

"Are you for fucking real?" she asks.

Ana's reaction catches Fish helpless. He waits for her to proceed further, which she does.

"That's the fucking symbol for Jesus Christ, you idiot!"

"Really...?" he postulates, half-expecting Ana to start laughing and confess on bullshitting him.

"Yes, fucking look it up!" she challenges.

Freakshow has turned to the television and is evading the situation by pretending not to hear the argument, and expecting Fish to be too proud to express his doubts vocally. If Ana is bullshitting, she's choosing to take it further than she normally does. Fuck, maybe she *is* telling the truth. Fish calls it.

"Yeah, I knew that! Everybody knows that, right Show? But it's not like it's..." Fish's brain works overtime to recall the word. "*Copyrighted* or anything," he blubbers out, trying to save face.

Ana lifts a book entitled *365 Sudoku-A-Day* and angles it on her lap before calling Fish's bluff. "You're so full of shit, Fish."

Then, picking up a ballpoint pen, Ana sets to work trying to restore any brain cells she may have lost in the needless dispute. She doesn't even get to establish where she left off in her puzzle before being interrupted once more.

"Here we go again," Freakshow announces with annoyance as he raises the volume on the television. It's another news bulletin.

Pension-ready Channel 4 daytime anchor Trevor Brently jogs papers on his desk. A face, which seems incapable of frowning, sits atop a Windsor knot and is framed in a baby blue collar. His silver hair is flawlessly set parting right with the miniature tidal whorl of follicles swooping over his forehead.

"And thanks for that Jeneane," he says out of habit. "New developments in the ongoing investigation into the death of Jesse George Shane of 17 Independence Parkway. Police have released residential security footage of a masked tattooed man exiting the passenger side of a 1997 black Honda Civic. What we are about to show may disturb some of our viewers."

Ana drops her pen in shock. The three watch the black and white footage, from what looks to be taken from a camera positioned within the front landing's lighting enclosure. An uncomfortably close shot of Freakshow from the waist up fills the screen as he approaches the front door. Feints of a raised weapon turn out to be just the diligent ringing of the doorbell, but the video is silent. Finally, Freakshow's masked head bobs in speech and black clothing flashes white before he saunters away, kicking at the lawn. With the door still open, the car speeds away. The photo of a telephone hanging off the hook is displayed as Trevor Brently narrates through the information hotline screen.

"Again?" Fish cries.

"Shut the fuck up!" Ana shouts as she wrestles the remote from Freakshow's hand and toggles the volume.

The feed is switched to Abby O'Neill standing before 17 Independence Parkway using journalism's "puzzled concernment" facial expression preset. She holds a peculiar object in her right hand. It is a very familiar black and silver toothy wrestling mask.

"Thank you, Trevor," she says out of habit. "The killers, recognizing themselves as 'Operation Freakshow,' were filmed wearing masks very similar to the one I hold in my hand now."

Abby, placing the mask over her hand, raises it to the camera and tries to maintain its shape by keeping it rounded over her fingers. She turns it to and fro.

"With Halloween nearly a month away, these masks of the once popular Mexican luchador Manuel el Monsturo Jr. can be purchased at any costume shop or discount store. The police neither have had luck in tracing the sales of these masks, nor the killers, though they are currently following a number of leads. Melvin Nordstrom, a resident of Hembridge, was one of the first who contacted police."

The camera pans left to an established-looking man with a robust tea-colored beard who is wearing a shirt screen-printed with the words *Nova Scotia*, advertising his last summer's escapades. The TV is muted once more as Abby begins conducting her interview.

"Well, it's a good thing Luiz set us up with those masks," Ana says with false relief.

Wearisome, Fish twists his bottom lip down in skepticism.

"I wonder...," Ana muses, unsure of whether or not to finish her thought. "Does Luiz have a camera for that computer?"

LIII.

Clouds roll across the sky.

Sober, showered, bandaged, and heavily cologned, Mike Bua stands with hands cupped below his belt buckle. Matt Mashburn wears an unsuitably-genial expression as the stern-faced Captain looks forward to face the crowd. The landing of the stone steps in front of the police station give them more vertical advantage than a stage would. Chief of Police Paul Fulara finally discourages the eagerly-raised hands by indicating the time and makes a short closing statement from the podium before walking away. Unencumbered, the questions resume in a frenzy of reporters still starved for answers.

A reporter juts her microphone forward. "What stance are you taking regarding the growing public support for Operation Freakshow?"

Now a man shoves himself forward. "What about the numerous reports of masks turning up in mailboxes?"

"Is this connected in any way with the disappearance of gubernatorial hopeful, McCleary, and his daughter?" A barely audible holler from the back drifts past other reporters lining the front.

The crowd is a sea of voices and is growing into a free-for-all. Another faceless person asks, "Are there any other charges being filed against Sal Solak?"

The Q and A went nearly ten minutes over, but was obviously not enough for some. Fulara's eyes desolately look over a bandaged and bag-eyed Bua, a stupidly grinning and pale Mashburn, and the austere gray-headed captain. He pauses to nod to the Captain before impotently stepping down toward an awaiting vehicle parked in the street. Camera flashes weakened by the daylight flicker in a last ditch effort to capture profiles of the three as they turn away to the station. The glass doors resist to shut against an escaping current of wind. Mike's yanks out his shirttails. His long sleeves cover up the self-inflicted wounds wrapped tightly in a bandage.

"This is goddamn ridiculous!" the Captain blasphemes. "These Freakshows are becoming overnight celebrities. I want this taken care of Bua!"

"I really don't see the problem if they are killing the scum of the earth," Mike confidently retorts.

"I know your position Bua. I know how you feel, but this has got to stop. These people getting killed have done their time and paid their dues by the letter of the law. Jesse George Shane served fifteen years! After that, he was a valued member of the community, not to mention a big contributor to our fundraisers! He paid for his crimes threefold with penitence."

Mike tenses his lips upon hearing this.

Matt Mashburn looks for a break in the conversation to squeeze in his own opinion. But not having decided on whom to back up, he continues to listen and vacillates his stance.

The Captain presses a button, calling an elevator.

"And what about Jesse George Shane's victim?" Mike coldly asks in parting.

The Captain ponders Bua's angle before continuing.

"Goddammit Bua. I saw one of those Freakshow masks spray-painted on the fucking wall outside the radio station today! Just get the fuck out there and catch them before this whole thing gets out of control. Nip it in the bud, that's what my father always used to say!" the Captain shouts.

The door to the lift opens, but the Captain ignores it entirely. Controlling his outburst, he lowers his voice to a near whisper and huddles in close. Mike and Matt mirror his actions by leaning their heads in.

"Listen Bua, Mashburn. That kid we found this morning, James, the one that called us, had curling iron burns up and down his arm. There were two shot in the kitchen and his guardian, Nigel Freed, was found in bondage in a soundproofed-room with said curling iron up his rectum."

"Oh, my God," Mashburn responds, cupping a hand over his mouth.

"Yeah, imagine the smell. And that's not the half of it. Burns all over his body. What was left of his genitals were covered in heat blisters. Time of death suggests that Freed was being tortured around the same time that camera picked up Shane's killer. It couldn't have been the sa-"

"Waitaminnit, how old is the kid?" Mike questions with imperative.

"Would you believe it?" the Captain smirks, acknowledging a sorrowful irony. "His birthday is today. Eighteen."

"What about the Santos case?"

"What about it?"

"Any relation?"

"I see where you're coming from Bua. Unfortunately we're not big town enough to have a medical examiner running DNA and cross-checking databases. All that shit takes time. For the time-being, all we've got is old-fashioned hunches. If you can prove that Jose Santos was the father of his niece's child then you got motive. Until then, we're going to treat it as a separate case. But the Santos hit was sloppy as all hell. You were there, so you know. These hits last night were by pros."

"Solak's still not talking?"

"Not a peep. And we can't hold him for much longer. The charges won't stick and he'll make bail either way."

"What about the kid, James?"

"Nothing since this morning's live snafu..."

The Captain breaks the huddle and raises his voice once more as he calls the elevator.

"Let me worry about the legalities. Just bring in anyone who has any answers to this! Top priority! If we can get someone to squawk, we can take down the entire operation."

The Captain steps inside. The closing doors end the meeting.

"Top priority. I'm on it!" Mike answers, his words resonating in the hollow shaft. He turns to Mashburn, who is still weighing out sides. "You know he's pissed when he starts using the word 'fuck.'"

"So, what are we gonna do?" asks Mashburn.

"Fuck catching them," say Bua. "We're gonna let 'Operation: Freakshow' take its course and collect bodies at the end of the night."

A branch of lightning streaks across the sky, illuminating the darkened halls. The following thunder and pouring rain have the press feverishly wrapping up their broadcasts and fleeing into their mobile units.

It's the sound of static as the falling water clashes with pavement.

"Looks like rain," Mashburn states in painful objectivity.

LIV.

The sampled phrase of a jazz flute loops over the subdued scratching of vinyl and the mellow tempo of a drum kit. A teenage boy wearing a white Linux penguin tee with unruly brown curls sits bobbing his head in rhythm before dual screens at a grandiose desk occupying the corner of his bedroom. A pornographic website opened in the browser gets shuttered behind a freshly opened tab. He speaks over his shoulder.

"By the way, you need to check out Reddit. Something on YouTube has sprung up to the first page in a few hours."

Jason, a boy whose pudginess would obscure his age weren't it for the uncontrollable acne, lies belly down on a bed. A lumpy pillow props his chest up. His fingers drag across the keyboard of a laptop as he answers.

"It's probably something stupid on TMZ about some pop star."

"No, it's about Operation Freakshow."

"No way! Send me the link."

"Just go to YouTube. It should be the top video."

Jason pops up a tab, concealing his incomplete and scathing response to a pretentious user, XXbrainiac13XX, on a comic book forum.

"...or are you still busy writing what'll get you banned

from the forum for another month?"

"I could care less!" Jason sharply answers, trying to convince himself. "This guy is a dick. Even the mods think he's a pain in the ass."

"I *couldn't* care less."

"Wha?"

"It's 'I *couldn't* care less', right?"

"Who cares?"

"Anyways..."

"Anyways this guy, XXbrainiac13XX, keeps saying 'DC Comics' this and 'DC Comics' that!"

Jason knits his brow after having made this point.

"Soooooo?" the boy at the desk asks with a frustrated drawl.

"So?! So?! No one says 'DC Comics'! DC stands for Detective Comics! It's like he's saying 'Detective Comics Comics!'"

"But no one says 'D-Comics' either..."

"Just say 'DC'! It's so easy! That's the whole reason they have the acronym! Why would you make it long again by saying the same thing twice? It's like people who say 'PIN number.' Fucking morons!"

"Dude, language. My mom's still home, you know."

"Dammit. Now I can't even remember why the hell I even opened this tab," Jason broods.

"YouTube."

"Oh, yeah."

Jason loads the page and clicks on the top thumbnail showing a grainy still of a silver trimmed wrestling mask under poor light. The video is titled 'Operation: Freakshow.'

"Holy shit."

"Language, dude!"

Jason rolls his eyes and apologizes sardonically faking a

speech impediment. "Sowwy Missus Gadd. Wittle baby Adam can't swear."

A thirty-second commercial that cannot be skipped has Jason wondering if he can finish writing and submitting his comment to the forum in the allotted time. By the time he decides he should, the commercial ends transitioning to the grainy footage of a bulky and frozen figure seated in front of a hardly distinguishable cinder block wall behind him. The video is just over a minute long.

"I wanna see too!" Adam shouts as he pauses his music and rushes over.

Jason taps a hotkey to turn up the volume. The voice sounds distorted and bleak.

"A lot of people in the media are calling us criminals or evil... like we're the bad guys. The truth is, we are not out to kill anyone except people on this list."

The masked man holds some stapled papers up to the lens. "We're just after sick people who have stolen the innocence of children, the ultimate sin. There are only a few of us, but there are thousands on this list. And this is just in the city where we live. We need your help. Get this list out in your city and help us rid the earth of this scum. We will not stop, but to defeat this enemy, we will need an army."

The bulky man shifts his weight.

"The law does not punish these villains enough, and some of them do not deserve forgiveness. Help us any way you can."

The man sits in silence, looking finished. The next person to speak sounds like a kid. "How do I turn this thing off?" he asks.

A pair of fat and full breasts circle around and engulf the lens in cleavage before the clip ends. Related and recommended clips show in the video frame.

Jason's hands are shaking in excitement. "Holy schemoly. This is freakin' awesome! I'm making this viral! I want this to be the most watched video in the history of the Internet. Our town is gonna be famous!"

"Okay, you can't swear, but you don't have to say 'schemoly' either. I'll tweet the link," Adam says, hastily returning to his electronic battle station.

"Vote it up on Reddit, Facebook, Digg, Google Plus, and that's just the start."

"I'm on it!"

The music resumes louder than before. A JBL woofer thumps the floor and satellite speakers tweet a melody out in stereophonic bliss as the two busily assume their duties.

LV.

The newsroom is in pandemonium with the recently-uploaded footage. Everything being communicated is done in shouts. The video counter lags behind at a pitiful 301 though the number of people who have seen it by now is currently speculated at quintuple digits.

Stanley Edwards tugs on the limp collar of his polo shirt as he does something in between a walk and jog toward Abby's desk. He twists his shoulders and sucks in his hips accordingly as he dodges other moving bodies in the room. No one ever seems to see him, or notice him for that matter, meaning he is at an increased risk for accidents. It is a simple fact of life for Stanley for as long as he can remember.

His parents never took particular notice of him among his four elder siblings and he never had the desire to be recognized or to want attention.

In elementary school, hardly any of Stanley's classmates knew his name, which could be attributed to the teachers who never took to him, so they never called on him. So no one had the opportunity to know his name through indirect means, and no one would dare directly ask his name because Stanley was not a very approachable person. His clothes were always faded and he wore the same oversized shirts year after year until he almost grew into them, almost, because he never quite did. He was a small boy who grew up to be a small man. And though he used to question and doubt his predicament, he now came to respect this seemingly natural order.

Ever since Stanley was assigned to work with Abby O'Neill, every day has been a waking dream for him. Her thin, beautiful eyes with eyelashes practically ready to curl in on themselves. Her breasts that look as if they could eject at any moment from her tight-fitting suits. Once, upon seeing Abby change in the van, Stanley was so affected with emotion he had to excuse himself to be alone and imprint the memory deep within his mind, dwelling on the special things so that they will not be forgotten. Every night before Stanley goes to bed, he replays the images of Abby in her black bra, hoping for the memory to be carried over to his subconscious where he can impose his will onto her as he pleases and freely exercise his boundless ego for a blissful and fulfilling sleep.

Abby sits at her computer.

"Hi Abby," Stanley says, fighting an urge to rest his hand on her desk. He is the only one who won't shout in the newsroom.

"Have you seen this, Stan?" Abby asks, gesturing to the monitor. "What do you think of all of this?"

"I don't think it's our job to think. It's our job to report," he wisely expounds in hopes of impressing her.

Abby laughs, showing her small and impeccable white teeth. "Says the guy who wanted to cover politics for FOX news!"

Stanley returns a timid smile, certain that Abby is confusing him with someone else.

Abby continues.

"As much as I'd love to follow bodies around town all day and collect the story, we've gotta come from a different perspective or else we'll be just like the other stations. We need to do a story about the potential targets of Operation Freakshow. The decent people who turned their lives around, but are at a risk of backlash because of this vigilante bloodbath. On the off chance that it slows them down or even ends ups stopping them, we'll be network heroes. Can you imagine the job offers?"

Stanley is distracted by a harbored question.

"Abby, are you hungr-"

A boisterous man with his sleeves rolled up shouts, "Goddammit Edwards. This footage isn't gonna edit itself! Get your ass over here!"

Stanley waves his hand and backs away from Abby's desk. He is mortified at not having been able to finish his question.

"Hey Stan. Let's get a bite or something after we get off," Abby says, her face absorbed into the monitor.

"Yes," Stan answers, then quietly excuses himself to the copy room before returning to edit.

LVI.

The room greys as moisture-heavy clouds engulf the neighborhood. Susan's blotchy complexion worsens.

"Wait. Please explain to me why you can't go home? Start with, 'because'..."

"Because... I'm on that list for some stupid shit I did a long time ago! And someone forwarded that Freakshow video to my work e-mail. Someone knows, Susan. I can't go home. They will look up where my registered address is!"

"How are you on that fucking list?" Susan shrieks, her trunk-like arms raising a pudgy finger to jab at Brett's chest.

"It was nothing! Seriously!"

"What the fuck was it, Brett? Seeing as these people are only targeting pedophiles..!" Susan crescendos to a grating volume. "I think I have a fucking right to know!"

"It was so minor, Susan."

"What the fuck did you do!" she demands.

"It was statutory sexual assault," Brett says, failing to make eye contact and instead, looks to the left to avoid Susan's icy stare.

"Statutory sexual assault!" Susan repeats in shattering dismay which Brett mistakes for a question. He begins elaborating, mistakenly hoping that he can improve the situation by doing so.

"Susan, I love you. Please! It was over twenty years ago! I was drunk at a family reunion. My half-cousin snuck up a few drinks and one thing led to another..."

He stumbles over his own words as he filters through the lewdness, trying to be as vague as possible.

"You fucking child fucker! I bring you into this house to start a family! I have a twelve year-old daughter living here and you weren't going to tell me?"

"I was a stupid twenty year-old!"

"How old was she, Brett?"

Brett avoids Susan's demonizing stare by looking to the left again. On the coffee table rests an issue of *Elle Decor*. "What does it matter?"

"Godammit Brett, how old was she?"

"Fourteen."

"God, what the fuck is wrong with you?"

"I told you, we were both drunk."

"Yeah, it's nice to know that you still drink too!"

"Susie, if it's *any* consolation, be happy that I didn't even put it in. Her dad found us right before she was about to go down on me. I was convicted for something I didn't even really do!"

"Yeah. How did that defense work out for you, you sick bastard?"

"Susie, please, I wasn't thinking. It was such a long time ago. And she was nearly fifteen, that's only a five-year difference!"

As the anger passes, Susan begins to feel the paralyzing effects of the crippling reality. The man with whom she's been raising her daughter for the past four years is a convicted sex offender. The beautiful house she's worked so hard to fill up with useless things that are nothing more than a superficial claim to a status that she doesn't really possess. The white carpeting and Ashley furniture throughout her home has been defiled by this stranger masquerading as an honest man with firm values and contemporary morals.

She thinks about her position on the Board of Education and how it now may be in jeopardy. She looks to Brett. The well-groomed Chevron moustache Brett wears over his lip, once endearingly regarded by Susan as a symbol of his individuality, has now become little more than despicable and a grotesque marker of his previous unorthodox sexual encounters. Brett has a sign of pain on his face. Susan only now becomes aware of the tears cascading over her many chins.

"This is why you've been putting off moving in for so long... Oh my God, and that job at your brother's restaurant!"

"Susie, I was going to tell you!"

"But it doesn't matter! It's over. I never want to see you again. Danielle is twelve. I can't trust you anymore..." she trails off, not knowing what to say.

"Susie, I never..." Brett says as he moves in to console her.

"Don't touch me!" she screams. Her chunky arms cut through the air like a whip. A heavy open hand contacts with Brett's aquiline nose. He doesn't bother to avoid the strike.

"Get the fuck out of my house!" Susan screams.

Brett holds a finger to his nose, too late to stop the blood from coming out. A crimson drop brushes his shirt and falls to the pearl white carpet of the living room. He remembers that his car is at the shop for repairs. He backs away from Susan and walks out of the house, forgetting to grab an umbrella. The heavy drizzle soaking his clothes seems to want to drag his body into the earth.

LVII.

Matt Mashburn types at his desk, trying to sift through the growing and already vast amount of minformation indexed online under 'Operation Freakshow.'

"I've never seen anything like this. This is absolutely unreal," he says to an oppositely seated Bua.

Bua glazes over the sexual offender's list, checking his familiarity with any of the names.

"Yeah, it's getting big, really quick."

"Is there a way to disable the Megan's Law site temporarily? I mean, isn't that the only way to stop this list from spreading like wildfire?"

"Mashburn, really?" Mike sips at his coffee, making a bitter expression. "By now that thing's all over the net. People are passing around hard copies of that list by now."

"What about a pattern? Did ballistics come back with anything from the club?"

"Ballistics?" Mike echoes irritated. "What are you, some kinda boot? We only sent those recovered bullets out this morning!"

The talking takes a brief intermission as Mashburn thinks of another way to address the mounting cases without losing any more of Bua's respect. Since his suppositions are negatively received—if not to say altogether farcical—

Mashburn tries only to concern himself with the facts.

"The Captain says that all these non-compliant sex offenders are turning themselves in. He says we don't have the manpower to process them all. Even the compliants are looking for a safe roof over their heads. Half-way houses aren't enough, I guess."

Mike puts his coffee down. Some of the mug rings on his desk are months old. He searches his drawer for a mint as he answers Mashburn. "At the risk of sounding much older than I really am, I will say that I never thought I would see the day when pedophiles would rather be behind bars than out floating free. Those Freakshow's must be doing something right."

"You still think that what they're doing is a good thing?"

"Hell, yeah I do. I only wish they didn't make that video asking for help. These copycats that are likely to spring up will have no idea what they're doing. They're gonna hurt themselves—or worse—someone else. Things are gonna be busy here for a while."

"We've gotta stop them!" Mashburn says, raising his voice in certitude.

Mike Bua lifts his eyes from his desk drawer. Trotting footsteps are heard originating from the front desk. An officer runs up with a look of urgency painted across his dark face. He leans on Mashburn's desk.

"Bua, we're having a wave of calls coming in about people in those masks vandalizing the former Shane residence! Some people at West End have been assaulted. Bodies are being dumped off in front of the ER!"

Mike's face glows with delight. "Davis! Nice tackling that Channel 4 cameraman! I caught the 12 o'clock replay," he compliments. "You ran across the room to tell me that?"

"Well, not exactly. I thought I'd pass this on to you."

Officer Davis slips a folded piece of paper to Mike and keenly rotates his head, checking to see if anyone is eavesdropping. "Here's some information that concerns you. Maybe you'd like to handle it personally, without uh... Matchburn here."

"*Mash*burn," Matt astutely corrects, not hiding a look of resentment.

"Sorry, *Mashburn*," Davis says in parting, though not really seeming to care.

Mashburn takes no time in continuing where he left off in the conversation. "Mike, we need to stop this tonight!" he says, raising his voice once more in certitude, though not to the same effect. Davis' intrusion seems to have stolen a great deal of oratorical momentum.

"Godammit," Bua curses.

"What?"

"I thought I had mints in here," Mike says. He rolls up his sleeves, exposing the fresh bandages wrapped up to his elbow.

"Jesus, what happened to your arm?"

Mike quietly gathers his jacket and readies himself to leave the room. He pushes the folded slip of paper from Davis into his pants pocket, not concerning himself with Matt's question.

"Let's get outta here, Matt. Like the Captain said, we don't have enough manpower."

LVIII.

Jason lies on his stomach, lazily swinging his crossed legs in the air as he waits for an angered reply from user XXbrainiac13XX. He refreshes the page for the umpteenth time.

"Adam!" Missus Gadd calls from the bottom of the steps.

"Wha-at..?" Adam shouts and then waits impatiently for a response.

"Adam!" she calls again.

"What is it?" he yells at the top of his lungs through the shut door.

This is the most common and frustrating form of household communication for him. His Mom doesn't answer so he tries once more. "What Mom?" Adam yells, even louder, stinging the inside of Jason's left ear.

"Derek is here," she says, her voice shrinking behind the wooden barrier.

"Damn, that was fast!" Adam exclaims as he jumps out of his computer chair and runs downstairs. 'Be back in a sec,' he turns to say, nearly forgetting Jason through his excitement.

Nearly three minutes pass with still no heated reply from user XXbrainiac13XX. Adam returns with jubilant countenance, and hands behind his back, waiting for Jason to pry.

"Okay, what is it?" Jason asks, rolling his eyes. He hopes that he isn't giving Adam too much satisfaction by still having to humor him at this age.

"Boo-yah!" Adam says, holding up a small black and silver bag.

"What?"

"Take a look at it," Adam says, tossing the lump of fabric onto the bed. Jason picks it up and unfurls the bag looking bored. His eyes widen as it begins to take a familiar shape.

"Oh, shit!" Jason exclaims.

"C'mon man. Watch the language." Adam scolds.

"Oh, my God! This is a Freakshow mask! Where did Derek get this?"

"The costume shop on Hudson. His brother works there. Saved the last one in stock for us."

"For *you*, you mean. What did you pay him?"

"Derek? Nothing."

"Nothing?"

"Well, no money at least. I made a trade for my Empire God III account since I don't play anymore."

"What's Derek gonna do with that?"

"He still plays."

"Who does Derek play *with*? That series is practically dead. The servers were a digital ghost town the last time I logged in."

"Yeah, I don't think anyone does play anymore, but he's confident everyone will be on again once the new patch comes out."

"No one's gonna go back to it, not with the Guilded Ages expansion coming out this fall! What a dumbass."

"Meh, his loss is my gain."

"Wow..." Jason runs his fingers over the slitted mouth, savoring the texture. "What are you gonna do with this?"

"I picked someone from the list!"

"What?"

"It's gonna be great," Adam says, kneading his hands together.

"You're not going to kill someone! Are you crazy?"

"I'm going to do this. I need to do this, and I need your help."

"I can't kill anyone!"

"We're not killing anyone."

"I hope not."

"I just wanna scare this one guy. I'll be in and out."

"Yeah? That's what the last guy said."

"Really? Who?"

"Figure of speech."

"Look, just drive me there and I will do it!"

"Why do *I* need to drive you?"

"This guy lives out past Chapsburg."

Jason shakes his head, deeply wishing he hadn't come over today.

Adam nearly finishes off with this weak argument: "Look, this is just something that I've gotta do."

"Why do I have to help?"

"Why? All you are doing is driving!"

Adam takes the upper hand and administers his final blow by questioning authenticity of their camaraderie that crushes any further argument Jason may have had.

"Aren't we friends? Remember when Slank was kicking your ass last year? Who jumped in and ended up getting his ass kicked with you?"

Jason sighs.

"You did."

"That's right," Adam states smugly. "You fuckin' owe me."

LIX.

Ana's arm begins to tingle. She uses her thumb to apply pressure just below the lump in the pocket of her tight-fitting pants and drives the translucent orange tube upward. Once high enough, she fishes it out with thumb and forefinger, pops off the lid, puts the rim directly to her lips, and swallows a few tablets.

Fish observes with worry.

"What's the dosage on that again?" he asks.

"Shut up, I'm self-medicating," Ana preparedly answers.

"So-"

"So there's no such thing as over-prescribing," Ana says, irritated.

Leftover slices from two extra-large pizzas lay on crumb-ridden plates blotted with orange grease. Two pizza boxes are stacked in the center of Luiz's work table. Freakshow pats his stomach in quenched satisfaction. Ana leans her head back and closes her eyes, waiting for the tingling to subside.

Footsteps.

Luiz enters the room, holding a half-empty plastic bucket sloshing with filthy water and stained rags. He places the bucket into the deep stainless sink, washes his hands, and then turns his attention to the worktable. Lifting the lid of a pizza box, he peeks under and grabs the biggest slice of the unequally divided pepperoni pizza—nearly twice as wide as the thinnest slice, positioned directly across from it. He takes an enormous bite from the drooping wedge before starting conversation.

"Anything new?"

"Nope," Freakshow answers. "I'm pretty sure the cops haven't got shit. They don't even know about the two that Fish did last night."

"I mean, is there anything new with your recruiting project?"

Luiz takes another bite and chews like a cow on cud.

"The video's got a lot of views, but nothing new has been on since twelve."

"Ah. Well anyways, I finished cleaning out your vehicle. I didn't have time to work on the stains." A small piece of half-chewed dough covered in saliva flies out of Luiz's mouth, landing near Fish's feet. "Sorry bro... As I was saying, at least the smell shouldn't set in now. You're all set to go."

"Thanks Luiz," Ana says.

"I also gave you my scanner. I don't know anyone in their right mind in your line of work who doesn't have one."

"Yeah, well, we'd better get going," Freakshow says, ignoring the cleverly disguised remark on his sanity. He braces his knees as he stands.

Fish rises to follow, Ana does so with difficulty.

"You wanna come with us?" Freakshow asks, watching Luiz's sluggard masticating.

Luiz takes his time to chew and swallow before responding.

"I'm sorry Michael, you know I can't," he says, enunciating the name as if he were speaking in his native Portuguese. "You know, I believe in forgiveness."

"Some people don't deserve to be forgiven," Freakshow

says, sizing up Luiz.

Fish and Ana sense a subtle turbulence. They wait by the door, not sure whether conditions warrant their attendance or absence from the room.

Freakshow's muscles tense.

Luiz stares into Freakshow's hollow eyes, attempting to solicit a remnant of the cold killer's long abandoned humanity. Freakshow's stone-like countenance is one of dead expression and unreadable motives. His eyes forever retain the frigidity and remoteness of his scarred psyche.

"One day, brother, someone may say the same thing about you," Luiz comments.

The corners of Freakshow's mouth jerk downward, but his hollow eyes do not respond. Luiz continues searching until Freakshow cuts his gaze away to head for the door. Fish and Ana oblige him and clear the doorway for his passage.

"Be safe, my friends," Luiz calls to the three.

Ana dissembles with an apologetic smile.

Luiz waves his hand at Ana in forgiveness, which she mistakenly interprets as a goodbye.

LX.

Evening. The clouds are thinning, though it's much too late for any sunshine now. Having noticed a small crowd gathered in front of Fat Freddie's Pulled Pork Restaurant & Eatery, Mike pulls around, making an unscheduled stop. He flicks off his windshield wipers and puts down the windows, flushing the cruiser with the cool but humid air, the vapor of which fills his lungs. The rain is letting up. A Dynasty Travel tour bus takes up the far end of the parking lot.

"Freakshow! Freakshow!" the crowd continuously chants. Someone shoulders a camera, though Mike doesn't see any news vans.

Standing toward the back, someone wearing a balaclava improvised from a black t-shirt looks to the approaching vehicle and notices the red-headed officer in full uniform sitting in the passenger seat. He taps the person next to him on the shoulder and points out the stealthily approaching unmarked cruiser.

He alerts the crowd. "Yo, cops!"

School kids stigmatized by authority pull out and run around the building to avoid reprimand.

Bua and Mashburn step out of the vehicle and walk toward the remaining group. Black, grey, and white-haired heads speaking in a foreign tongue and holding Fat Freddie's signature barbeque sandwiches are all huddling around something. Mike isn't sure what to expect. He can't make anything out of the simultaneous exchange of words in moonspeak.

"Excuse us!" Mashburn calls, parting the crowd. A few respond by what would be the English equivalent of oohs and aahs, sounding off in positive wonderment at the United States law enforcement in action. They snap pictures to document what will surely be a memorable event.

A svelte black teenager wearing an Operation Freakshow mask stands on a collapsed cardboard box, signing autographs on napkins and the back of receipts to the Asian tour group. He makes sure to fill all young female requests first.

Mike Bua cuts to the front of the throng with some of the tourists scoffing in disapproval. Mashburn's uniform attracts much attention as nearly the entire crowd has now begun recording video footage with their mobile phones.

The teenager, from the corner of his eye, notes the blond-haired man with the bandaged arm who has pushed himself to the front of the eager crowd. "What's up? You want my autograph?"

Mashburn advances from behind Bua, showing his badge.

The masked boy fights off a sudden twitch in his legs. He was too absorbed in himself to have heard the alarm earlier. Now, he regretfully calculates his prospects of fleeing, which are close to zero. He can't get away surrounded by all these people who wouldn't understand a command to move even if he asked them.

"Listen, you're not in any trouble, but you will be unless you take off that mask and go home, now," Bua says to the boy.

Members of the tour group begin elbowing each other as they point to their wristwatches. Assuming the entertainment to be over anyway, the crowd begins to disperse, heading towards the bus, with some disappointed at not having received a souvenir. Two young men carrying crisp knapsacks and wearing lanyards with student identification from a community college stay behind to film with a single camera.

"Yo, y'all need ta step offa my shine," the boy recites to Bua and Mashburn as he plays it cool in front of the camera.

"I understand you even less than those tourists that were just here. I'm not even gonna ask you your name or take any information. Just take off the mask, go home, and we can forget this even happened."

"Yo, we're doing this for class," the masked boy answers gesturing to the camera crew.

"I don't give a shit what you're doing it for. Pack it up!"

Mike turns and squints his eyes at the nametag of the boy behind him holding the camera, Jarvis Sherman. Mike secretly chuckles at the name.

Jarvis, wishing to avoid a criminal record of any sort, removes the camera from his shoulder, points it slightly downward, and pretends to toggle with the settings.

A group of high school students walking out of Fat Freddie's make their way to a purple Dodge Neon parked near a lamppost. The masked boy turns dismayed to a portable speaker unit holding his smartphone. He picks up a pair of earbuds laying on the ground and throws them begrudgingly into his backpack. Bua and Mashburn turn around, thinking things to be over, only to hear Herbie Hancock's *Rockit* being blasted on the portable speaker. The boy wearing the Operation Freakshow mask begins feeling for the beat before doing an impressively-executed stabbed windmill on the cardboard. The teenagers stop to watch the breakdancing, but dare not approach. They see the uniformed officer with a rapidly changing demeanor. Jarvis and the other student let out boisterous laughter and shout their approval.

"Goddamn kids!" Bua growls. He dives, pinning the boy down mid-backspin and flips him on his belly.

"Yo, what the fuck?" the boy angrily shouts.

The high schoolers begin pointing and taking pictures. Some customers from Fat Freddie's step outside to watch the outrageous ordeal.

"You're under arrest," Mike says handcuffing the black Freakshow. Jarvis and the other boy take a step back not wanting to draw attention to themselves. Jarvis checks to make sure the video is still recording and takes an even further step back, giving himself ample reaction time should one of the officers try to confiscate the equipment.

"Would you tell the Punisher to take off his mask and go home?" the boy protests.

"Punisher doesn't wear a mask, you idiot," Mike answers.

"What about Batman then?"

"Yes."

"Goddammit! No! I'm a hero! Long live Freakshow!"

Mike pulls off the kid's mask and flings it. It lands, upsetting the portable stereo. *Rockit* now only plays through the single-stressed speaker of the boy's phone.

"Black! Because I'm black!" the boy yells, feigning cries of pain. "Mah arm! Mah arm! Police brutality!"

Matt Mashburn wants to make a reference to *The Boy Who Cried Wolf*, but conscious of the cameras, can't figure out how to reword it to avoid any misconstrued racist connotation.

"Smile, I'm sure we'll be all over the evening news," Mike Bua says as he hands the boy to Mashburn who locks him in the back of the cruiser. Attracted attention from the restaurant and rubberneckers from the road begin snapping photos and recording video.

Mike decides to retrieve the mask and shoves it into the glove compartment. He sarcastically wishes the two students filming a good grade on their project before driving away.

LXI.

A thick wetness from the rain hangs off of the snarled trees and uncut grass. Cheap inflated rubber balls lie floating in puddles of deep mirrors that reflect the near-full moon in the night sky. Poor drainage transforms the land into a temporary swamp. On the highway, the black SUV nearly whizzes past, missing the gravel driveway. It brakes suddenly and does a wide turn onto the long weather-beaten path marked *Mavis Manor*.

"Goddamn, how many trailer parks do we have surrounding this fuckin' city anyways?" Fish mentions while trying not to drive in a manner that would be perceived as suspicious.

"You talk pretty high and mighty for someone who came from one himself," Ana says and points to a rectangular area of packed dirt ahead. "Park over there."

"Who the fuck told you I come from a trailer family?" Fish asks, surprised that Ana knew.

"Who do you think?" she matter-of-factly returns, though still leaving ambiguity in her answer.

Fish pulls the SUV in headfirst and shuts off the engine.

Everyone has worked the masking-up part of the job to a routine now. They pull the material over their heads, absent of any awkwardness or hesitation.

"Most of these trailers are dark. These people probably aren't even home," Fish argumentatively states in a increasingly sour mood. "So which trailer is it?"

"Jeez, hang on a sec... two, three, four, six, eight, twelve— shit, forgot nine—and... fourteen."

"Eight?"

"Yeah, eight too."

'Yeah, I know, I meant, like, altogether?"

"Sorry. Yeah, eight altogether."

"I'm not gonna remember all that!"

"Well, then fucking write it on your arm!" Ana throws Fish the communal ballpoint pen.

"How many people do you think own guns out here?" he asks.

"I don't fucking know! Just try to get it over with quick! Write it down this time: two, three, four, six, eight, nine, twelve, fourteen! Let's just fucking go!"

Ana unlatches the door and slides down, making a mucky splash from her side of the vehicle.

Freakshow and Fish pop their doors, climb down, and hunch over with trigger fingers itching. The mask begins to adhere to Fish's face in the humidity.

LXII.

Danielle goes through her digital rounds, sifting through one webpage after another, updating her mood, changing her few-days old profile pictures, and remarking on her hatred of swimming and fourth period Mr. Buck's Biology class. After having made her updates, she starts from the beginning all over again, counting her likes and responding to any comments received. A boy in her classes named Chris King seems to have been the first to comment on everything. In addition, he asks her if she's still coming to the basketball game on next Friday. Danielle replies with a wholehearted "yes!", locks her phone, and holds it to her fluttering chest.

A song she likes comes on the radio. She reaches to increase the volume but notices her mother Susan's hands clumsily moving over the steering wheel. Her mother is holding back a flood of tears. Wrinkles Danielle has never even noticed before seem like decades-long pronounced furrows on her mother's oxen face. Though Danielle hates to think it, her mother is ugly. She is often embarrassed, not only by her mother's large figure, but by her short-snouted face and podgy cheeks sagging to decimate what is left of her receding chin.

Perhaps it is a blessing in disguise, for Danielle never takes for granted her own maturing beauty and popularity.

She only prays that Chris King never discovers that Board of Education's Susan M. Poole is her own mother. Yet, despite all the concealment and slight repulsion, Danielle still loves her mother dearly. Susan has never been anything but caring and open with Danielle. Her insecurities as a parent only come from the unknown reasons as to why Danielle continually tries to put a distance between them. Danielle rests her left hand on her mom's fleshy shoulders.

"Mom? What's wrong?"

Susan pulls the car over, terribly worrying Danielle. The keys are left in the ignition and the volume is turned down on Danielle's song.

"I've got to ask you..." Susan spouts. "I've got to ask you Danielle."

"What happened? Did I do something?"

"This is about Brett..."

"Oh Mom, Brett already told me! Congratulations. I am totally happy you two are getting married!"

"Let me finish!" Susan screams, turning the heads of a couple crossing the street. Danielle slouches in her chair feeling, for the first time, a fear of her own mother. "You need to be honest with me now! Has Brett ever touched you?"

"He's given me hugs and stuff, but Mom he's never ever hit me. Honest!"

"No, Danielle. Has he ever *touched* you, sexually?"

"Are you serious? You mean like, *molest* me?" An explosion of air leaving Danielle's sealed lips imitates the sound of flatulence as she bursts into laughter from the incredibly absurd question.

"Dammit Danielle! I'm serious! Has he ever touched you? Has Brett ever molested you?"

Susan bangs on the dashboard repeatedly. Her clumsy hand knocks off an immaterial stack of paper clipped business contact information and memos from the sun visor. They scatter like a flying deck of cards. Danielle is successfully silenced.

"No, Mom! Never! What's wrong?" Danielle recoils in fear from her mother's rage.

Susan places her forehead against the steering wheel, sobbing.

"Danielle, are you telling me the truth?"

"I swear to God Mom. Brett would never do anything like that."

Susan's rolled layers of fat overcome the steering wheel as she curls into a ball. Danielle leans over to the driver's seat and holds her mother.

LXIII.

Fish jogs the length of a few abandoned trailers toward Freakshow and Ana.

"Four and nine were empty," he reports, half-relieved at not having had to kill anyone.

"Twelve was empty too," Freakshow says as he throws his shoulder into mobile home fourteen expecting the same disappointing results. He carelessly sticks his head inside and casually looks from left to right. "Well whaddaya know, this one's empty too."

"What the fuck? Are we being set-up? Or is this just one big coincidence?" Fish asks foolishly trying to flatter himself.

Ana sucks her teeth.

"Dumbass, all these people probably heard about us on the news and hauled ass."

"They must have heard that the Fishman was coming."

"Yes, I'm sure that's exactly what it was. Everyone is running from some pubescent bitch with an awful color job."

Fish, now self-conscious, pats his hair. "Shut the fuck up! What's wrong with you Ana? I'm just joking."

"Both of you shut the fuck up and let's go. What a fucking waste of time," Freakshow says, tucking his gun into the waist of his pants.

"It doesn't have to be," Fish says, grinning underneath his

mask.

"Yeah? You got any bright ideas?" Freakshow asks, his patience wearing thin.

Fish yanks both of his pant legs up, revealing three pipe bombs duct-taped above each of his ankles.

"Yeah, that's real smart. Luckily you haven't blown your legs off yet," Ana starts once more.

"I didn't wanna leave them in the car and couldn't think of a better way to hide them on me."

Fish slowly pulls off the duct tape. His legs are hairless, eliminating a great part of what would have been pain.

"I have never gotten to use these," says Fish. "Please, let's at least put on a show before we leave. I mean, no one is in those trailers anyway, right?"

"Have it your way," Freakshow replies.

"Thanks Show. I'd kiss you if I could know for certain that there aren't any security cameras around here as well."

"Funny man," Freakshow offers in a rare compliment. "Go do what you've gotta do."

A station wagon that's color is obscured by the darkness speeds around the bend and tosses gravel in the air as it skids to a stop. Freakshow, Ana, and Fish see it just in time to duck behind one of the many abandoned mobile homes in the park. Fish sees one of the pipe bombs left behind in plain sight. He curses to himself.

The station wagon switches gears as the ass end of the car whips around in circles. Three people inside the car shout hedonistically as the car does doughnuts on the lot. A floodlight from one of the trailers at the far end of the park kicks on and showers the station wagon in beams of blinding light. Green glass bottles glow in the hands of the car's occupants. They're only kids.

"You damn hooligans! Why can't you just leave me

221

alone!" A man with a crooked back shouts from the trailer with the blaring halogen lamp. "All my tenants have left, no thanks to you!"

"AhPeraShen FreeKSShowe!" a boy in the backseat cries, using every ounce of strength in his drunk lungs. His voice oscillates as the wagon swings around for another full rotation.

"What the fuck?" Ana reacts, looking to Freakshow and Fish. They are completely hidden behind one of the trailers with no visibility.

A bottle flies from the spinning vehicle and impacts the side of trailer fourteen. The car shuts off as its ancient drivetrain begins to feel the strain of youth behind its wheel.

"Wuh heppen'd?" someone from inside the vehicle asks.

"This fucking piece o' shit Chevy!" someone else yells, perhaps the driver.

The man on the porch disappears into his trailer and shuts off the floodlight, leaving the lot once again in a thick darkness.

"Nick, what the fuck?" one of the boys exclaims as he jumps out to kick the tire of the overworked automobile.

"Chill out bro. Have another."

Three clicks are followed by the gentle hissing of gases escaping from aluminum cans. Loud gulps are heard. After a hearty belching, the cans are respectively crushed underfoot and kicked, or smashed against the head and thrown.

"D00d, my fuggin hed!" the heaviest-slurring voice announces. "AHPerAShin FreeEKsshOW!"

"Fuck yeah!" the two others shout.

"Hang on. Lemme look at the car. This is my grandfather's."

Fish peeks around the corner wishing to see the hilarious performance of what everyone else can only hear—three stupid and drunk teenagers playing immortal. A kid swaying in the backseat, and an extremely upset boy standing at the passenger's side, both having the identical black and silver masks with a toothy frown. A boy opening the hood of the car is the only one who isn't disguised. There's no light for him to be able to see anything. He blindly reaches for the chassis and throws his hand back, screaming hotly.

In the pitiful situation, Fish cannot help but see his own stupid yesteryear self.

"These guys are wasted," he snickers to Freakshow and Ana. "Let's go say 'hi.'"

LXIV.

DiPaolo's Italian Cuisine, a family-owned business for more than sixty years, was first established by Leo DiPaolo Sr. following his release from an Italian-American internment camp at Italy's surrender in the late summer of 1943.

Leo DiPaolo Sr., who hailed from the culturally-wealthy region of Tuscany, had been a dental student studying in the U.S. at the time. On December 20th, 1941, nine days after Germany and Italy declared war on the United States and only five days before Christmas Day, Leo DiPaolo Sr.—at that time only known as Leo DiPaolo—was apprehended as he was attempting to flee his small dwelling on the upper west side of Woosterton. Leo never spoke much of his time spent in the internment camps, but upon his release, it was an undeniable fact that something had changed within Leo.

Leo ignored his father's wishes for him to continue in dentistry, consequentially destroying his familial relationship. Having lost his possessions, a place to stay, and his father's support, Leo started work immediately at a local kitchen owned by a second generation Italian-American. He took to the job immediately. He was incredibly bright and had a knack for all things culinary. His constant adjusting of the recipes infuriated his boss though it brought wide praise and won the loyalty of many customers. His self-confidence was quickly established and Leo's boss, realizing Leo to be a valuable asset, paid him graciously.

Having a formidable amount saved by the end of the decade, Leo was able to open his own restaurant. In autumn 1949, DiPaolo's Italian Cuisine opened. The following years entailed his marriage to a stoic Protestant woman, siring three children with her, and seeing his first two grandchildren born. On the night of May 17th, 1987, Leo, having not fulfilled his final wish of visiting beautiful Tuscany once more, passed away from coronary heart disease. His eldest son, Leo DiPaolo Jr., took over the business and has been maintaining the DiPaolo legacy since.

Abby O'Neill and Stanley Edwards sit opposite one another at a rectangular table. The white cloth placemats are an elegant touch. DiPaolo's Italian Cuisine never boasted a gourmet menu for those with refined tastes. Instead, Leo Sr.'s cooking philosophy was one of democratic virtues and authentic taste for authentic people. The atmosphere is relaxed. Celeste Aida performed by Enrico Caruso trickles through a speaker mounted on the wall at a volume so light you have to lean in to be able to identify the music. David DiPaolo, Leo DiPaolo Jr's middle son, takes Abby and Stanley's order and disappears through the springing portholed kitchen doors.

"What a crazy day. Man, all those people are friggin' nuts," Abby says, brushing her hair behind her shoulders.

Stanley, not sure what to do with his hands, keeps them under the table on his lap. "Can I ask you a question Abby?"

"You just did. Wow, it sure is a good thing you're behind the camera. Someone could get hurt." Abby wonders why she didn't order wine as she takes a sip from the ice water. "All right, ya big baby, ask away."

"I've seen you cover a lot of criminals," he proceeds testily. "You always had a tough-on-crime attitude. It's one of the many things that I have always respected about you."

"Go on," Abby cheerfully says.

"Well, why are you against the Freakshows? It seems like they would be right up your alley."

"I'm sorry Stan, but I have no sympathy for masked murderers."

"No, the Freakshows are *against* the criminals," Stanley points out.

"Murdering people on a list does not make you a crime fighter."

"What about Batman? Isn't he a crimefighter?"

"God damn it, Stan. If I have to hear another Batman comparison today I'm gonna scream. This isn't a comic book. This is real life."

Stanley wishes to drive home with his point.

"Abby, you remember last winter? We did that story about the woman who took revenge on her husband who always beat her?"

"What about it?" Abby asks as she chews on an ice cube.

"You said it was justice, remember? What's the difference between that and the Freakshows?"

"You wanna know the difference?" Abby asks.

"I am curious," Stanley replies.

"It's because my mother is a horrible bitch."

David DiPaolo reemerges from the portholed doors. Abby imprudently raises an arm to flag him down.

"Can I get a bottle of red? Whatever the house is," she orders loudly enough so that David needn't trouble himself with the trip to their table. He once again disappears himself into the kitchen.

Abby crosses her arms on the table and leans in, gaining intimacy.

"Stanley, what I'm about to tell you can never leave this

table."

Stanley's heart is overworking. Abby is so close. He cannot remember the last time he was this close to a woman. He lies to himself, saying that it has been years, though a more accurate estimate would be to say never.

"I won't tell anyone," he responds.

"Promise?"

"Promise," he says. He's never had to promise anything before and answers, entirely oblivious as to what stipulations a promise even entails.

"I haven't told anyone this since I was fourteen."

"I swear I won't tell anyone," Stanley replies, repeating himself. He feels a noble duty in guarding something that is being entrusted to him, especially something of Abby's.

"My mother cheated on my father when I was real young," Abby says.

Just at that moment, David DiPaolo emerges once more with two wine glasses and a bottle. He cautiously sets the glasses down onto the table and removes the loosened cork. As he lifts his arms to pour, Abby steals the bottle into her own hand and begins liberally filling both glasses. David smiles, guilefully disguising his dislike for this who sees herself as a privileged local celebrity; he slips away undetected.

Abby, not doing the honor of raising her glass, tips it into her face, swallowing the acidic liquid in a single gulp. She then immediately pours herself another. Perhaps it is just enough fuel for her to finish her story.

LXV.

Black Freakshow sits on top of his gangly arms, bringing his cuffed hands around his feet and to the front of his body.

"This is fucking bullshit, man! Gimme back my mask! I'm on the side of the heroes! All you are is a pig! A fat fucking no good pig!" he belligerently yells as he leans back and begins trying to kick out the steel partition.

Mike pounds on the cage in warning.

"Shut the fuck up back there!"

"You can't shut me up! I'm motherfucking Wolverine, Shaft, and Rorschach combined, you fucking pig!"

Mike Bua sifts through Black Freakshow's wallet. The kid carries no official identification.

"Oh, what's this?" Mike says holding up an Edy's Grocers Group shopper's club card. He brings it up to the steering wheel and angles it to catch the streetlight.

"Julian Hampton?" he asks, reading from the raised silver letters on the card. "Classy. What a peculiar name for a boy like yourself."

"Peculiar? Peculiar? Whatchu mean pe-culiar? Fuckin' racist-ass honkey! Gimme my shit back!" the boy shouts.

Mike searches for Julian Hampton's name in the computer. Staring at the screen, unmindful of what it displays, he begins chuckling to himself. "Who did you say you were again?"

He turns around, ignoring the road for a split second. "According to your file here, you're no hero, you're not even close."

"Huh?" Julian asks, acting as if he is suddenly hard of hearing.

"Dumbass kid, you're on the fuckin' list," Mike states.

Matt Mashburn gives Mike a cocked look of suspicion.

"Whatchu talkin' about?" the boy asks, becoming upset.

"Seventeen years old with a thirteen year-old... This doesn't ring a bell?"

Mike turns back to the road, continuing conversation instead with the boy's small reflection in the mirror.

"What? That's gotta be a glitch o' somethin'! I didn't touch no thirteen year-old! I ain't never been arrested!"

"Tell it to the judge," Mike counters.

He makes a sharp left, heading toward East Bumble. Mashburn is feeling nervous. This isn't the way back to the station. Julian has become quiet in the back of the car.

"I'll tell you what, Julian... Freakshow, whatever the hell you call yourself. I'm gonna let you go, but only because you're safer out here than you would be in a cell."

"Really? Man, but I swear I really didn't do nothin'."

"Really. Here, hang on a sec, lemme drop you off around this corner."

Mike stays close to the high curb as he pulls around and stops the car. He steps out and opens the door for Julian. Neighborhood fathers sitting on their elevated porches scratch their stubble, pull the beer cans away from their faces for a moment, and stand up to see what the commotion is about. Mike has Julian about-face and uncuffs him.

"Thank you so much, uh... sir," Julian says with sincerity as he massages his wrists. "Maybe you cops ain't that bad after all."

A few men with hair long due to be cut and feeling that a black boy being uncuffed in their neighborhood is their concern, step off their porch steps trying to listen in.

A dirty black mullet belonging to a man with sunken eyes and heavily sun-damaged skin approaches Mike.

"Is there a problem officer?"

Mike looks questioningly at the man's choice in novelty t-shirts. He reads: "My tummy sticks out further than my dickie-do?"

"Eh-heh, you like this shirt, huh? My wife got it for me."

"It's nice," Mike responds, lying.

Julian, oblivious to police procedure, stands around wondering if he has to fill out any forms for his release or perhaps if he should just stroll away?

More men, gaining their confidence from watching the first man with the dickie-do shirt, walk up to the squad car to make conversation. Mike gets back in his vehicle and hangs his arm out the window.

"Anything wrong officer?" a well spoken man with thick glasses and golden walrus moustache asks.

"Have you gentlemen been watching the news?" Mike asks in an unsettlingly-polite manner.

The five gathered men nod their heads and answer "yes" or "yeah" multiple times, each wishing his voice to be the last that answers in hopes of being the first to be addressed by the figure of authority.

"Those Freakshow guys. They've got that list...," Bua says.

The men continue nodding. Julian feels the instinctive twitching in his legs once more. Surely, what he thinks is happening couldn't be happening.

"This young man here is on the list and I figured I'd hand him over to you men."

The clairvoyant twitch in Julian's legs was right all along.

He starts booking up the street before Mike even finishes his sentence. It takes the men roughly two seconds to fully comprehend the situation and transform their neighborly expressions into looks of contempt for the young man. Though their physicality wouldn't permit them to actually catch up with Julian, they chase after him anyway, slanderously shouting up the block.

Mike muffles his laughter and pulls away in the opposite direction.

Mashburn is furious.

"That was really fucked up, Bua!"

"Oh, we're not on a first-name basis anymore?" Mike composedly asks.

"That kid wasn't on the fucking list! You know how many laws you just broke?"

"Wanna know how much I don't give a shit?"

"You had better hope nothing happens to that kid or it's gonna be your career. What the hell is wrong with you?"

"Didn't you see him run? Black boys can run, trust me. The kid will be fine. Besides, I didn't see you try to stop me. It'll be your career as well as mine."

Mashburn's vigor is arrested by Mike's disheartening counter-argument. He is crippled from his lost momentum once more. "God damn it, Mike... Don't you give one shit about your life?"

"I don't have a life."

LXVI.

Second bottle and Stanley has yet to take a sip.

"...We had these thick drapes. Thick dark green drapes. You could probably fit two adults behind them without anyone noticing..."

Abby, failing to announce that her story is officially beginning, catches Stanley ill prepared. Stanley draws the wine glass to his mouth and finally sieves a few drops through his pinched lips. He was not expecting David to bring two glasses. Abby didn't ask for two glasses; neither did she raise her fingers or make any other gesture of the sort aside from her initial raised arm to catch David's attention. Stanley wishes to point out the mistake of the extra glass, but figures it is much too late, seeing as how it has already been decanted. Even later still is the fact that the glass is raised and he is timidly quaffing from it.

"I always used to go back there and play with my dolls. It was supposed to be their island getaway or something. I was behind the curtain when I heard my dad drag my mom into the living room. I was on my hands and knees and the couch peeked out just enough so that I could see what was going on. I knew it was serious because my father never swore and he was cursing up a storm that day. The fight was about mom. She slept with my dad's boss, who wasn't even that good looking. He was this pale and bow-legged Finnish guy with one of the squarest faces and highest foreheads I'd ever seen. I don't know when it happened or how many times. Hell, I don't even know how dad found out."

Abby attempts to wipe away the lipstick mark on her glass, but only succeeds in smearing it.

"Work was so hard to find in our area at the time since they moved the docks further up north. My mom made some clever excuse, first saying that it was because my father was always working, then a less clever one saying something about how she thought it would help dad at work."

Stanley grips his glass in suspense.

"Jeez, never in a hundred years would I have thought I'd ever be telling all this to *you*," Abby continues.

She pours herself another glass and savors a mouthful.

"I thought my dad was about to beat the living shit out of my mom. He had his hand up in the air, but he froze. Then, he said that it was over, but my mom convinced him that they had to stick together for my sake. Heh, *my* sake."

Abby looks up to Stanley. Stanley's lips are pursed from the sour wine, nevertheless he is responsive.

"What happened then?" he asks.

"So it's my mom's great idea for my dad to get a prostitute, and once he was done, they would never have to speak of it again. They'd be even. Forgive and forget. Eye for an eye. That kind of thing."

"That doesn't sound like a very good idea," Stanley says, surprised with his own frankness. Are the effects of the alcohol already taking hold of him?

"What happened then?"

"The story gets worse."

Abby's eyelids lazily shutter closed.

Says Abby, "The police were in the middle of this big

bust. There was a prostitution ring at that time that was funneling in a huge number of runaways, all underage of course. Remember the Hotel Blanche? Well, the night my father went to get his 'lover' was the same night they decided to bring the hammer down on the entire operation."

"The Blanche Pedophile Ring?" Stanley blurts out, then hunches over, embarrassed at his outburst. Abby is certainly too wrapped up in her own passions to care about confidentiality anymore. Stanley looks to the green bottle that won't even provide Abby with another full glass.

"The girl was only sixteen or seventeen or something. My dad didn't know jack shit about getting hookers. Right place, wrong time or wrong place, wrong time. I don't fucking know which it is..."

"What happened then?" Stanley asks, sounding much like a broken record.

"The charges were intense. My dad was at a known house of child prostitution and had no way of proving that he didn't know it was anything other than that. He didn't handpick the girl, but that was about as shitty a defense then as it would be now. The lawyer was bad and the D.A. was out for blood."

"I'm sorry."

"Don't be. It's not your fault. You weren't there. You know, even if my dad was found not guilty, I don't know how it would've went over in the court of public opinion. Anyway, he was ruined either way. Do you remember the most peculiar thing about the Blanche Pedophile Ring?"

"I don't remember."

"HIV, almost half of those girls had it. No one was using protection. And would you know? My father, the man who blushed when my uncle got him a *Playboy* for his 40th birthday, contracted HIV."

"Oh dear..."

Stanley is feeling terribly awkward at this point. His feelings can be contributed to Abby's watering eyes and stammering words.

"Mom took everything from him, including me. Years later, after dad got out, he was found in some ditch with his head bashed in. That's all that was in the newspapers at least. Once I did my own fact-checking, I found the truth, or 'omitted story', wasn't much better. On top of the head-bashing, the coroner's report lists his eyes being gouged out, pieces of wood lodged in his colon, and his penis and testicles missing."

Abby's mascara is running and makeup smearing.

"My mom didn't have the balls to stand beside him and defend him in court! She didn't testify on his behalf because she didn't wanna sound like a whore who fucked the bow-legged Finn! She left him to rot! She didn't really give a shit about staying together!"

Stanley extends his hand to touch Abby's, but she excuses herself from the table and rushes to the restroom.

LXVII.

Fish, Freakshow, and Ana approach the three inebriated teenagers. Fish fetches the pipe bomb dropped earlier and inspects it, not quite sure what he's inspecting for before he forces it into his narrow back pocket.

"This beer tastes like shit!" the masked boy hanging on the passenger door shouts.

"I hope we don't look as stupid as they do," Ana says.

The crunching of gravel on the lot catches one of the boys' attention.

"Hey! More guys like us! Yeah! Operation Freakshow," the same boy hanging on the passenger-side shouts. He directs an immaculate finger, yet defiled of labor, toward them.

"What are you guys doing?" Fish affably questions.

"Fightin' motherfuckin' crime!" says the masked boy in the backseat as he suppresses his spasming gut.

The boy hanging on the door thrusts his fist that clutches a can of beer into the air.

"And putting the man in his place! Woo!"

The most articulated of the three stands just out of sight in front of the popped hood of the car. "Do you guys have any flashlights?" he asks hopefully.

"Nope," Fish answers in disinterest. "What kind of weapons do you guys have?"

"We got some TP and bottle rockets," says the boy in the backseat, his constitution looking none the better.

"TP?" Fish repeats, perturbed.

"Toilet paper," Ana clarifies for him.

"No shit! I know what the fuck TP stands for!"

"Dur! Well, you looked confused!"

Freakshow steps forward. The three boys turn their heads upward, all the better to behold the masked giant.

The boy who was tinkering with the hood looks to an inked serpent twisting itself around the thick mast that is Freakshow's left arm. "Um, what kind of weapons did *you* guys bring?" he asks, suddenly feeling unprepared.

The boy hanging off the door looks to Ana and feels the immediate effects of a crippling euphoria. His groin begins to tighten and the blood in his body circulates at an increased rate.

Fish's speech, already distorted by the mask, is further warped by his twisted grin. "Come this way my warriors. I've got something to show you," he says keeping mind not to sound too eager.

The masked boy behind the car, finding it prudent to feign an upset stomach to conceal his explosive erection, follows behind the other two.

"BLARGGGH!"

"Jesus Christ, Nick!" shouts the maskless boy.

Nick, previously only known to Freakshow, Ana, and Fish as the queasy boy wearing the mask and riding in the back seat, releases a stream of pumiced vomit through the slitted mouth hole on his mask. Fish raises his arms as if to protect himself from any splatter, though he is well out of distance.

"O God..." Nick gurgles, lacking any strength. He tears off his mask. Residual drips of half-processed beer, bile, and cheeseburger macaroni hang off his inflamed lips.

"Dude, that is some fuckin' nasty shit! Ha-ha!" says the boy with the protruding erection as he jumps around Nick and the other boy in celebration.

"Is your friend gonna be okay?" Ana asks the maskless boy.

"He'll be fine. He always overdoes things."

"Iwannago-ome," Nick begs.

"What's your name?" Ana asks, again addressing the boy without a mask. It's so dark she can't make out any defining features on his face.

"I'm Tony," he introduces. "Rich, is that a fucking boner? You are fuckin' gay!" Tony shouts, turning to the boy sporting a short and sharp point in his crotch. "Rich, if you don't calm the fuck down, I'm gonna sack-tap you again!"

Rich stops jumping, but continues giggling to himself not wishing his fun to be suppressed entirely.

"C'mon, let's get this shit over with!" Freakshow commands over the disorder.

Digestive acids mixed with drool swing from Nick's lip. Tony and Ana hoist him off the ground. Rich walks behind, rubbing himself through his pocket as he watches Ana's buttocks shift with each step.

"Shit," Fish says as realization hits him, "Is our car gonna be okay?"

Freakshow acknowledges by falling back toward the SUV. The engine turns and the black vehicle follows behind, cloaked in darkness.

Fish settles on an arbitrary spot a distance away from the main lot and sits cross-legged on the ground.

Freakshow steps out of the SUV and squats down with the rest of the already-seated five. Fish pulls off the loosely-hanging duct tape from his legs. Ana scoots away from Rich.

"Shit, how do I do this? Just light and throw?" Fish asks, looking to Freakshow.

"Just light and throw... and don't hold onto it too long," Freakshow replies.

"What are those?" Rich asks, pointing to the six large steel vials placed at Fish's feet.

"Don't touch those!" Fish snaps before quickly controlling his temperament. "Here, I'll show you."

He produces his clear purple lighter and holds the pipe bomb directly level with his eyes. He brings the lighter to the fuse. His thumb is delicately balanced on the flint wheel. Everyone's eyes are focused on Fish's hands. Fish's thumb snaps back. A snake-like hiss calls forth an orange flame. The flame licks the fuse and triggers a crackling sound. Though the preliminary pyrotechnics are measly, Fish finds himself so easily mesmerized by the shortening fuse.

"Fucking throw it you idiot!" Ana screams.

Fish shoots up, and with great force, casts the pipe toward the trailer park. He loses its line of flight.

The others stand in expectation. Fish leans in, trying to hone in on the sparkling fuse.

An immense flash of light followed by another sees the instant disintegration of two trailers. Twin fireballs wrapped in black cinder rise into the air with a deafening howl, discarding any smaller material surfing on its glowing plumes. The sound is amplified in the night air. Fish flinches, feeling the wave of heat hit his face.

"Lukslikkyehittaprohpntnak,"Freakshow says, though his voice is unintelligible.

"What?" Fish shouts.

"I said it looks like you hit a propane tank!"

Nick's rapidly declining condition doesn't permit him any further surprises. He is stricken with horror. His eyelids drift closed. Tony hurriedly drums the cheeks on Nick's unresponsive face.

"Oh, my God!" Tony shouts.

Fish, going off of nothing but adrenaline, picks up two more pipe bombs, lights them, and blindly catapults them into the park once more.

Tony tries to speak again. "Are you guys fucking craz-"

Two consecutive explosions nullify any ongoing speech and all ongoing thought. Thick clouds of smoke stampede through the air. The scattered puddles from the day's rainfall reflect the incinerating sky. Fish busily shuffles to light the remaining three and throws them.

"Oh, my God! Nick! Talk to me!" Tony pleads to his unconscious friend.

"What happened to N-," Rich tries to ask.

If there was anything that was going to bring sobriety to Rich, it would have to be the three remaining explosions. The fiery displaced air brings a hot breeze from underneath the SUV, toasting the boys' exposed backs where their shirts are riding up. The rising fire engulfs the night sky. The trailer at the back from which the old man had emerged has now vanished. Also missing is Tony's grandfather's station wagon. A single roll of flaming toilet paper plops onto the hood of the SUV.

"Ha-ha! How do you like that?" Fish laughs.

"What the fuck!" Rich screams with shallow streams running from his eyes and soaking into his mask.

"My pap's car! Oh, my God! What the fuck did you do to that old guy's trailer!" Tony screams, reluctant to believe in whatever truth Fish may tell him.

"Operation Freakshow, right?" Fish appreciatively answers.

"You're really them! You guys fucking killed all those

people!" Tony backs away slowly, conscious of the immeasurable danger he and his friends are in. "What the hell happened to Nick? He's not moving?"

"He'll be fine. He's just in a bit of shock. That and he drank entirely too much," Ana assures them. "Emergency services will be here soon, I imagine," she says, looking to Freakshow and Fish.

"Let's get the hell outta Dodge," Fish says, gunning for the driver's seat. "Hey kid, don't forget your toilet paper," he says, beating the flaming ball of tissue off the hood. Fish slips his trusty purple lighter back into his pocket before climbing in and turning the engine.

"Don't run over Nick," Ana reminds Fish as he pulls away.

"I'm all right. I got it."

The black smoke blanketing the air dissipates as it spreads itself thinner and thinner, obeying the command of the wind. The SUV speeds down the highway. Fish reminisces on the evening's exploits, loudly applauding himself. "Oh man, that toilet paper line, what did I say? 'Don't forget your toilet paper!' or something? That's gotta be in the comic book."

Freakshow laughs wearily.

"Sure *Fishman*, you tell the story any way you want."

LXVIII.

Susan M. Poole's cashmere pearl-colored Chrysler Town & Country has to park a ways down the street this evening. The distant parking would normally imply a minimal cardiovascular effort while walking back to the house. Unfortunately, any lost calories are being reconstituted by the enormously stacked ice cream cones that both Susan and Danielle are holding in their hands. The reason for their having to park so far from the house is addressed by Danielle first, only due to her faultless teenage self-centricity.

"Why are there so many cars here?" Danielle asks, sneering.

"I'm not sure sweetie. I think the Griffith's may be having their family reunion."

"Well, why did they have to take up the whole block? You should tell whoever to come and move their cars."

"It's okay sweetie, it's only for tonight. It's no trouble," Susan says as she tries to save a drop of mint chocolate chip from landing on her plus-size designer dress.

Danielle pivots her neck as they pass the Griffith's residence, curious and hoping to catch a peek of the ongoing festivities behind the lace curtains, but there is nothing to be seen.

"I love you Danielle," Susan says, then draws her tongue

up the side of a melting slope.

"I love you too, mom." Danielle lovingly responds. "What are you gonna tell Brett?"

The amount of time it takes Susan to finish pondering this question is coincidentally the same amount of time it takes them to reach the front steps of their porch.

"I'm going to tell him that I'm sorry... And I'm going to tell him that I love him."

"I love him too! You guys are so perfect for each other," Danielle says, turning to open the front door.

"Nuh-uh-uh! You finish that ice cream out here. I'm not going to have you dripping chocolate ice cream on our carpets."

Susan is then reminded of the single drop of blood on the carpet left from Brett's nose.

Susan and Danielle sit on the stoop, quietly devouring their frozen treats. Danielle's pocket vibrates, indicating an incoming message on her phone. Choosing to view the text later, she waits for her mother to finish her ice cream cone before leading the way to go inside. She uses her key to unlock the front door, only to find it already unlocked. The door swings open and Danielle stands with arms and legs spread, blocking the doorway. Susan is discomfited by Danielle's inappropriate timing.

"C'mon Danielle, now is not the time for g-"

Susan is stopped mid-sentence by a tall dark figure waiting under a horizontal beam marking the division to the living room. She is shocked to a paralysis. The only thing that seems to have not failed her is the functionality of her eyes. Danielle screams. A green polo shirt and pleated brown khakis make this man waiting under the beam to resemble Brett. A moustache perched on the upper lip looks slightly distorted from the open and drooping mouth. The man's bulging eyes look down to his feet which float from the ground. The waxen face captures his final languishing moments. An empty plastic painter's bucket is kicked to the side. A spot of urine is on his pants. Susan looks once more to the grim expression and then first sees a shimmering nylon rope anchoring Brett's neck to the horizontal pole.

A memo advertising allergy medication hangs out of Brett's left breast pocket. The ballpoint pen marks are too light to read at their distance and neither Susan nor Danielle wish to approach the body to see what it says.

Susan regains function of her muscles and pulls Danielle away from the horrific scene. Danielle's breathing is excited and she forgets to blink. Susan draws her large arms around her daughter and releases a jagged scream, triggering the concern of a neighbor to phone for the police.

LXIX.

9:15 PM. Bua and Mashburn are responding to a report of malicious mischief on Main and Tuscarora. The car is silently steering through the narrow streets of downtown. Mike turns onto Main; both sides of the one-way two-lane street are crammed with vehicles. A live band plays on a portable dais in front of Jolson Records. A small ripple of people fleeing from the nearby disturbance take no mind to respect that the sidewalk and street serve two separate purposes.

A young boy looking behind him as he runs bumps into the slowly oncoming cruiser, quickly recovers, and hurries away without making eye contact. The band of musicians, composed of middle-aged men with long yet thinning hair, stop playing to turn to the growing commotion from only a block away.

Mike's foot is overexcited against the gas. He turns on the flashers, gets on the horn, and tries to squeeze through the surrounding vehicles, but no one is budging or listening. Mike can get there faster on foot. He goes up just a little further, hoping to be able to pull up onto the sidewalk, but a car attempting a left turn is gridlocked, blocking his path. The commotion grows. A metal trash can is lifted into the air and thrown into the storefront window of Gustav's Handmade Knickknacks & Curio Cabinet Collectibles. The cruiser's dashboard vibrates violently to the frequency of the decelerating engine as Mike brings the car to a halt.

"Secondary responder my ass! I'll handle this. Mashburn, you find some place to park this piece-of-shit car!" Mike says, shifting to park before he exits.

"Bua dammit. Let me go instead!" Mashburn calls out, but Bua is already gone.

Mike sprints toward the sound of shattering glass and banging metal. A crowd of over a dozen people covering the entire spectrum of the body mass index have their face's concealed with the silver-toothed grin of black Freakshow masks. Their numbers are focused mainly on the cobbled sidewalk with some spilling out into the streets and seeking cover behind parked vehicles. A 95-gallon square trash container lies upturned in the road with its contents trailing over a cherry red pickup. One of the Freakshow's holds a slingshot, another with a crowbar, another with a wooden bat, nunchuks, pepper spray. They are too spread out to assess, or even successfully, count at this given moment, though no one seems to be carrying any firearms. Mike can only hope Mashburn, or whoever the hell the primary responders were supposed to be, show up soon.

Mike draws his weapon.

"Police! Nobody move!" he yells while waving a single arm in the air.

A weight usually occupying his pocket and not so usually hanging from his neck is no longer with him. A pang of regret is felt upon realization of where his badge lies relinquished—the graveyard. Perhaps Mike would get more immediate results if he flashed that instead of waving his arms looking like an uncommunicative fool. Further up, and the result of the congested traffic, a jeep with a smashed window is abandoned, blocking one-and-a-half lanes. A silver Porsche, whose driver bet on sound passage, has somehow managed to catch his wheel well on the jeep and is pinned, blocking the only escape route.

Booming laughter bounces off the historic brick and mortar buildings that line the narrow street. A buzzed blond giant donning a single-cartridge gas mask emerges over the far side of a black pickup. He sends a volley of two-by-fours aimed at the Freakshows in the street. The wooden plank arsenal travels with tremendous speed and rattles loudly upon being deflected off of automobile hoods and hitting the ground. One successfully launched slat is sunken into the windshield of a parked sedan on the opposite side of the street. Mike doesn't need to give anyone instructions. The remaining occupants of any nearby vehicles flee out of concern for their lives. The giant man's insect-like features disappear as he bends over behind the pickup truck once more, only to reemerge lifting a fallen Freakshow with one arm. He slings the limp body over his immense shoulders.

Bua, in one of his rare moments of true surprise, wishes to express himself with a "What the fuck?" but only ends up repeating himself. "Police! I said nobody move!" He hopes that this finally catches the attention of whoever he assumes to be the primary aggressor.

The Freakshows do a double-take to the new challenger bearing a pistol, looking incredibly serious, and presenting himself as authority.

The giant laughs once more. Compensating for the decibels absorbed by his gas mask, he completely expends his breath with five cavernous and taunting ha's. If it weren't for the realism of Mike's drawn weapon, onlookers wouldn't be foolish in thinking this whole ordeal is merely just another performance piece done in poor taste by the eccentric community theater group that occupies a building only a block away.

The giant speaks.

"I am The Predator and I fuck little girls! No one can stop me! Not even you!" he says, pointing his thick-skinned finger menacingly at Mike.

"Freeze!" Mike commands behind his steadied pistol. The situation is surreal. If it weren't for the very clear and present danger, this ridiculous behemoth claiming himself to be The Predator and hurling construction materials would be no more than a local laughingstock. Where the hell did those two-by-fours even come from, Mike asks himself. The Predator's position behind the pickup makes for a challenging shot. The unconscious Freakshow draped over The Predator's left shoulder leaves Mike's only viable shot for the right.

The Predator is unflinching. He kicks at something or someone stirring at his feet. The amount of force exerted is most certainly breaking whatever is lying there.

"Oh, you're here to stop me, little man?" he says, addressing Mike once more.

Bua, moving slowly, lowers his weapon and returns it to his holster. He shows both his hands and cautiously sidesteps onto the cobbled sidewalk to close in on his target.

"Look, you're the boss! I just wanna talk, that's all. What's your name?"

"I'm The Predator!" the man says, raising his arms in his delusional pedophilic glory.

"I just want to talk," Mike's says again, assuming one of many roles that he was instructed to take in situations like this, as if there were anything such as situations like this.

The rest of The Predator's body comes into view. A black t-shirt with the letters 'RKO' in lower-case is paired with frog skin camouflage pants. He stands somewhere near seven feet tall and, if Mike has to guess, well over three-hundred pounds. There is no way Bua can subdue this man alone.

The Freakshows courteously clear a path for Mike to approach the pickup. The mangled body of one of their comrades lies facedown at The Predator's feet. There is a small amount of blood, looking as if it's coming from a head injury. "Is that man okay? What happened here?"

"I know your tricks, you fucking pig! You just had a gun pointed at me! If you take another step I'll stomp this man's head in like a grape! You will provide me with the following things: one Toyota RAV4 as a getaway vehicle—and don't try to bullshit me, I want a full tank of gas!—two brunette virgins, $1,000,000 in unmarked bills..."

There is no sense in reasoning with this imbecile. The demands being made are well out of league with anyone operating at a normal mental state. Is this man on drugs? Or perhaps someone who was teetering on the edge of sanity to begin with and took the final plunge after some media-triggered traumatic event? The Predator is insistent on listing all ten of his demands now, even though he hasn't quite settled on what they are yet. After his sixth and equally unrealistic demand to occupy the Playboy Mansion, The Predator pauses to sift through his shallow imagination for any further material wants. He thinks with eyes rolling upward, perhaps in hopes of pulling an idea from the sky.

Mike sees an opportunity and throws his bulky bandaged hand into his jacket pocket and withdraws a taser. He pulls the trigger. The electrodes miraculously penetrate the thin cotton shirt and lodge themselves into The Predator's abdomen. The Predator is stunned. He drops his shouldered prisoner and falls to his knees, but not before letting his arm fall like a pendulum over the wires cutting off the incapacitating current.

The Predator quickly recovers, looking particularly unpleasant, and entirely unforgiving. Mike's cognitive functions are still trying to fact-check through the ridiculously-paced chain of unfortunate events unfolding before his eyes. The Predator digs his heels into the ground and charges at Mike. Mike's instincts kick in and he reaches into his jacket to draw from his holster, but the gas-masked villain has already made contact. A sudden pressure on Mike's ribcage has him eject a large amount of air in a forced cough. His teeth rattle in their sockets as he flies backwards. His head contacts with a large iron tree grate shaking his skull, and being reminded of his sinuses excellent resonating abilities.

Mike tries to reach for his gun once more but it isn't there. A thrusting sensation overcomes him and he cannot seem to distinguish direction anymore. He feels weightless. He is being thrashed senseless by a baneful gorilla who thinks he's some kind of comic book villain. Mike's chest tightens. He wonders what ever happened to the help that was supposed to come. He looks up and is only able to see the ground as a spinning vortex.

Looking straight forward, a blur of silver and black masks move in, shouting and taking the offensive. Mike swears he caught a glimpse of his pistol in one of their hands. Mike, now a whirling human centrifuge, feels the blood being pulled to his head. A thick exhaustion comes over him. Three shots are fired. Bua is released and tumbles to the ground. His arms extend to break his fall. He lands safely and pulls himself up, but his inner ear is sending him mixed signals.

The Freakshows sound off in victorious laughter before vanishing from the scene with the sound of hustling feet. The sound of weighty metal falling on cobblestone has Mike turn his head to see his gun abandoned on the ground, and near it, The Predator lying face down, dead with two gunshot wounds—one under his jaw, one behind his ear.

The two injured Freakshows from only moments ago

must have been carried away. All that remains as proof of their presence is a single blood stain on the smooth stone. Mike needs to make a call but cannot locate his cellular phone, meaning it must have been ejected from his pocket as well.

Mike stumbles, looking for something to grab on to. His head is still wildly spinning. "Bua!" he hears from afar. "Bua! What in the hell happened?" someone asks, bracing his shoulder. It sounds like Mashburn. "They can't get an ambulance in here. We're gonna have to sit tight and guard the scene."

"The Freakshows are gone and some whackjob calling himself The Predator is lying dead from two gunshot wounds to the head," Mike gurgles out in malaise.

"You saw the Freakshows?"

"Not Sal's Freakshows, I don't think. Kids," Mike says, trying to keep his vocabulary to a minimum.

"Where the hell are they?"

"You didn't see them?" Mike asks, confounded.

"No, which way did they go?"

"I don't know. I couldn't see."

"Just sit tight, Mike!" Matt Mashburn turns to his shoulder and gives a muffled report of the situation to his handheld transceiver. A static-laden response comes through, but Mike chooses not to listen. "Shit, where the hell are Barnes and Hayes?"

"That's what I'd like to know," Mike says closing his eyes, allowing his senses to recalibrate.

"Jesus H. Christ, Mike. I don't know how you managed to come out of that with barely a scratch on you. It's a fucking miracle if you ask me."

"They fuckin' shot him with my gun."

"That means its evidence now, right?"

"Don't care. I got more."

LXX.

Theodore Leonard Pratt's perspiring left hand runs over the light polymer surface of his Glock pistol's slide. His bedroom is brushed with shifting hues of blue and grey as his eyes slowly adjust to the absence of light. He sits on the floor feeling neither much better nor safer. The carpeting in his room, specifically marketed as outdoor, is stiff and scratchy against his bare feet.

At the moment, Theodore seeks cover. Cover from whatever may spot him through the window. Cover from what he knows is hunting him. An unfamiliar car is parked in front of his home. The door opened and shut only seconds ago. The sound of wet grass being trampled underfoot heightens Theodore's age-deteriorating senses. Whoever is approaching the house is not interested in taking the walkway leading to Theodore's front door.

If he could only get to his phone to call for help. Theodore peeks over his bed and at the window. The old home's windows and doors are long warped from compromised frames and improperly sealed woodwork. His bedroom window is unlocked simply because the latching mechanism is no longer flush anymore. He can only hope that the stiff and swollen wood of the window is enough to discourage tonight's intruder.

Theodore wonders if hiding in the bedroom was a good idea after all. He needed to get his gun, but what is he to do with it? If he ends up having to use it that will be all the proof necessary to send him back to prison for illegal possession, but he has to protect himself. He has unfortunately placed himself in a situation where he is left with very few options.

The sharp scratching sound of metal against wood is followed by the pop of the stiff window giving in to the simple lever of a crowbar, or perhaps a knife? The squeaking wood stubbornly slides up halfway before refusing to budge any further. The labored breathing of someone wishing to enter fills the room. Feet kick against the siding searching for a suitable foothold to provide an ample boost. A second person whispers something from the street. How many people have come tonight? Theodore's grip on his gun tightens as his level of fear rises. He disengages the safety.

Something forcing more and more of its mass through the window blots out a majority of the light coming from outside. The room is incredibly dark and Theodore's eyes struggle to adjust once more. Theodore stands up and turns toward the window. A masked man with chest wedged in the narrow opening of the window sees movement and looks up at Theodore.

"Oh, shit. Wait!" he says, fidgeting in the narrow opening though it cannot be ascertained whether it is to enter or escape.

Theodore raises his weapon, but does not give the masked intruder enough time to react appropriately. Theodore pulls the trigger once intending only to scare the man away. The man's body lies limp in the window frame. It's too dark for Theodore to tell where the bullet penetrated, if it even did. Theodore prays that he missed but his already strained breathing is in anticipation of the worst. He aimed to miss. He couldn't have hit. Expecting a response, Theodore uses his sockless foot to nudge the man. The body rolls out of the window. The streetlights cast onto the body, revealing it to be much smaller now. Blood pours from a wound at the base of the masked man's neck staining his penguin graphic tee saying *Linux*. Theodore cringes at the discovery of his doing. The body twitches with fleeting life. It's a kid.

"Adam!" the immature voice of a boy cries from the unfamiliar car parked on the street.

Theodore squints, looking to the driver of the vehicle, perhaps in hopes of recognizing a face, but the car starts and quickly peels away. The driver's strangely infantile features strike Theodore with dread. His hand relaxes, allowing his gun to fall to the floor. He runs toward the living room to phone the police.

LXXI.

Crickets are chirping. Ana kneels underneath the paint-peeled windowsill of a two-car garage off Grant Parkway. Absent of any vehicles, inside a single incandescent bulb hangs from the center of the ceiling to illuminate four men seated around a poker table in an orange aura.

"I still can't believe that last guy just blew his own head off," Fish jabbers to Freakshow as they cut through the backyard to meet with the already-positioned Ana.

"Will you shut up!" Ana yells in almost perfect silence. The only audible sound being from the escaping air through her teeth on the pronunciation of the S and H.

Fish silently shapes his mouth in apology to Ana.

The three huddle underneath the window, hugging their knees like cramped and overconfident toddlers plotting against their adult oppressors. The men inside tending to their game begin glibly conversing. A man calls and pompously splats his fan of cards onto the table.

"Read 'em and weep, cocksucker!" he taunts.

All four men are dressed in their decades old high school football jerseys. The faded navy blue hue of the East Bumble Hedgehogs.

"Lucky prick! Can somebody else please fucking shuffle!" a pygmy-like man shouts as he grooms his goatee with motor oil stained hands.

"You shur we shoul' even be playin' today? I mean, given the see-choo-way-shun an' all."

"Jumpy fuck you are. Not even gonna give me a chance to win my money back? It's Friday. We always play on Friday."

The conversation continues inside with no hope of them divulging any information as to their identities.

"Show, there are four guys in there, but I have no idea who is who," Ana says, concerned.

Freakshow looks querulously to Ana then, staying low, crabwalks toward a decorative stone placed within the backyard garden. Digging his fingers into the soil, he pries the stone loose and hoists it over his shoulder like an Olympian.

"There's only one way to find out," he says in pragmatic flair. Neither Fish nor Ana could have anticipated his hurling the stone through the garage window announcing their arrival. The rock crashes through the window landing directly on the game of cards. Overturned beer bottles hit the concrete floor pinging like an alarm.

"Jee-zhus!" the pygmy man shouts. "I tol' you they'd be comin' soon'r lat'r! I tol' you didn't I?!"

"Shut the fuck up!" Another man rages. "Get your shit!"

Freakshow, pistol drawn, kicks down the garage door beside the window. The four men, having weapons of their own, open fire first. Freakshow dives to the left and finds himself back under the window. A bullet whizzes past Fish's ear. He manages to get off a single shot before diving to the right, seeing himself on the opposite side of the door to Freakshow. Ana works out three shots, sinking a bullet directly in someone's eye.

The rhythmic gunfire from the garage weakens with one less shooter. The man brandishing the rifle let's out a hearty "fuck" before tipping the poker table for ad hoc cover. A man hit by a bullet compresses his hand against a bloody gash on his neck and follows ducking behind the flimsy foldable card table. The pygmy man with a goatee covering himself from behind a work table on the far side of the garage now pulls out a shotgun.

He releases a round that throws his arms back. Ana feels the propulsion against her chest as she flies backwards onto the thin strip of pavement running through the yard. Fish feels a warm and heavy wetness hit him in the face. The stench of gunpowder carried by the shot is ever-prevalent in the wind. Ana lies on her back, immobile and gasping for air.

"I fuckin' got the bitch!" the man enthusiastically announces.

Freakshow's senses are lost. Screaming, he quickly gets to his feet and rushes into the garage, unperturbed by the speeding bullets. Fish sees the second blast of a shotgun and smaller explosions from 9mm's being fired flicker as white across the lawn. Indistinguishable grunts of pain come from inside the garage.

Within seconds, the gunfire has ceased completely. Fish, still sitting with his back against the wall, peeks his head around to see the aftermath. There is barely any movement.

All four men are lying on the floor spotted with blood. Freakshow's body is sprawled out as if he casually fell backward onto a bed, desiring nothing more than sleep. Fish stands up and enters with weapon drawn. The pygmy man's breaths are short and quick. The man looks more like a wounded rodent. With one eye open, he looks to Fish and strains for his dropped handgun just out of his reach.

"I juss came over t'play cahrds," he says, talking through the curdling blood in his mouth.

Fish gives an emotionless gaze before shooting the man in his face and ending his life. It is a kill absent of the passions and absent of any thought given to consequences. He feels nothing anymore, neither sorrow nor pity. Nothing previously regarded as a threat moves. That's all that matters now.

The garage is still.

Freakshow's bloodied arm imitates Ana's injury from Sal's. His leg is caked in red from the shotgun blast. Blood trickles from his shins. Fish kneels by his side.

"How's Ana?" Freakshow asks, reserving his strength.

Fish looks just outside the door to Ana's body lying on the pavement. What he used to think were real breasts are shredded and Ana's bandaged arm is steeped in blood. Ana no longer struggles for breath. Ana's chest no longer rises to replenish her bloodstream with oxygen. Ana is dead. She is dead. Fish clenches Freakshow's hand in his own. The faint sound of sirens begin to pan out the sound of crying crickets.

"We've gotta get outta here! The cops are coming!" Fish says.

Freakshow pinches his eyes shut to stifle his flushing tear ducts. Seeing Freakshow in this state is an entirely new experience for Fish.

"Ana's dead Show, c'mon! We've gotta get out of here!"

Freakshow neither demonstrates the willingness to move, nor does he provide Fish with a verbal response.

"Show! We need to get the fuck outta here!" Fish says.

Instinct directs him to quickly turn his head to look behind.

"No, I can't walk," Freakshow says flatly. "You've gotta leave me here."

Freakshow cranes his neck to view Ana's body, only wishing that he could be closer to it, to be able to hold her. A deluge of hopelessness displaces what physical strength he has left.

"Take Ana!" he commands. "You've gotta bury her. You've gotta make sure no one finds out about her. No one, you understand? It's what she wanted."

"Bullshit 'you can't walk'! I've seen you much worse!"

"Listen up, you shit! Take Ana! You gonna fuckin' leave her here? You gonna fuckin' pussy out like always? Take fuckin' Ana!"

Fish glances at Ana's corpse.

"Okay! Okay! So you *can't walk*! I'll take Ana. Then what? What's the fuckin' plan then? Or do you not have one as usual?"

"God dammit, Fish! You have even less time to argue than me! Take Ana. Get rid of her! She cannot be found, ever! Go back to the Brazilian. Ask him about an envelope. Inside there will be instructions as to what to do."

"Envelope? What the fuck about you?!"

"This isn't about me Fish, it never was." Freakshow lowers his gaze. "Forget about me Fish. It's over for me. Just go. Get Ana the fuck outta here now!"

The answer that Fish gets isn't good enough to satisfy him, but he doesn't have any more time to argue. Fish bends his knees and cradles Ana's body in his arms.

"I'm sorry it had to go down like this," he says to Freakshow.

Freakshow raises a hand in absolvement. "No worries." he says, and closes his eyes.

Fish dashes with Ana's combined weight through the backyard toward the SUV. He places Ana in the backseat. Taking advantage of the convenience, he shuts the door behind him and squeezes himself in between the front seats to sit down and drive. The engine causes him momentary worry groaning almost as if refusing to ignite. On the second turn, the engine catches, and Fish inconspicuously drives away, pouring sweat from his forehead. The sirens are closing in with a flicker of blue and red from only a few blocks over. A helicopter's stroboscopic whir sounds off in the distance.

LXXII.

11:00 PM. Police cruisers squeal to a stop in front of 2036 Grant Parkway, residence of Phillip Henry Clarke. Detective Mike Bua has the passenger-side door opened ready to deploy himself before Mashburn even fully stops. Mike pulls out a fresh pistol and runs to the backyard shouting out a confusion of orders only comprehended by a few of the officers on the scene. A rookie and veteran pair run up the front porch to secure the home. The neighborhood houses are lit up like it were still only the early evening. Curtains stir and some front doors are left open with the dim silhouette of curious residents standing in the doorway. What's happening tonight will be water cooler fodder for weeks to come.

Mike is told that the paramedics should be here shortly, if "shortly" were only an acceptable way to measure time when dealing in life and death situations. But at this point, Mike can't know whether there would even be anyone worth saving.

Freakshow lies in silence, though he makes subtle movements indicating from a distance that he is indeed still alive. The tattoos are unmistakable. Mike Bua immediately recognizes him as the same masked man from the Shane video and approaches Freakshow with extreme caution.

He has deliberately tossed his gun well out of reach.

Freakshow's leg is shot and badly bleeding. Bua identifies himself before drawing any closer. The pistol tense in his hands is surprisingly the exact opposite of his relaxed psychological state.

"It's really you, huh?" he asks, lowering his voice.

"It's me," Freakshow says.

"Where are your buddies?"

"I don't know what you're talking about."

Mike smiles. His shoulders jerk upward with silent laughter.

"You're nearly as big as that Predator fuck."

"Predator?"

"Just some nut job. Got himself killed downtown. I swear you guys probably share the same shoe size."

Bua looks to the nervous officers crossing the lawn behind him.

"Yeah, he was one of the bad guys though," Bua cleverly adds, making his alignment known.

Officers gather behind Bua, awaiting instructions.

"Cuff him," Mike says.

"Do we really have to?" an officer asks. Mike doesn't justify the question with a response.

A helicopter cuts through the air overhead arbitrarily swinging its blinding spotlight on the surrounding blocks. The paramedics arrive. The two officers hesitantly walk into the garage and handcuff Freakshow. They go through all necessary motions of a police arrest per Bua's orders. A third-year officer dramatically unmasks Freakshow, making an over exaggerated arc with his arm. Freakshow's large bleached and short-spiked hair stands up straight on his head. Light brown stubble shows on his face. No one shows a look of surprise.

Bua looks to the four lifeless bodies. Bicycle playing cards, beer bottles, and cigarettes litter the floor. Overall, it's not the climactic ending that Bua would have expected. A quick string of murders targeting pedophiles which became nothing more than a small town media fad, all ending with a poker shootout in a tight two-car garage. Sure, the body count is anything more than this semi-populous suburb has ever seen, and not to leave out the dynamic series of explosions that consumed the trailer park on Fox Way, yet, Bua feels unsatisfied with the ending. A call to arms by true killers ended up being little more than an early Halloween for the immature inhabitants of the city.

Mashburn steps behind Bua with his arms on his hips.

"Mike, about the Freakshow driver..."

"Yeah?"

"I think we may have lost him."

"You *think you may have*?" Bua asks, putting a noticeable strain in his tone.

"We lost him," Mashburn states with certainty.

Bua lets out a very deceptive sigh.

"All right. Call off the damn search. We'll have better luck with interrogation."

Freakshow is placed on a stretcher and rolled away.

"Funny," Freakshow says to Bua and Mashburn in passing.

"What's that?" Bua asks.

"My name is Mike too."

LXXIII.

Detective Michael Bua slips his jacket off in the cramped space of the ambulance heading toward the city hospital named after some Danish saint whose venerate deeds are overshadowed by his celebrated name. The paramedics have Freakshow's pant leg slit up to the crotch. Bright red liquid seeps out from numerous blackened red holes from his thigh down to his shin. It's been a while since Bua has ridden in an ambulance and it seems to be shakier than he remembers. He braces himself, hoping that whatever painkillers they give the suspect won't knock him out for questioning.

For the moment though, Freakshow is very lucid. The fluorescent white, along with the smell, reinforces the atmosphere's cold sterility. The pain in his leg is immaterial, he's been in much worse, and in complete honesty, he just doesn't give a shit anymore.

"Looks like the press caught wind of this!" the driver shouts from the front.

News lights pointing from behind a shifting crowd cast a menagerie of shadows on the side of the ambulance. The raised voices of reporters penetrate through the rigid hull. Lights are feverishly flashing. The ambulance stops. Bua can feel the presence of the encroaching fanatic citizens and reporters from just outside the rear. He opens the doors and does his best to push the crowd back. Someone chants, "Free Freakshow!"

The media rushes him with microphones, his tiny dark and convexed reflections seems to mock him through the lenses directed at his face. He pays no attention to the audible information attempting to be processed by his brain. He needs focus to get the primary suspect inside the hospital and away from the media stampede. The flashing is optically disrupting. Bua has trouble locating the main entrance to the hospital.

The staff from the E.R. run to meet the ambulance. A stocky nurse with a pencil-thin moustache who fancies himself a fullback forms a path by cleaving the crowd in two. Bua looks past the sponge windscreen microphones and sees a few familiar faces, some from the press conference earlier today, one of Abby O'Neill's.

"Are you the *real* Freakshow?" she hopelessly shouts at the heavy stretcher being carried away.

Freakshow shouts something that no one understands, even after they go through the playback and filter the noise.

Mike sticks his hand in the Channel 4 camera kindly answering, "Sorry, no comment at this time."

LXXIV.

Fish questions his luck. On top of not getting hit with any bullets, he has luckily made it as far as the highway. The cops are all over the city and surrounding areas tonight. The attacks are out of control and emergency services are up to their necks in phone calls from criminal mischief to homicide. Fish is on edge, twitching at the slightest shift in light within his peripheral vision. He drives with his eyes to the rear-view mirror, seeing the road behind him go pale as if a vehicle were just on the verge of breaking over the horizon, but nothing surfaces.

He decelerates to allow his mind to catch up with his actions. The narrow dirt road should be somewhere around here. To think, it was only two days ago on Wednesday when Fish was in the back seat, with Ringo behind the wheel, and Freakshow riding shotgun. Only two days ago, when he did not know about killing a man and the dreadfully hollow satisfaction that it brings. After fifty yards, Fish locates the age-old clandestine path leading to the lake. Ana's arm falls of the seat with the sharp turn, causing Fish to jump out of his seat in shot nerves.

The SUV glides over the path with its darkened trenches on either side. It would only take one strained nerve to wind the steering wheel in the wrong direction, thus stranding himself in the middle of the woods with a dead body in the car. Fish realizes that he is still wearing his mask, and that Ana is still wearing hers. He breaks to the clearing and drives the vehicle up to the edge of the aptly named Bridge to Nowhere. Situated nearby is the fire pit.

He turns off the engine and headlights, feeling much safer to work in the dark, at least for the moment. Fish sits in the eerie silence for a minute, attuning his ears to the still woods.

There is no one here tonight, not with what's going on in the city. Fish exits the driver's side and walks around, dragging out Ana's gunshot-ridden cool body. He'd wish nothing more than to show Ana the respect that she deserves by carrying her, but his long-expended reservoir of stamina can only serve enough energy for him to hold her head up as he tows her body across the light ashen dirt surrounding the pit.

He stops to regain breath before cricking his knees in a low squat and rolling her body over the stone encirclement. Ana's masked head is cast face-down into the fire pit, her body disposed of without so much as a forethought alongside scorched beer cans.

The air is thick with disturbed ash. Fish can faintly make out a sharp bulge protruding from the side of Ana's front pocket. He reaches his hand forward to retrieve it in sheer curiosity. Surely she wasn't mad enough to bring along any identification when the three of them were making hits. Fish steps over the stones and the sole of his shoe sinks into the ash. He pinches the curious rectangular object in between his middle and forefinger and draws his hand back with the necessary force to overcome the weight resting on it.

The wallet is dislodged. The fat bi-fold is much bigger than he expected. Perhaps Ana snagged it off of one of the hits from the Freed house. Fish flicks it open and parts the leather, looking for any considerable denomination of bills. He finds a fifty and twenty and promptly pockets them. As he thriftily begins shuffling through the assortment of cards, before he is even fully conscious of the fact, his eyes register in a peculiarity. He flips the cards back, unable to see a connection, with neither Freed nor any of the hits that Ana participated in. Squinting, he holds the cards close to his face for scrutiny. His fingers come across the smooth plastic gloss of a D.M.V. issued license. He tilts the card, catching a stray beam of light that reveals a rainbow hologram of the state seal.

He walks back to the vehicle and pops open the door for a small radius of light. The wallet is filthy with the grime of ash. Fish, now squinting until his eyes adjust once more, tilts the card, casting off a shadow from its surface. The driver's license reads: *Michael Andrew Starr*. The face lacks any familiarity to Freakshow's; the high cheekbones, and green deep-set eyes, the pale complexion. Fish now fights an unsettling feeling in his gut as he looks to the date of issue, then to the height, then back to the name; Michael Andrew Starr. Upon the chilling revelation, the wallet slips out of Fish's grasp and falls to the ground. Refusing to investigate any further, Fish nudges it into the fire using the tip of his shoe and walks back once more to the SUV to get two cans of gasoline.

Surprised by their unexpected weightlessness, he shakes them against his ear, measuring the volume before pulling off the cap and dousing Ana's body in the sweet-smelling fuel. His work is much quicker than he gives himself credit for. He isn't even engaged in conscious thought as he pulls out his lighter, woos a flame, and throws it on Ana's terminant body. A fire whips itself in the air, consuming the fossil fuel-laden cloth and flesh.

Fish sits on a fat stump, soaking in the heat of the potent

fire. He reaches in his pocket pulling out the cloudy sandwich bag. It didn't contain enough bud for a decent high. He stands up, shifting his hands in his pockets, looking for the lighter that was in his hand no more than seconds ago. He steps to the fire. Tightening his face from the heat, he sees his purple lighter being singed at the base of a large flame. The sandwich bag is re-categorized in Fish's mind as nothing more than rubbish. He flings it into the fire hoping to capture with his nose the newly infused aromatic quality, but he can smell nothing more than the percolating oils being cooked off of Ana's skin.

No, not finished yet.

Teeth, he thinks. Someone somewhere will know, *from the teeth.*

Fish walks back to the SUV. There is no shovel, but there are pliers.

Pulverizing the teeth should do. Afterward, though.

"I'm sorry, Ana."

LXXV.

It's a cloudy, windy, and chilly August morning. Freakshow lies handcuffed to the bed with thick bandages wrapped around his leg and arm with the bottom half of his bed inclined. Two guards with the same short-cropped brown hair watch a television mounted on the wall while munching breakfast burritos brought up from the hospital cafeteria. The smell of bacon grease lingers in the sterile room. Freakshow has been awake for the past two minutes but keeps his eyes closed listening to the sounds coming from the TV.

"A male suspect in the recent string of murders that has been receiving national coverage has been arrested last night after a bloody shootout at the residence of Phillip Henry Clarke, who was targeted due to his name being listed on the National Sex Offender Registry. Police are unsure as to the extent of the apprehended suspect's involvement. Chief of Police Paul Fulara issued a statement after the arrest late last night identifying the detained man as the shooter in the Jesse George Shane video. No further names of those involved have been released. Chief of Police Paul Fulara was quoted as saying that local police will 'be transparent in their investigation' and are handling the situation with the 'utmost care'. The suspect, further alleged to be the author of the call-to-arms video uploaded on YouTube titled 'Operation Freakshow' is currently in custody at Saint Canute's Memorial Hospital and is in stable condition. The President has not yet issued a statement regarding the surge of similar violence that has spread to surrounding states. The Governor says the National Guard remains on high alert."

"This fuckin' news makes me sick! They put the National Guard on high alert for what? To protect a bunch of pedophiles? There's your tax dollars at work my friend. I'll be damned if I ever vote Democrat again," one of the officers says. He packs the remains of the burrito into his mouth and attempts to ease digestion with a sip of coffee before chewing.

"I know whatchasayin. I hear a lot of these poor bastards are offin' themselves to spare themselves the pain of what they've had comin' for a long time. Good riddance!"

The officers finish their breakfast in silence. The door clicks and swings open to a nurse dragging in a wiry mess of mobile computing technology. Her forearms cradle the sides to stabilize the top-heavy machinery. It's as if her arms are fused to a slightly more maneuverable adult walker. She has the voice of a chain-smoker and steps in with an energetic morning greeting to the two uniformed officers. She then walks over to Freakshow to check his vitals.

"Big guy you got here," she says out of conversational habit. Her scratchy hand brushes Freakshow's thick forearms in adoration. Her nursing scrubs smell of stale tobacco. The computer mouse purrs as she scrolls through the screen. "John Doe, eh?" she says, turning her face to the guards.

"The most famous John Doe you'll ever have the pleasure of meeting," one of the men says.

She makes a brief entry into her computer before asking the officers whether they'd like any more coffee—to which they decline—and then exits the room, walking the same way she did when she came in, dragging the jumbled mess of cordage from her cybernetic frame beneath her.

As soon as she closes the door, the officer shouts with excitement. "There's the has-been!" He makes a sharp gesture, nearly upsetting his empty Styrofoam coffee cup. The volume swells on the television.

"... Well, whether it be positive or negative, one of the people on the receiving end of all the Freakshow publicity is Juan Cervantes, or, as he's known in the world of professional wrestling, Manuel el Monsturo Jr. or Manuel the Monster, whose signature black and silver wrestling mask is being used as a tool for anonymity in the Operation Freakshow attacks. Our correspondent in Santa Fe, Stephanie Porter, got a chance to sit down with Mr. Cervantes last night for an exclusive interview. Here is the recap."

> "Mr. Cervantes, I can't help but notice that you still wear your mask..."
>
> "Please call me Manuel. I cannot be called 'Mr. Cervantes', not as long as I wear this mask."
>
> "Manuel, what are your thoughts on your mask being adopted by the members of Operation Freakshow?"
>
> "I am honored. Operation Freakshow seeks to eradicate a great evil in the world. I do the same."

"What a joke!" one of the officers snarls at the television. "Self-righteous prick."

Freakshow, unable to quell his curiosity, opens an eye and directs it at the television. His cheeks tighten in queer gratification. Manuel el Monsturo is indeed masked and wears a suit. He sits composed with hands crossed over his lap, only occasionally lifting his arms for a grand gesture as if he were still standing in the middle of a ring. Stephanie Porter makes a sigh that is picked up by the microphone. Manuel lifts his arms, shapes an invisible globe between his upheld hands, and starts a curious riddle of a monologue, with the illusion of promulgating some great truth.

"It's all in the mask. One does not choose the mask; the mask chooses you. The mask transforms you. The mask gives you strength. Even the ancient cultures believe in this. When I take this off, I am a normal human being who cries, who sometimes suffers. A human being that makes sacrifices, and these sacrifices have created Manuel el Monsturo. And now one can no longer exist without the other."

"I dunno Hayes. This guy sounds pretty deep," the officer comments.

"Are you kidding me? He's a washed-up has-been." says Hayes. "This Porter chick is asking him about Operation Freakshow, not his fuckin' mystic hero origin, criminy."

Stephanie Porter's voice is saturated with irritation. The clip cuts to the end question of the interview:

"What do you have to say to the members of Operation Freakshow, if anything?"

Manuel el Monsturo, in an unorthodox news interview move—though perfectly accepted in wrestling interviews— stands up out of his chair, puffs up his chest, and points fiercely at the camera. The unexpecting cameraman staggers as he pans back the shot, capturing Manuel's full figure and the interviewer's exquisite crossed legs. The camera shakes slightly.

"Never give up for what you believe in. Fight until the last ounce of strength has left your body and you can fight no more. My match this weekend against The Red Gizzard for the championship belt will serve as a symbolic offering to the efforts of Operation Freakshow. May I smite my enemy as you smite yours. *Pelear le buena batalla*! Fight the good fight!"

LXXVI.

Freakshow no longer feels the need to hide the fact that he's awake. His eyes blink morosely as he looks from the tubes and wires running from various equipment to his body. He lifts his head to view the horizon outside, but can only see the treetops of recently-planted saplings and guesses himself to be on the second floor. The two officers seated in Freakshow's room give gestures of jubilation upon seeing the newly-awakened national celebrity. One of the officers stands and fiddles with the brim of his hat, looking as if to speak. He advances slowly toward the bed and lowers his voice.

"Name is Barnes... Mr. Freakshow, you've done this community a great service. I've got kids, so I know. Now, we're not supposed to show favoritism, but if there's anything we can do for you personally, don't hesitate to ask."

The far seated officer widens his gaze at Freakshow's lips, waiting for him to speak, but Freakshow only nods his head.

Barnes continues, "Now, I've gotta call the detective in charge of the investigation and tell him that you're awake, but if you need a couple more minutes to think and get your story straight, that's fine. And I know a good lawyer if you need one, Shapiro. They call him the shark! You tell him that I referred you."

Freakshow closes his eyes as if in prayer before answering

275

Barnes.

"Let me talk to the detective," Freakshow says in a scratchy voice.

"You sure?"

Freakshow nods again.

Without turning, Barnes orders in the façade of rank, "Hayes, go get Bua."

The other officer steps out, pulling the door closed behind him, but with not enough force. The door latch fails to catch and remains partially open.

Not even a minute passes before Hayes returns with the familiar face of Detective Michael Bua.

Barnes quickly turns to greet Bua.

"I told him to call Shapiro, but he said he wanted to talk to you."

"Thank you Barnes. May I have some time alone with him please?"

Barnes would like no more than to squeeze another word or two in on Freakshow's behalf, but soon changes his mind and is the last to exit the room behind his partner Hayes. The door is pulled shut, closing the room off in a momentary vacuum of silence.

Freakshow, in a roundabout manner, expresses his gratification.

"My leg wasn't that bad. Why the hospital?"

"Well, I've convinced the doctor not to release you to us yet. Apparently he sympathizes as well."

"Yeah? Well I thought that last guy was gonna give me a handjob."

"Barnes?" Bua says in a grin that bears his teeth. "Well, there's something about cops. We don't anger easily when a guy knocks off a bunch of sexual predators."

"Sexual predators? How ironic. They just all owed me

money..."

Bua calculates Freakshow's sarcasm, unsure whether or not he should proceed with the interrogation in an honest manner or not.

"Mike?" Bua says. "Can I call you Mike?"

Freakshow tightens his face. "I'd prefer you didn't. I mean, I'm a Mike, you're a Mike, I have friends named Mike. It's an overused name."

"*Who is like God?*" Bua quips.

"I guess all of us," Freakshow answers in a disinterested way.

"Then what *should* I call you?"

"The other guy called me Mr. Freakshow. I dunno, Mr. Show or-"

"How about just *Show*?"

"That will do, sir. That will do."

"I'm Bua."

"Okay, Bua. Look, I don't wanna draw this thing out into a long court battle or whatever the system does nowadays to people like me. I did it. I killed them all. I just admitted to it. There's your confession. I'm ready to sign whatever papers you brought with you and say it on camera. I did it all by myself, and I am in no way being coerced into this confession of my guilt."

"C'mon, you know it's not that easy..."

"I waive my right to counsel."

"Why take the fall all by yourself?"

"Because everyone who helped me is now dead and gone."

"Now we both know that's not true. You had a driver last night who sure as hell got away."

"Yeah? Well what does that say about the force?"

Freakshow takes a breath allowing his brain to process

his words to follow.

'The driver last night was a for-hire, nothing to do with any of the other attacks. I'm the last one. I'm on the video online. I'm on the Sal and Shane footage. I am The Freakshow. And there's nothing and no one else."

"So you did Santos and Sal's thugs?"

"Yeah."

Bua scratches his head. "You did Freed, Davidson, and Hill?"

"If those were the other two guys' names, then yes."

"You did Shane, Williams, and Botton?"

"Yeah," Freakshow answers.

"And last night's Clarke, Petrovic, and the two other fucks."

"Guilty."

"Hmm, what about Dutroux? Did you kill him too?"

"You bet I did."

"Dutroux was murdered this morning on his way to work while you were here in the hospital."

"Well, it was me."

"How did you manage to pull it off then?"

"Via magic."

Bua's frustration is mounting.

"Goddammit! You know they'll fuckin' crucify you! There isn't a judge or politician in this state that didn't get elected without help from Jesse George Shane's family. That's old money. They're gonna give you the death penalty! They may make sure that you don't even live long enough to see trial."

"That's why I'm confessing."

"Well I'm trying to help you! Why couldn't you just fuckin' run last night?"

Bua's attitude is almost that of an upset parent concerned

over the welfare of a child. Freakshow, irritated, asks, "Why the hell do you give a shit about me anyway?"

"Because aside from your one slip, the one innocent guy you killed last night, all those sick fucks got what they deserved. I wish I could do the kind of thing that you did."

"If anyone can do it, you can. Anyone can. That's the whole point. Isn't it your fuckin' job? I did what I did because fucks like you who are supposed to uphold the law weren't there. Because you let pedophiles live with kids who can't defend themselves. Because the people that were supposed to protect them ended up being the same people that abused them."

Freakshow's face is rosen with malice.

"Look, I can't fucking fix the broken system overnight. But you can't just go out with pipe bombs and blow up neighborhoods either. Innocent people get killed."

Bua raises his voice to match Freakshow's

"Have you seen the news?" Bua asks. "Some kid was killed last night impersonating you!"

Freakshow yanks his cuffed arm upward, pulling the chain taut on the bed pipe. He speaks through his teeth.

"Well, you said it yourself. It's better than growing up and being part of the system that is fueled by people like Shane. You'd better check who you work for before feeding me lines of your bullshit. At least I'm actually helping people. You only exist to keep the flawed system running."

Bua's eyes are animated with a mania. He brings his gaze to Freakshow's, but, unable to hold it, he quickly breaks away. His hands shake with a fury that he does a poor job of hiding. He walks out of the room in a brisk stride and slams the door behind him.

LXXVII.

"This is Abby O'Neill reporting for Channel 4 News. Protestors gathered in front of City Hall are requesting the governor grant immediate clemency to the alleged leader of Operation Freakshow, though he still remains to be officially charged with anything. The group, operating anonymously, has been responsible for numerous acts of vandalism and multiple homicides over the past two days. All targeted victims are persons listed on the National Sex Offender Registry. The violence has since spread to surrounding states with the Governor having dispatched the National Guard at noon. The leader of Operation Freakshow's identity has yet to be disclosed by officials. He is currently in stable condition at Saint Canute's Memorial Hospital. Signing off for Channel 4 News, this is Abby O'Neill."

The Brazilian mutes the television and makes his way towards the cabinet lining the wall around his workbench in a proportionately perfect L. He pops a lower cabinet door open with a bent steel latch which once accommodated a padlock. He contorts his arm upward in a small acrobatic feat, which apparently requires him to stick out his tongue in concentration. He locates the envelope; his tongue retreats. He pulls his hand out, bearing a packing-paper brown document envelope ridden with the dried crust of duct tape and hands it to the expectant Fish.

Fish turns the envelope over in his hands, noting the cleverly marked black lettering with two simple words: The Plan. He untwines the string binding the seal to the bottom flap and, feeling through the heavy protective paper, guessing at what could be contained within. He flips it over, dumping the contents onto the table. There is a yellow sheet torn from a memo pad, a strained paper clip holding together around a dozen $50 bills, and two travel vouchers for the Cayman Islands.

Fish and the Brazilian look to the scant contents with little enthusiasm. He picks up the letter, recognizes the atrocious handwriting, and carefully reads the letter in Freakshow's voice.

> Congratulations to whoever is left. This is it. This is the end. If you are reading this most of us are either dead or completely fucked. We've done some fucked up things together, but now it's time to leave the past behind and start something new. Use the tickets and money to go to the First People's Bank Cayman in George Town, Grand Cayman.
>
> Give them this number: 08050-33709
>
> And then give them the password: heaven

The money in the account should be enough to live a better life and forget about the sins of your past.

That's the plan. May God or whoever the fuck you believe in be with you.

The Brazilian looks at the letter with a lavish wonder.

"I always wondered what that envelope was all about," he says revealing a disappointment not at all suggested by his expression.

"There are two tickets here," Fish says, not quite sure what to make of it.

"Yeah, but that's all for you. I'm not going anywhere. I have my first love, the gym, right here. Take your girl or somethin'," the Brazilian answers proudly.

"Jesus Christ, Show!" Fish curses in a burst of emotion as he throws down the letter to the table.

"Tell me, where is she?" the Brazilian asks in a somber tone.

Fish hesitates. The only answer he's able to give is an unsatisfactory one. Which also happens to be the truth.

LXXVIII.

It's late. Barnes and Hayes have been sleeping upright on the sofa positioned toward the entrance of Freakshow's hospital room. The television is off. The completely unnecessary beep of something monitoring something else steadily pulsates. The only other distraction is a little lamp too bright for its size on a nightstand far from reach. Freakshow tries to close his eyes, but cannot seem to fall sleep. He calls the names of the guards, but they have irresponsibly fallen victim to exhaustion.

Freakshow lifts his right arm, but the handcuffs quickly clink against the bed pipe, restraining his movement. He shuts his eyes and meditates, trying to relax the muscles in his body. Timed with the bleeping of the ECG monitor, the door clicks and softly swings open. Freakshow's eyelids twitch with the amount of conscious force he has to exert just to keep them closed. He opens his eyes to ask the nurse for something to help him sleep.

Sal Solak stands at Freakshow's bedside, gripping a pair of suture scissors in his hand with his taunting lazy left eyelid. Freakshow glances to Barnes and Hayes. He lifts his head to see Barnes' arm hanging over the armrest. The light Styrofoam cup just out of finger's reach is suspended within a small puddle of dark brown liquid on the linoleum floor. A brief inspection of the further seated Hayes shows his abnormal posture and a second spilt cup of coffee.

"Hey Sal," Freakshow says.

"Hello Mike. I wanted to use a scalpel, but all I could find was this," Sal responds, tilting the stainless steel in the light. He turns of the monitor.

Sal moves fast. He places a pillow over Freakshow's head and leans all his weight onto it. The scissors are driven into Freakshow's abdomen three times before enough strength is lost to confidently finish the job by running it twice into his heart. Sal leaps back, his orderly scrubs stained with fresh blood. The serpent wrapping itself around the mast of Freakshow's left arm dangles lifeless off the side of the bed. The pillow covering Freakshow's face slowly rises, erasing Sal's handprint in its center.

Sal removes his shirt and wipes the handle of the scissors that he chooses to leave lodged in Freakshow's chest. Sal removes his sodden shirt and washes his bloodied hands at the small sink in bathroom.

No gloves. Must wipe everything.

His breath is heavy and he leaves the smell of sweat lingering in the room. Sal dashes to turn off the light and exits the room, gently clicking the door behind him. He throws his sodden shirt into a laundry bin, showing only a slightly stained t-shirt underneath.

Skeleton crew, and no one saw him.

Sal smiles to himself as he exits the hospital.

LXXIX.

Chief of Police Paul Fulara stands at the podium situated in front of the station. A cool wind sweeps through the low buildings allowing the thin sweat formed on everyone's back to evaporate. The Captain, Bua, and Mashburn stand at ease in the background. Paul Fulara pulls up his cuff to check his watch before approaching the microphone with an air of confidence. He clears his throat too close to the podium. The grit of phlegm in his 52-year-old throat is picked up and resonated through the loudspeakers in an unpleasant introduction.

"Excuse me," he begins. "Earlier this morning at approximately 1:30 AM, the leader of Operation Freakshow, whose true identity is still unknown to us, was murdered last night in his bed at Saint Canute's Memorial Hospital. The two officers stationed to guard him were incapacitated shortly before the killing took place. As you already know, the National Guard is ever-present in our city to ensure the safety of our citizens. A curfew is being issued for all the residents within city boundaries. Anyone caught with *any* facial covering will be regarded as a person of suspicion and *will be* detained.

"As you may know, the violence born of our beautiful city has spread to surrounding areas. I am asking that you all

285

cooperate and please report any suspicious activity immediately."

Fulara tightens his tie and puts up his chin. He continues, "Now I know everyone is in an uproar. People may think that vigilantism is the answer, but it is not! These people are a threat to society, the principles this country was founded upon, and well, these vigilantes usually wind up dead! No matter how you paint the picture, these people operate beyond the law and lack the proper procedure, and because of this, innocent people have died. The system is in place for a reason: to keep people safe and to fairly enforce the law."

Paul Fulara finishes and stands back.

The crowd comes back with a mixed response. Quite a number of boos are heard from faceless people in the back. The reporters and cameras swell forward with questions that fuse together in a soundscape of nonsense.

A man with a polished head and glasses hanging on the tip of his nose steps forward with a patronizing smile. "I'm sorry," he tells the reporters. "We won't be taking any questions at this time!" His crooked upper teeth protrude past his lips, exposing his offensive red gums.

Much like last time, Paul Fulara is hurriedly escorted to an awaiting vehicle. He looks to the Captain, Bua, and Mashburn affirmingly before descending the stairs, entering his vehicle, and being driven away.

"I never could understand why that prick isn't stationed here. Where the fuck is he always going? Rubbing shoulders with dirty politicians." the Captain grumbles through dancing lips.

"Planning out his political career," Mike says.

"At his age? Who is he kidding?"

Bua and Mashburn smirk at the Captain, relieved by the

shared sentiment.

"And neither of you are leaving the station today until I get those reports," the Captain adds, prodding the air with his finger.

Bua and Mashburn turn to enter the station as the Captain stays behind to handle questions from a few trusted news reporters.

"What a fuckin' week," Mashburn sighs. "I need a damn vacation."

"Yeah, well this whole thing is long from being over, I'm sure," Bua tiresomely says.

"Where are they gonna bury John 'Freakshow' Doe?"

"They won't. They're gonna keep him on ice just long enough to grab his dentals. Then they'll incinerate him."

"Who do you think did it?" Mashburn asks, eager for Bua's speculation.

"It could have been a number of people, other members of his group, a sex offender, family member of a victim, Solak..."

"You really think one of those pedophiles could have killed him?"

"Why the hell not? They've got as much motive as anybody."

Up the hall, Officer Davis parts ways with a bald-headed man with an advancing beer-belly. The man looks distraught but Davis maintains his ever-genial expression. He hails Bua and Mashburn from the far end of the hall. "Hey, what's going on? You crack the case yet?" he cheerfully asks.

"Captain says we've got a shit-ton of paperwork," Mashburn answers.

Davis is noticeably unsated by the responding Mashburn and averts his gaze towards Bua.

"Hey Bua, did you ever check out that tip that I gave

you?"

"Damn! You know, I never did. We got so damn backtracked out there. You know how it is. I didn't even get a chance to read it."

"Well, you'll wanna give it a look-into. It concerns you, Bua."

Davis' expression changes drastically, making Mike uneasy.

"All right, thanks Davis," Mike answers, feeling somewhat vulnerable and perhaps not so thankful after all.

Davis visits the restroom, leaving Bua and Mashburn alone in the hall.

"What was that all about?" Mashburn asks.

"I dunno, but something doesn't feel right. You head back to the office and get started on that paperwork. I left something in the cruiser."

"Oh yeah, speaking of which, did you hear? The department's getting new cruisers! Hell, someone even mentioned an armored vehicle. How about that? Things are looking up!"

Bua ignores Mashburn's parting statement and sprints to the garage. He realizes he's wearing the same pants as yesterday. Bua fishes into his pocket and produces the folded piece of sticky memo. He steps into the vehicle and carefully unfolds the paper, uncertain with himself.

Brother-in-law working at Halford Correctional
says Emily's killer is going to make parole.
Davis

Mike Bua's heart drops into his stomach. His hands instantly go numb from a perceived cold.

He holds the note with a frozen face and dead gaze. He

nearly swallows his swelling tongue. His hands tremble, searching for the torn photograph tucked into his breast pocket. He pieces it together and holds it pinched between thumb and forefinger trying to reconstruct the memory.

"Emily..."

The picture seems older than he is. He brings it everywhere with him. Emily's gaze is directed to Maki who stands to the right, outside of the shot. Emily's youthful smile illuminates the glossy photo paper. Mike leans on the center console and reaches over to open the glove compartment.

There was something that he left inside and forgot about.

He pulls out the mask with the biting silver grin and spreads it on his lap. His fingers trace the large black sockets.

"Game on."

About the Authors

Ray Fisher is from Northeastern/Central Pennsylvania. He studied music in California and currently resides in Tokyo, Japan.

Dave Koco, originally from the United States, served in the Marine Corps Infantry for four years. He now lives in Tokyo, Japan with his wife and three children.

Operation Freakshow is their first novel.